I0647839

DARRYL ANKA

SHARDS
OF A
SHATTERED MIRROR

BOOK 1

· CRYPTIC ·

"Shards of a Shattered Mirror," by Darryl Anka. ISBN 978-1-947532-13-7 (softcover), 978-1-947532-14-4 (eBook).

Published 2017 by Virtualbookworm.com Publishing Inc., P.O. Box 9949, College Station, TX 77842, US.

CHAPTER ONE

THREE ROCK MOUNTAIN

"After open contact occurred between humans and extraterrestrial Hybrids, technology was introduced to Earth that proved the existence of parallel realities. As humans and Hybrids mingled over time, their offspring exhibited the ability to perceive these alternate realities directly with their natural senses. With further practice and training, our human-Hybrid ancestors developed this skill into a science that gave rise to the Cryptics, Nocturnals, Shapeshifters, Sages and Wraiths that exist in our society today, seven hundred years after The Landing."

Excerpt from "A Hybrid History"
by Holly Cotton

*

"IF TIME IS an illusion, isn't time-travel an illusion too?" Willa prodded in her soft Irish brogue.

Willa Hillicrissing, a slender, blossoming thirteen-year-old human-alien Hybrid, sat on the soft meadow grass, legs crossed. Her larger-than-human butterscotch eyes gazed up at her mentor, Holly Cotton, who was also a descendant of the Hybrids that came to Earth in the dimly remembered twenty-first century.

Actually, Willa was staring at the back of Holly's head, which was capped with long, silver-white tresses that gleamed in the late-afternoon sun.

Holly turned away from the nano-glass computer screen that floated in the air in front of her, glanced at Willa's eager elfin face, which was framed by a wild cinnamon mane that always reminded Holly of fox fur.

"So," said Holly in an accent far more ancient, "you've been listening all along."

"I listen," Willa protested.

"But to what things? There are many things to ken in the forest besides the sound of my voice."

Willa cocked her head toward the dense grove of willow trees at the edge of the meadow. "Birds, insects, wind in the leaves, water rushing over rocks," Willa offered.

Holly humphed. "You still hear so little, Willa."

Willa bristled. "What else is there?"

"Listen," said Holly.

Willa stared at the largest willow perched on the bank of the meandering stream. A section of loamy soil had eroded away, exposing a tangle of roots that reached toward the life-giving water as it burbled by, just out of reach.

Willa knew that her great grandmother had been named after the willow. The tree was also Willa's namesake but it had taken only four generations for the name to evolve, as names often do, from Willow to Willa.

Most off-world Hybrids had adopted a name from nature after The Landing nearly seven hundred years ago and the custom eventually crystallized into tradition.

"Willa!"

Willa's attention snapped to Holly's ice-blue eyes.

"Daydreaming isn't a lesson you need to learn," Holly remarked.

Willa straightened her posture. "I was thinking about how different Earth must have been before The Landing, before Deconstruction and Restoration. Thorn told me most of the world was paved in stone."

"Concrete and cement," Holly corrected. "The world wasn't exactly covered with it but, well, it might as well have been I suppose. Cities of concrete and steel sprawled over deforested ground, connected by a web of hard, black roads that stretched for thousands of miles in all directions. Once off-world tech was gifted to the human population and they spread out among the stars, plus with the rising sea level, it all began to change. Now, Port Paris, Port New York, Port Beijing are mere villages compared to what they once were, only a million or so in each. But this isn't a history lesson, Little Fox, and you're changing the subject. We were talking about listening to the trees."

"Actually," said Willa, "we were talking about time."

Holly smiled. "So we were. Let's see what else you recall. What are the five levels of mastery?"

Willa sighed, resigned to the lesson. "Everybody knows that. Cryptics, Nocturnals, Shapeshifters, Sages and Wraiths."

"Oh, everybody knows that, do they?"

"Well… don't they?" Willa wondered if this was one of the trick questions Holly often used to test her grasp of the lessons.

"The titles are obvious," Holly said. "The skills that go with them, not so much."

"Okay," Willa nodded, accepting the challenge. "Cryptics can communicate with nature; with Elementals, trees, and even rocks. Nocturnals can see alternate realities and learn things about them. Shapeshifters can, well, change their shape. Sages are like the ancient human idea of wizards and witches. They can alter physical matter. And Wraiths are kind of like living ghosts."

Holly gazed at the tall Yew trees that lined the edge of the meadow and slowly shook her head.

"Isn't that right?" Willa said, slightly annoyed by Holly's cool demeanor.

"You make the skills sound like magic tricks," Holly said. "They're much more than that. They require a deep understanding of the nature and structure of parallel realities, of space and time, of existence itself." Holly shifted her gaze to the sun, low in the sky. "And speaking of time, let's call it a day."

Holly tapped the nano-glass screen three times. It shrank to the size of a marble and fell into Holly's outstretched hand. She tucked it in one of the many pockets in her flowing, knee-length tunic.

Willa stood and stretched in the golden sunset light, then ran to catch up to Holly as her mentor strolled across the meadow.

"What do you hear when you listen to the trees?" asked Willa.

"Stories," replied Holly. "Stories of the past, the present and the future."

"Do the trees tell each other stories?"

"They do," Holly nodded. "In fact, they do far more than that." Holly bent down and gently caressed the caps on a patch of mushrooms growing near the base of a Yew tree. "The roots of every tree in the forest are connected by fungal filaments that not only deliver information, but can also be used to share food and water where needed. It's called a mycelial network." Holly stood and gazed at the forest in awe. "In essence, the forest is one tree."

Willa cupped her ear in the direction of the grove. "I don't hear any stories, except the tall one you're telling me now."

Holly smiled. "Then you're listening with the wrong ears."

"These two are all I have," Willa said.

"On the outside," Holly said with that same enigmatic smile. "You need to listen from within."

"Why are Cryptics always so… cryptic?" Willa said.

"My job, as your mentor, isn't to answer your questions, dear Willa, but to teach you how to answer them yourself. You'll do the same for your own apprentice one day."

"You must be eager to finish tutoring me," Willa said, slightly downcast.

"Why would you say that?"

"So you can move on to become a Nocturnal."

"That may not be my path," Holly mused. "Not everyone wants or needs to master all five levels. I could spend a lifetime learning about nature and still not know everything about being a Cryptic."

They walked along the bank of the stream, listening to the rippling water as it coursed over smooth stones. Willa tried to match Holly's gliding stride without looking conspicuous.

"I suppose the stream has a story, too," Willa joked.

"Everything does," said Holly. "For example, I know that, in your story, you like Thorn very much."

Willa stopped dead in her tracks, thunderstruck. Holly kept walking as though she had commented on nothing more important than the weather. Willa shook off her surprise and ran to catch up.

"Yes, of course I like Thorn," Willa sputtered.

"You met him yesterday after sunset in this very grove. And the day before that and the day before that," Holly said.

Willa's face blushed red as her hair. "No one knows— "

"The trees know," said Holly.

"You're saying the trees told you that we… "

"Trees can tell you lots of things," Holly said, "if you know how to listen."

Willa locked eyes on a Yew tree as they passed, scowled in suspicion at the tall tattletale.

Willa and Holly walked in silence until they crested a small hill with a mass of large, grey boulders on top, three of which rose above the others, bestowing the name Three Rock Mountain upon the area since long before The Landing.

Holly and Willa strolled down the gentle slope toward the Shaddok, a spiral structure similar to Stonehenge, but fashioned from large, shimmering blocks of nano-glass. There were ten wide gaps between the upright slabs, spanned by thick lintels. Nine of the spaces rippled with transparent rainbow hues, like oil on water. The tenth was empty, a simple passage that allowed entrance to the center of the spiral. Willa followed Holly through the entry passage.

"Tomorrow, then," said Holly.

Willa nodded, afraid to speak lest Holly raise the subject of Thorn again.

Holly favored Willa with a reassuring smile, stepped through one of the shimmering portals and vanished.

Willa exhaled with relief but before she could step through a portal on the opposite side, her eye caught a glimpse of a fox sitting on a nearby low hill. It had a white chest, black feet and red fur that matched Willa's hair. The fox stared at Willa with intense curiosity. Willa smiled and held its gaze for several heartbeats before the fox turned and vanished in a grove of Ash trees. Willa faced the Shaddok and disappeared through the portal that would transport her home.

*

Ashgrove cottage was more accurately described as a large, ash wood arbor that served as a scaffold for thick vines blooming with violet Cathedral Bells that swayed gently in the evening breeze. A soft, warm glow emanated from several Luminaria globes that floated in the air inside the arbor.

Rowan Ashgrove regarded his younger brother Thorn with the large, velvet-black eyes that ran in their Hybrid family. Though he was only seventeen and a mere two years older than Thorn, Rowan had worn the mantle of adulthood ever since their father, Kale Ashgrove, vanished a year ago on an exploratory mission to the Orion nebula, the third such mission to vanish without a trace. Several of Rowan's classmates began calling the region the Orion Triangle and the name soon stuck.

Had Earth been in a less enlightened age, many would have considered the Ashgrove family to be cursed due to the fact that Kale's absence mirrored the mysterious disappearance of Rowan and Thorn's mother, Celandine Ashgrove, three years before.

"So that's where you've been going every night," Rowan said to Thorn in a fatherly tone when he learned of his secret trysts with Willa. "Do Willa's parents know?"

"Willa and I haven't told them and neither will you," Thorn said.

Rowan caught the hint of a nervous plea buried in Thorn's imperious tone. He would never betray his brother's trust, of course, but that didn't mean he couldn't tease him to within an inch of his impetuous young life.

"Just her mother, then," Rowan said, suppressing a mischievous smile.

"No!" Thorn shot back. The plea was more evident this time.

"I wonder what father would have thought," Rowan mused, "of one of his sons wanting to learn to be a Cryptic and a Nocturnal at that. We've been a family of explorers for generations."

"I am exploring, just not out among the stars. I think father would be proud and happy that I'm following my dream."

"And yet you don't want anyone to know." Rowan fixed his obsidian eyes on Thorn. "Is it your dream? Or is this more about Willa?"

Thorn averted his brother's bottomless gaze. "What's wrong with that?"

"Nothing," Rowan admitted. "You may be making the right choice, but is it for the right reason? The path of Mastery isn't for everyone. What if it's Willa's path but not yours?"

"Willa and I can still be together, Rowan."

"Can you?" Rowan shot back. "Do you ken what it really means to become a Cryptic, a Nocturnal, a Shapeshifter… a Sage? What if Willa chooses to go further than that? Will you still be together if she becomes a Wraith?"

"That's just a myth," Thorn said.

"Many myths contain a seed of truth," Rowan said. "I've heard that a Sage who becomes a Wraith can sometimes forget who they once were and can transform into a Banshee, trapped between the world of the living and the dead."

"You're holographing!" Thorn said, though his confidence was beginning to waiver.

"I'm not saying you can't have a life together," Rowan said more gently, "just that you'd better understand what that life would be. I'm sure father, wherever he is, would be happy and proud that you're following your dream. But in father's absence, it's my job to make sure your dream doesn't become a nightmare."

Rowan selected a blue nano-glass bead from the download dimple on the countertop. He tapped it and it expanded into a tablet. Rowan did a quick check of the data, tapped the tablet again. It shrank back to a bead and Rowan headed out.

"Where are you going?" Thorn asked.

"To Andromeda Spaceport. We're finally starting first contact simulations tonight. In three years, I'll be wearing the sigil of a First Contact Specialist." Rowan flicked the bead in the air, caught it and tucked it in a small pocket.

"Rowan?" There was a wavering tone in Thorn's voice that made him sound more like a lost child than a boy of fifteen. Rowan stopped and waited. "You'd never go to Orion like Father, right?"

"Don't worry," Rowan said, "the Triangle's been quarantined."

Thorn nodded, relieved. Rowan pushed down his own sad memories and hurried out into the cool night air.

*

Willa's family lived in a spun nano-glass spherical tree house perched high in an ancient oak. In the early morning light, it looked like a giant, glistening cocoon. The Nest, as her mother dubbed it, contained several large chambers that served as rooms, with Willa's at the very top, where she had the best view of the verdant countryside.

Willa awoke to the muted drumming of a black-and-white Great Spotted Woodpecker as it searched for breakfast outside her room. What was once a rare bird in Ireland now populated many of the forests and groves on the outskirts of Port Dublin. Willa tapped the frosted nano-glass wall next to her hammock. A large, transparent circle appeared in the wall and framed the Woodpecker like a spotlight. Willa gazed at the bright red cap on the nape of the bird's neck that identified it as a male. The bird continued to hunt for food as Willa listened to its staccato beat.

"Willa... morning meal!" Her mother's melodic voice hung in the air as the walls softly reverberated like crystal wind chimes.

As Willa rose from the hammock, her gossamer blanket formed to her lithe frame and transformed into a one-piece garment that covered everything but her head, hands and feet. She placed her bare feet on the smooth, cool floor and stepped onto the spiral nano-glass staircase. The stairs instantly lowered her to the floor below like an escalator.

Lily Hillicrissing, Willa's mother, was dressed in a buff-colored, long side-slit kaftan with pajama pants and soft brown suede-cloth slippers. She didn't look a day over thirty, though she was nearly twice that age. Her graphite-colored hair was woven in a long, Celtic braid that hung down her back to her trim waist. Her eyes were large, cool pools of deep lapis. Lily watered the herbs in the hydroponic garden that made up half of the small kitchen.

Willa padded into the room, still half asleep, her fox-fur hair tousled like a thistle top. Lily glanced over at her daughter and nodded to the hollowed-out bubble in the kitchen wall that served as the breakfast nook. "'Mornin' Pooka," she chimed.

Lily started using the nickname ever since Willa announced her intention to become a Cryptic like Holly, Pookas being nature spirits that long ago bestowed the secret of shape shifting to Hybrids who were skillful enough to curry their favor. Willa also heard rumors that Pookas can sometimes be difficult and mischievous creatures, which made her wonder if that was the real reason her mother had chosen the pet name.

Willa sat at the table before a small plate of ripe melon slices and popped one in her mouth. The cool, sweet juice always helped her wake up.

"Where's Father?"

"Out collecting a few herbs, sage and leeks, mostly."

Willa sat up. "Are you making Mimzy soup?"

"Holly said she's waiting for you at the Port Dublin Shaddok," Lily said as she tended her little garden with the greatest of care.

Willa looked up from her plate. "Port Dublin? Not Three Rock?"

Lily smiled. "Do you know me to be hard of hearing?"

Willa bolted for the spiral staircase, which lifted her up to her room as smoothly as it had brought her down. A change of location always meant that Holly had a new adventure in store for Willa. At this point in her training, it could only mean it was time for Passage, an important step on the path to becoming a full-fledged Cryptic, hence the Mimzy soup, which Lily only made for special occasions.

Willa was back in the kitchen in less than sixty seconds, dressed in a slick cinnamon-hued nano-suit and boots that perfectly matched her hair and accented her golden eyes. She kissed Lily on the cheek, snatched two more slices of melon from her plate and walked straight toward the curved wall of spun glass. It opened like an iris at her approach and Willa stepped out onto an enormous oak branch that wound its way down to the ground. In a flash, she was off through the grove with all the exuberance of youth.

Up in the Nest, Lily watched her daughter until she vanished among the trees. With a nod, the door shrank to nothing. She walked over to a

Luminaria sphere floating nearby, tapped it twice. Holly's face appeared like an apparition in a crystal ball.

"She's on her way," said Lily. "Are you sure she's ready for Passage?"

"The purpose of Passage is to find out if she's ready," Holly reminded her.

"I ken that," said Lily, "but she's only thirteen."

Holly fixed her ice-blue eyes on Lily. "Then she's about to grow up very quickly."

*

Dozens of spectators were gathered around a large game court, cheering several teens that stood on two-foot wide hexagons of various colors that made up the playing field. A large nano-glass screen replicated the field and displayed symbols for each player.

Poppy Rousseau, an intense, human girl of thirteen with smooth, mocha skin, coal-black hair and deep brown eyes, stood on a white hex and studied the screen with single-minded focus. She wore a deep green jerkin and skin-tight black leggings down to her knees that left her calves and bare feet exposed.

Braelan, a Shunzai alien about the same age, stood on an adjacent white hex. He wore his culture's customary silver neck ring inlaid with his family's five-moon crest and little else. His entire body, including his long tail, was sheathed in small, delicate crimson scales. His large violet eyes blinked at Poppy. "Gold's got to appear in the grouping over there."

Poppy shook her head. "No, that doesn't feel right."

A gong rang out from the display speaker. The players jumped into the air all at once, some straight up, several to one side and a few sprang diagonally. The hexes shifted colors under them and they landed, some on white hexes, some on colored ones, a couple of players on black. The players who landed on black hexes moaned and left the field. Poppy, Braelan and a handful of other teens remained.

Braelan pointed to a position a few hexagons away. "I'm telling you it's a fractal progression."

Poppy ignored her friend and stared at a nearby black hex. The ghost of a gold, six-pointed star appeared in her vision. The gong sounded again. Braelan went one way as Poppy took a leap toward the black hex.

The field shifted and Poppy landed. The black hex had turned into a gold star as she had envisioned. The gong repeated six times, announcing her as the winner.

The spectators cheered as Poppy raised her arms in victory. Braelan, smack in the middle of a black hex, fixed on Poppy. He huffed through his flat nose slits, exasperated.

"How do you always know?"

"Women's intuition," Poppy said with a wink.

"You're thirteen!"

"Don't be a stick. Everyone knows that girls mature faster than boys."

The crowd dispersed and the teens congratulated Poppy on her win. She caught a glimpse of Willa in the nearby field, waved goodbye to her friends and ran to catch up.

"Willa, wait!"

Willa slowed her pace until Poppy joined her and they continued across the field together. Willa glanced back at the game court.

"What's that make it, Poppy… ten wins in a row?" Willa said.

"Twelve," Poppy said with pride. "I'm going for lucky thirteen next month."

"Do the other players know you cheat?"

"Mom says it's not cheating to use your natural ability."

"Sounds like something a Nocturnal would say."

"Green-eyed?" Poppy prodded with a wicked smile.

Willa returned the smile. "Me, jealous of you? I'll pass you soon enough."

"You'll be old as Holly by then."

"And as wise," Willa quipped.

Poppy shook her dark locks. "I never thought you'd be the type to go through the training."

Willa stopped, taken aback. "Thanks."

"I don't mean that in a bad way," Poppy said quickly. "Just that, most of the Cryptics and Nocturnals I've met have sticks up their butts."

Willa raised an eyebrow. "What about your mother?"

"Her most of all," Poppy said.

"Sticks up their butts," Willa repeated. "Humans have such charming expressions."

Poppy smiled. "You love us."

"I know. What's wrong with me?"

The girls laughed.

"Holly can be frustrating sometimes," Willa said, "but she's not stuck up. Maybe a little annoying."

"She's a Cryptic. Annoying's part of the job description."

Willa smiled. "Then you'd make an excellent one."

Poppy accepted the remark as a compliment and bowed. "Thanks, but I won't be walking the rocky road to the Port Dublin Lodge anytime soon, if it's all the same to you. Besides, Shapeshifters give me the creeps."

"Walk me far as the Shaddok?" Willa said.

"Soul swear to come to my next game?"

"Promise."

They locked arms and headed across the field, then skirted the edge of the Yew grove in silence.

"Your mother," Willa began, reluctant to voice her next thought, "was it difficult for her?"

"The training? Why, because us lowly humans don't have your fancy Hybrid genes?"

"That's not what I meant," Willa said.

"It's okay. It is tougher for humans, which is one reason I don't mind 'cheating' at Hexes. Maybe you should join in, even the odds."

"Thanks, but I've got no tick for games."

"Now who's got a stick up her butt?"

They reached the Shaddok and shared a hug.

Poppy's eyes locked with Willa's. "Word of advice? Human or Hybrid, the training changes you. My mom's not the same person she used to be. I'd hate for you to lose yourself."

Poppy's words unsettled Willa. "Don't worry, I'm not going anywhere," she said with false bravado as she stepped through the Shaddok portal and vanished.

CHAPTER TWO

THE BLACK LEAGUE

"The Empire has cast a shadow over our lives and given birth to a great irony: That we must search within that shadow to find the light that will dispel it."

Darva val At'n
Founder of the Black League

*

THE ROGUE GAS-GIANT planet floated through the black expanse of space, not tethered to any star. Deep blue storms of swirling gas were driven, not by the heat of a sun, but by radiation emanating from deep within its titanic core.

Orbiting the nameless giant was a coal-black moon the size of Mars. Its staggered surface was tiled with dark crystal outcroppings that reflected the dim indigo light of its parent planet.

Deep within the moon, a network of chambers and tunnels had been carved in the obsidian rock that served as a secret sanctuary for the Black League, a literal underground resistance movement dedicated to overthrowing the oppressive Overlords of their home world, Xos.

The League had been fighting the Overlords for as long as Brim could remember and tomorrow would be the sixteenth anniversary of his naming. Brim had grown into a strapping young man, with the green eyes and golden-brown skin that was typical of his people. He was almost too tall to lie comfortably in his cot that, along with a work desk and a small game table and two folding chairs, were the rock-hewn room's only furnishings. Brim's father, Dennik, and his mother, Alarra, had been members of the League for over thirty years. Brim had been born within the deepest chambers of the dark moon and had never set foot upon Xos, nor even seen the planet other than on the tactical screens in the central command chamber.

Brim would sometimes download images of Xos onto his personal tablet and study them for hours. Scenes of the lush forests and crystal clear seas of ancient Xos, as it was in the days of his distant ancestors, would clash against recent recon images of the dark steel towers that loomed over the stark expanse of grey stone apartment blocks that housed the downtrodden population.

As foreboding as the towers were, none matched the ominous presence of the Citadel, a massive steel mountain that rose from the center of Arcana, Xos's capital city. Ensconced within the Citadel's peak was the Aerie, a hive of surveillance monitors and quantum computers constantly sifting through trillions of data-points per second in the relentless search for any sign of dissent or discord among the enslaved populace.

Brim knew that an unspeakable beast was sequestered in the black heart of the Aerie, its pale eyes fixed on the monitor banks, as though feeding on the streams of data that poured into the Citadel all hours of the day. The beast's name was Xos-Asura, the Archon of the Overlords.

Even at a distance of thirty light years, Brim felt a slight shiver of fear as he gazed at the Citadel's imposing image on his tablet. After his sixteenth naming day, he'd be old enough to officially join the resistance and accompany his parents and other League members on their clandestine missions, most of which were extremely dangerous. Many of Brim's friends in the League had lost at least one parent in the struggle, if not both, so Brim considered himself lucky to still have a mother and father.

A knock on Brim's airlock-style doors interrupted his reverie. He rose from his cot. "Come."

Gar, an older man of military bearing, with close cropped white hair and a weathered mahogany complexion, entered and plopped himself down in front of the metal Tactics game board on Brim's table. He wore the dark grey tunic and pants with black, knee-high boots that was the typical garb of the resistance. Brim's own garb was just as utilitarian.

Several red, white and black hexagonal stone pieces were spread across the playing surface of the Tactics board. Gar studied the layout with his one good eye. The other eye, milky white in the center of an angry crimson scar that slanted across his brow and cheek, made Brim's skin crawl whenever Gar looked at him.

"Your grasp of strategy is coming along nicely. A few more lessons and you might even win a game."

"Any word of my father?" Brim asked the elder soldier.

"He'll be back when he's back," Gar said, never lifting his gaze from the game board. He reached out with one thick, gnarled hand and moved a red playing piece to block a white one. "There. Let's see you get out of that one."

A klaxon sounded through the tunnels outside Brim's chamber, alerting everyone to the approach of a ship. Within moments, the doors parted to admit Brim's mother, Alarra. Her bright green eyes matched the flight suit that blazed against her smooth, cocoa skin and straight black hair. She stood framed in the circular doorway.

Gar stood at attention. "Alarra," he said with a slight bow of respect.

"At ease, Gar," she said and turned her attention to her son.

"It's your father's ship," she said. Her voice trembled very slightly. Brim could tell she was holding her emotions in check until she knew for certain that his father had made it back alive.

Brim tapped his tablet off and they all moved briskly down the corridor toward the docking bay, the three of them on pins and needles.

The docking bay was a large, circular chamber surrounded by several smaller circular bays, each capable of servicing a hundred foot diameter starship. Dennick's ship, a gunmetal-grey disc nicknamed The Shield, lowered into one of the bays, its gravitic drive field discharging intermittent bolts of electricity as it came into contact with the steel ribs that reinforced the bay walls. A thick airlock dome sealed overhead once the ship settled into its berth.

A smaller airlock opened into the larger central chamber where Brim waited with his mother amid several others eager for news of Dennik's mission. Brim's father, a tall, lean, muscular man with mahogany skin, a shaved head and a heart-melting smile strode through the airlock in a crimson flight suit along with his flight crew. His pale, blue-green eyes locked onto Alarra and Brim. Without breaking stride, he headed for them and enveloped them both in a crushing hug. He planted a kiss on Alarra's full lips and another on the top of Brim's black locks.

"I have a gift for you, son." He dug into a pocket and extracted a small, flat rock divided equally into a black side and a white side. He held it out to Brim, who took it, slightly puzzled. Alarra was astonished.

"You made it to the Forge without being detected?"

"I don't understand," said Brim, "it's a rock."

"It's a piece of Xos, a piece of our home world," Dennik said with the awe and reverence usually reserved for rare gems, "a symbol of what we're fighting for. I got it for your naming day."

"It's a rock," Brim repeated, doing his best to sound grateful.

"Not just any rock," his father assured him. "It's from the Forge, the place where the Resistance began on Xos after the Overlords arrived. Plus, it's a very rare polarity stone, perfectly split into black and white, symbolizing our struggle against the forces of darkness who've stolen our world from us." Dennik glanced at the other League members surrounding him. "Gar. Call a Council meeting, I have news."

Gar gave Dennik a crisp, military nod and hurried off at a pace that belied his advance age. Dennik and Alarra headed across the docking bay toward the airlock that led to the Council chamber. Brim remained where he was, turning the polarity stone over in his hand, trying to feel the importance his father had placed on it.

Dennik glanced back, rested his gaze on his son. "Coming, Brim?"

Brim's emerald eyes snapped upward. "Me? Attend a Council meeting?"

"You're turning sixteen tomorrow, or have we miscounted?" Alarra teased.

Brim clutched the stone in his palm and ran to join them. They passed through the airlock and led the other League members down a long corridor cross cut with tunnels that led to several chambers. They had been laboriously carved from the black basalt of the volcanic moon with plasma beams.

One of the side tunnels ended in a thick steel door outfitted with a DNA scanner, keyed only to admit Dennik and Kara val At'n, head of the resistance. An extra layer of security was provided by Vodnik, an imposing guard in black armor over six and a half feet tall, a tranquilizer rifle in his vice-like grip.

Behind the door was the League's communication chamber. Not a single message was transmitted or received without Dennik's or Kara's approval, thus insuring the League's location remained secret. The only other communicators were aboard the ships and were hard wired to transmit ship-to-ship or to the base and nowhere else. If anyone tampered with the circuits, the com system would self-destruct in seconds.

Brim eyed Vodnik as they passed on their way to the Council meeting. He'd never been inside the communications chamber, nor would he ever enter unless he eventually rose to his father's rank of Captain or took over as base Commander. Brim shook the thought off because, should that ever happen, it would most likely mean his father and mother were infirm, severely injured or even dead.

Alarra looked back at her son. "Let's not keep the Council waiting."

Brim realized his pace had slowed and he hurried to catch up to the others.

*

Xos-Asura stood on the balcony of his Aerie on the uppermost level of the Citadel. His pale, alien eyes scanned the surrounding city of Arcana, a monotonous patchwork of dull stone and steel cloisters that stretched to the horizon in all directions, punctuated here and there by tall, black sentry towers manned by ever-vigilant security drones. His pallid grey skin was stretched tight over a cadaverous frame that stood over six and half feet tall, held together by an iron will more than by mere muscle and bone.

He was dressed in titanium military armor rather than the black tunic, leggings and knee-high boots favored by the Overlords under his command. Xos-Asura believed it was his duty, as Archon, to present nothing less than a powerful and unwavering image to the populace, lest they perceive any hint of weakness in those that ruled over them.

Constant vigilance, to ensure that order was maintained in the face of the threat posed by the Resistance, was a small price to pay for the nearly limitless power the Overlords wielded for the past thousand years.

However, Xos-Asura was no idealist. He knew full well that every Archon that had come before him and every one that would come after would face dissent from a small but vocal minority. The Black League, despite their frustrating talent for remaining hidden, was still just a minor annoyance in the long history of the Overlords' rule.

The planet Xos was the center of an ever-expanding empire, presently in control of the wealth and resources of twenty worlds within a hundred-light-year sphere. Those worlds, and the subjects upon them, had been hard won, annexed by the Empire slowly over time, often after long, bloody battles that took a heavy toll on ships and resources, not to mention the cost of growing thousands of new bio-synthetic soldiers in the genetic tanks. But now, a gift from the Elder Gods had been placed in Xos-Asura's hands, along with an opportunity to expand the Archon's reach far beyond the present borders of the Empire.

Strangers from over a thousand light years away, possessing a powerful, previously unimagined technology, had been captured by a sentry patrol. Their ship had been damaged by the Maelstrom, a swirling, anomaly of violent electromagnetic storms and ever-shifting gravity waves that formed the farthest border of the Empire and could tear a starship apart in seconds. Only the strangers' advanced technology had saved them from annihilation. The crew and their crippled ship had drifted between the stars of the Empire for a year, their supplies nearly depleted, before being found and transported to the Citadel.

Granted, the survivors had been reluctant to divulge the secrets of their tech to the Overlords, but Xos-Asura's interrogators were particularly persuasive. As the Archon gazed out over Arcana, he knew it was only a matter of time before his legion of scientists adapted the strangers' tech to their own ships, allowing them to cross the Maelstrom intact, and traverse the thirteen hundred light years to the planet the strangers called "Earth."

Capturing such a prize and vastly extending the borders of the

Empire would consolidate Xos Asura's prestige and power in ways no Overlord had before, thus cementing his rule and rendering him impervious to the power-hungry machinations of the other Overlords who constantly plotted to usurp his throne.

However, ruling such a vast Empire wouldn't be easy. The Archon knew he'd have to rely on a few trusted Overlords, one most of all, to maintain order across the light years between Xos and Earth. Xos-Asura had been grooming that Overlord for years for just such a task. He knew it would be foolish to assume his protégé was without ambition or beyond plotting her own rise to power and would have to make sure his bribe was sufficient to buy her unwavering loyalty.

*

Dennik stood before the League Council as Alarra, Brim and Gar sat in the stone amphitheater that surrounded him. The domed chamber and the tiered gallery were hollowed out of the moon's black basalt heart and lit with glowing blue-white crystals embedded in the chamber walls. Presiding over the meeting on a raised dais was an elderly woman whose mahogany skin was in stark contrast to long, snow-white hair wrapped in multiple braids. This was Kara val At'n, the daughter of the League's long-dead founder, Darva val At'n. Though her green eyes burned with the vibrancy of youth, Kara was over a hundred and fifty.

"Your plan is risky, Dennik," Kara said.

"The risk is far greater if we don't mount a rescue," Dennik responded. "Our spies say the prisoners are from outside the Empire… that they possess technology far more advanced than ours. That tech is already in the Archon's grip. We need to know how to combat it and to do that, we need to rescue one of the captives."

Kara nodded at Dennik's logic. "Then you have the Council's blessing. Assemble your crew. We will be free in this life or the next."

Dennik repeated the oath. "We will be free in this life or the next, I so swear."

The meeting broke up and, as Dennik and Alarra headed back up the entry corridor, Brim was right on their heels.

"I want to volunteer!"

Dennik and Alarra stopped and pulled Brim into a side tunnel.

"I appreciate your resolve, son, but just because you're old enough to attend Council meetings doesn't mean you're ready to go on missions. Especially not one as dangerous as this," Dennik said.

"How else am I supposed to learn?" Brim protested.

"I agree that experience is the best teacher," Alarra said. "But without proper training, your first experience could be your last."

Brim leaned against the rock wall, crossed his arms and sulked. Dennik and Alarra exchanged a glance.

"I'll make you a deal," Dennik said. "I'll ask Gar to accelerate your training while we're gone and you can go on the next mission that doesn't involve a trip to Xos or any of the Empire's security outposts."

"You mean a supply run?" Brim grumped.

"A mission's a mission," Alarra said in the tone that Brim had learned from long experience meant his mother would brook no further dissent.

Brim nodded and Dennik placed a hand on his son's shoulder. "Every mission, no matter how small, is vital to the survival of the Resistance, Brim."

"We're never more than ten orbits away from starvation," his mother reminded him. "Every member of the League must do his or her part if we're to survive."

Brim let the harsh reality sink in and managed a weak smile. "I promise to make you proud."

Dennik smiled and ruffled Brim's hair as Alarra wrapped him in heartfelt hug. "We already are, my son."

CHAPTER THREE

PORT DUBLIN

"Strangely, after The Landing, it took much longer for humans to accept the Hybrids into their society than it took to accept the Grey beings, who we sometimes refer to as Whelks, or other extraterrestrials. For all their inherent xenophobia, humans were far more suspicious of the half-human Hybrids that could blend in among them than of the alien beings who clearly stood out."

Excerpt from "A Hybrid History"
by Holly Cotton

*

PORT DUBLIN STRADDLED the wide river that was once known as the Grand Canal, a narrow channel that, hundreds of years ago, transported boats from the inland villages to the sea. Long before Deconstruction and Restoration, the oceans had slowly risen due to a warming global climate, inundating all coastal cities. While enormous numbers of the population moved farther inland, many remained to rebuild their homes into multi-level villages anchored to the remaining island clusters, with connecting bridges and wide walkways high above the surface of the sea.

Willa and Holly strolled across the broad Marrowbone Bridge amid the daily throng of Hybrids, humans and aliens that populated the coastal village. Living in far country, interacting mostly with family and friends, Willa was a bit overwhelmed by the mélange of alien races that populated Port Dublin.

A Whelk glanced at Willa with its large, black eyes as it passed. The odd nickname was bestowed on the diminutive aliens by the locals due to the similarity of their grey skin to the large, local sea snail of the same name.

Three amphibious Nommos from the Sirius star system, looking a bit like slick-skinned salamanders, were hunkered around a table on the shady veranda of the Stargazer Inn, flexing their feathery gills, sipping water and awaiting cooler temperatures.

Even other Hybrids similar to Willa and Holly were a mix of traits that hinted at more exotic alien genes somewhere in the family lineage.

Here and there, a human would stand out among the interstellar inhabitants. As Willa had learned, even they were an ancient genetic recipe composed of indigenous hominids and a long-lost race of extraterrestrials called the Anu that visited Earth hundreds of thousands of years ago.

"Isn't the Lodge in the other direction? Where are we going?" Willa prodded.

"As far as we need to," answered Holly in typical Cryptic fashion.

Willa sighed with mild exasperation and figured she'd know soon enough. She continued to gaze at the fascinating denizens of Port Dublin. A being at the far end of the bridge caught Willa's eye. A being so odd, so unusual, it reduced the potpourri of alien beings around it to a single race by comparison. It stood at least eight feet tall. Its muscled body was covered with smooth brown and grey fur like a sea otter, except for its broad face, the palms of its enormous hands and the soles of its huge feet. The creature possessed a prominent brow ridge, deep-set brown eyes and flaring, leonine nostrils. It ignored the unabashed stares from all other beings that skirted around the behemoth and fixed Willa with its unwavering gaze.

Willa discretely tugged on Holly's sleeve. "What is that?"

Holly glanced at the being. "Ah, there he is. That's Argus, your new mentor."

Willa gaped. "My what?"

"I'm still your sponsor," Holly explained, "but different mentors will guide you at each level of your apprenticeship. Argus is a Divinorum Master. He can teach you how to open your senses to a larger world than can be seen with your eyes."

Willa couldn't take her eyes off Argus. "I've never seen anyone like him."

"Argus's people are ancient and known by many names," Holly said. "Almas, Narcoonah, The Old Ones, Yeti, Susquehannock, but most used to call them Sasquatch in the days before The Landing. They're the natural people of the Earth who evolved from the early hominids not altered by extraterrestrial genes."

Holly and Willa stood before Argus, who lowered his intense gaze to meet theirs. Holly bowed her head in greeting. Argus did the same, then waited until Willa caught on that she was to follow suit. Willa bowed and Argus responded in kind.

Without a word, Argus turned and, in three giant strides, stepped off the end of the bridge onto a wide, wooden walkway that led to the Northern Lodge, a large, three-story timbered hall anchored by a massive stone chimney that rose above the slate-shingled roof. The Lodge was used exclusively by the local Quorum of Cryptics, Nocturnals, Shapeshifters and Sages for social gatherings and important meetings, although it rarely hosted all members of the Quorum at once. The Sasquatch, also a Quorum member, ducked under the heavy crossbeam of the high entry doors. Holly and Willa followed him inside.

A great fire roared under a huge copper cauldron in the giant hearth. A thick, brown liquid bubbled in the cauldron and filled the room with a pungent aroma that wrinkled Willa's nose.

An intricate, circular Celtic design ringed with five symbols – a triangle, a wavy line, an arch, a circle and a dot - was inlaid in the wooden floor in the center of the great room. Argus made a point of walking around it as he crossed to the far wall and disappeared into an anteroom.

Willa pointed to the symbols. "What are those?"

"They symbolize the five levels of mastery," Holly said. "Land, sea, sky, space and spirit, representing the Cryptics, Nocturnals, Shapeshifters, Sages and Wraiths."

Holly stood by the crackling fire and inhaled the steam that rose from the bubbling brew. She wrinkled her nose and nodded her approval. "Good batch. Very potent."

Willa sniffed at it and recoiled. "That's a manky stench. I hope that's not lunch," Willa said with mild disgust.

"No," Holly said, "that's Divinorum. It's used in sacred rituals. Argus is a master brewer. You're lucky to have him. My mentor wasn't so good at it. I couldn't hold down any food for three days."

Willa blanched. "You mean I'm supposed to drink that?"

"It's essential to the rite of Passage if you wish to become a Cryptic."

"What does it do?"

"It opens doors deep within the mind," Holly said. "Doors to other realms that can't be unlocked any other way."

For the first time since her training began, Willa wondered if she'd chosen the right path in life. She'd heard stories, mostly vague snippets and hints, about the mysterious rituals of the Nocturnals and Shapeshifters, but had always assumed learning to be a Cryptic was more about studies and maybe a few meditation exercises. It was one thing to sit in the woods by the stream at Three Rock, listening to Holly's lessons on time, space, parallel realities and other esoteric concepts that Willa found fascinating. Even Holly's tall tales about talking trees were preferable to ingesting some foul-smelling, mind-altering brew cooked up by a mysterious, furry giant.

"Maybe I should talk to my parents first," Willa offered.

"They know," Holly assured her. "I explained the ritual to them before I took you on as my apprentice."

"Why wasn't I told?" Willa asked, trying not to sound hurt.

"Part of being a Cryptic is to expect the unexpected. Part of being a mentor is to see how you respond to the unexpected."

Argus ducked under the anteroom door as he strode back into the great room. He carried a small, golden cup that looked like a thimble in his gigantic hand. Argus looked at Willa and pointed to the ornate ring in the floor.

"Argus show, you go," the Sasquatch grumbled in a voice that grated like gravel.

Willa glanced at Holly, who nodded her assurance at Argus's instruction. Argus repeated his gesture. Willa walked over and sat dead center in the circle.

Argus carefully dipped the cup into the steaming brew and handed it to Willa. "One sip only."

Willa glanced at the huge cauldron, then at the diminutive cup in her hands. "All that for this?"

"You're not the only apprentice going through Passage today," Holly commented. "Just the first."

Willa stared at the brown liquid in her cup. "What if I don't pass the test?"

"Not everyone's cut out to be a Cryptic. There's no shame in taking another path," Holly said. She sat on the floor on one side of the hearth. Argus set his huge bulk down on the other side. They both closed their eyes and sank into silent mediation.

Willa looked at them, a pair of wildly mismatched bookends. She took a deep breath of courage and brought the golden cup to her lips. She sipped the Divinorum, winced at the taste and gently placed the cup on the floor. Willa closed her eyes and waited for the unexpected.

*

Thorn paced in a wide circle around the base of Willa's tree house to the point where he was wearing a rut in the grass. Lily peered down at him now and then during the past few hours, wishing there was something she could say to put Thorn at ease. Truth be told, Lily was just as nervous, waiting for word from Willa regarding her Passage.

Lily filled two cups with water, stepped through the iris onto the oak branch and descended to the base of the tree just in time to meet Thorn as he completed his latest lap.

"You sure you wouldn't rather wait inside?" Lily said as she offered him a cup.

He stopped and took a sip. "Thank you, Mother Hillicrissing, but I'm hickory," Thorn replied.

"I've asked you to call me Lily."

"My father would think it impolite," Thorn said.

Lily sat on one of the large, twisted tree roots, felt the cool grass between her toes and allowed her concerns to float away on the gentle, afternoon breeze. She gestured to another large root across from her. "Please join me."

Thorn hesitated and forced himself to sit. Lily gathered her thoughts, but noticed Thorn's legs bouncing with nervous energy. Thorn caught her glance, crossed his legs to quiet them and took another sip, self-conscious.

"Do you mind if I ask you a question about your father?" Lily asked.

Thorn would have preferred any other question but nodded rather than rebuffing Willa's mother.

"What was the last thing your father said to you before he left?" Lily asked.

The question took Thorn by surprise. He'd tried to push that memory from his mind but Lily's inquiry pulled his thoughts back to that day at the spaceport over a year ago. He swallowed the lump in his throat and took a deep breath.

"He had the fizzies about the expedition to the Orion sector," Thorn began. "The region's still mostly unexplored. He said there were reports about an anomaly he wanted to investigate. Something about how it might prove certain theories of space and time." Thorn hoped that would satisfy Lily.

"Go on," Lily prompted.

Thorn struggled through the pain. "I was worried because he'd never traveled that far from Earth before. He told me, 'Never be afraid to explore the unknown because that's where all the secrets live.' But... I think the real reason he went out there was to search for Mother."

Three years ago, his mother, Celandine Ashgrove had been on a diplomatic mission to the planet Shan, a new member of the Interstellar Alliance, when her ship, the Phoenix, mysteriously disappeared with all hands before reaching their destination.

There were dozens of confusing and contradictory stories about Celandine's fate after she vanished. One said she had gone undercover on a covert mission for the Contact Council, a rumor they adamantly denied. Another tale emerged that the alien inhabitants of Shan had hijacked the Phoenix for some clandestine purpose, which their government also denied, and an even more unlikely theory was proposed that Celandine's ship had unknowingly passed too close to a recently-formed black hole and been caught in the gravitational prison of its event horizon.

Thorn couldn't bring himself to believe that any of the rumors were true, but was at a loss to explain his mother's absence. Now that he and his brother had been orphaned by the disappearance of their father, Thorn was just as likely to feel that a family curse was as good a theory as any.

Lily felt a pang of empathy for Thorn and Rowen and began to regret opening the old wound. She sat quietly next to Thorn and placed a reassuring hand on his shoulder.

Thorn lowered his gaze to the ground. "I guess Willa's exploring something similar. I hope that…" he trailed off as his throat caught.

Lily gently lifted his chin until his moist eyes met hers. "Don't worry. Willa's a strong girl. She'll be fine."

Thorn wiped his tears away. "Are you sure? Rowan said… I mean, what if she becomes a Wraith, or worse, a Banshee?"

"Rowan told you rumors. But even if that were the case, it wouldn't stop Willa. If there's one thing I know about my daughter, it's that she always follows her heart." Lily smiled at him. "I've grown fond of you as well," she teased.

Thorn managed a soft smile, slightly embarrassed. "When do you think we'll hear from her?"

"Passage is different for everyone. It could be minutes, hours or even days. We must trust the timing," Lily said. "Aren't you supposed to start your own training soon?"

Thorn hesitated, looked down at the ground.

"What is it?" Lily pressed.

"Rowan said… maybe it's not my path," Thorn admitted.

Lily understood. "You wanted to be with Willa."

Thorn nodded, eyes still downcast. "Yes, but…"

Lily laid her hand on his shoulder. "She's not the only reason you want to become an Initiate. Your mother, and now your father, both missing in space, your brother following in their footsteps, hopefully not literally… you feel safer on the ground, don't you?"

Thorn wiped at his tears. "But what if Willa wants something… someone besides me?"

"Sages may be able to manipulate time and space, but know one knows for sure what the future will bring," Lily said. "Give Willa some time to figure out who she is and what she wants."

Lily took a sip from her cup to help her think. She took Thorn's cup and set it next to her.

"Hold out your hands and make fists," she told Thorn.

He frowned, puzzled, but obeyed. Lily poured some of her water onto his hands. It dribbled onto the ground.

"Now open and cup your hands together," she instructed.

Thorn did so and Lily poured water into his cupped hands.

"Drink," Lily said.

Thorn sipped some of the water.

"What've you learned?" she said.

"That it's easier to drink from a cup."

Lily laughed. "Love is like water. You can only hold onto it if you don't squeeze too tight."

"And if I open my hands too far?" He spread his palms and the water poured onto the ground.

Lily glanced down at the puddle. "Well, it's a balancing act."

Thorn sighed. "Thanks, Mother Hilli... Lily. I feel better... sort of."

She patted his hand. "You think I did this for you? I'm shaky as a willow in a wildfire." They both laughed. Lily stood. "All that pacing, you must be hungry."

Thorn suddenly realized he was starving and nodded.

"I have fresh berries."

Thorn smiled, followed Lily up the winding branch into the Nest and hoped that, with her mouth full of berries, she wouldn't ask any more questions about his father or mother.

CHAPTER FOUR

SHARDS

"Information is like water or electricity. It will flow along the path of least resistance, through whatever opening it can find."

"The Book of Paradox"
by Sassafras the Sage

*

WILLA STOOD ON an endless plane of deep blue light suspended in an infinite black void. She slowly turned in a circle. The view was the same in all directions, except for a tiny glint of white on the horizon that slowly grew larger. Willa squinted to bring the object into focus. It resolved into a clear crystal sphere rolling toward her on the plane of light.

Willa found it difficult to judge size and distance in the abstract landscape but, as the sphere came closer, it quickly grew to the size of a mountain. She turned and ran, the sphere closing on her by the second. Now the size of a small moon, it filled the horizon.

Willa ran, legs straining, her heart threatening to burst. As the crystal sphere bore down on her, Willa opened her mouth to scream but it engulfed her before she could let out a sound.

Inside the sphere, Willa floated in a liquid thick as honey. She drifted toward the center of the titanic orb, open mouthed, suspended in a silent scream. Her heart pounded in her ears and sent ripples from her chest through the liquid. She fought through the terror, called upon every ounce of will power and broke the deafening silence with a scream born in the depths of her soul. The sound froze the crystalline liquid. Enormous cracks raced through the sphere from its heart to the outer edge at the speed of light. The sphere's interior shattered into billions of shards, each a prismatic rainbow, brilliant as a diamond. The shards spun and twisted around Willa as she tumbled through them like a ghost. Thousands of crystalline inclusions reflected her image like an infinite hall of mirrors. Slowly, Willa began to notice that some facets showed her as a child, although it took her a few moments to realize that other shards revealed how she might look several years in the future.

Fear was replaced by fascination as Willa floated through the fractures, absorbed by the tableaus that filled the shards. Scenes from her life paraded before her eyes along with images of people she knew but also many she didn't.

Thorn was reflected in dozens of shards, like secret windows into private moments in his life, past and future, as well as scenes with his brother Rowan, his father Kale and several with Willa. Even their clandestine trysts among the trees at Three Rock were reflected back to her in a shard. She was surprised to find she didn't react with embarrassment as the intimate exchange of their first, passionate kiss played out before her, but felt the promise of love between them as a sweet and precious thing, like the blooming of a flower at first light.

Willa's life continued to unfold in the shards. Glimpses of her as a baby in her mother's arms, the discovery of how soothing the cool water in a stream felt on her bare feet when she was three, her father chasing and tickling her around the tree that supported the Nest. Emotions ran deeply through Willa as she relived the memories, feeling them as though for the first time.

The warmth of those moments abruptly evaporated as other shards came into view. Her attention was drawn to one razor-sharp shard that displayed Willa a few years hence, her body lying in the dirt, battered, bruised and bloody, with a tall, cadaverous grey alien with pale eyes clad in titanium armor standing over her in triumph as Port Dublin burned to the ground around her.

Willa was aghast but had little time to absorb what she was seeing as another shard tumbled into view. She saw the face of Kale Ashgrove, Thorn's father. Her spectral body turned ice cold as she witnessed Kale being brutally tortured by the tall, grey alien. As Kale screamed in agony, the shard shattered into smaller fragments with a loud crack, piercing Willa's ghostly form like shrapnel. She gasped in pain and dissolved in a blinding flash of light.

*

Willa blinked, disoriented, as she found herself back in the great room with Holly and Argus standing outside the circle, peering down at her. She tried to stand but her legs folded under her.

Argus caught her arm and gently lifted her off her feet. "Willa not stand, Argus give hand."

The Sasquatch carried her over to the hearth, leaned her against the wall and rubbed the stiffness from her thighs.

She nodded her thanks then frowned as she glanced outside through the entry doorway. It was night and the Marrowbone Bridge was lit by the warm glow of dozens of floating Luminaria.

Willa looked at Holly. "How long?"

"Several hours," Holly said. "Do you remember your name?"

"What? Of course."

"What is it?" Holly asked.

Willa stared at Holly, her mind a blank. "It's… it's… Willa," she finally managed to blurt, puzzled by her faulty memory.

"Thank the ancestors," Holly said, relieved. "Sometimes, the Divinorum can shatter one's identity, especially after being immersed in its thrall for so long. Can you remember what you saw?"

Willa closed her eyes in concentration. It was like trying to recall a dream already beginning to fade. Her eyes snapped open as a memory flooded back into her mind. "Kale!"

"Kale?"

"Kale Ashgrove, Thorn's father, I saw him in a dark place. He was being…" Willa's voice abandoned her as an overwhelming sense of dread permeated her senses. She ran out the door and threw up over the side of the bridge.

Holly went out and stood beside her, rubbed Willa's back until the heaving stopped. She carefully led Willa back inside the lodge, ignoring the curious glances of passers-by.

Argus brought a small stool from the anteroom, set it in front of the fire with a deep booming chuckle.

Willa scowled at Argus as Holly lowered her onto the stool. "This is funny to you?"

The Sasquatch nodded his huge, shaggy head and offered her a dipper of cool water. "Big funny. Willa looks like ghost."

Willa drank the water, stared into the fire and slowly regained her composure.

Holly sat on the floor next to her. "You saw Kale. Are you saying Thorn's father is alive?"

Willa blinked, caught off guard. "Are you saying the vision was real?"

"It's possible. The Divinorum collapses time and space, sometimes allows one to see farther than usual. What did you see exactly?"

Willa thought back. "I saw him being held against his will. Tortured for information. Somehow, I could hear his thoughts, feel his pain, his despair, like they were my own."

"Did you see where he is?" Holly prodded.

Willa searched her memory in vain. "It was a dark place. It could be anywhere. I didn't recognize the alien who interrogated him. He was tall and lean, with grey skin and pale eyes. But even through his pain, Master Ashgrove thought of Thorn and Rowan, of all of us." Willa looked up at Holly, her eyes haunted.

Holly knew Willa well enough to read her expression. "What aren't you saying?" Willa swallowed the fear that rose in her throat like bile. "I caught a brief glimpse of the alien's thoughts, too." She locked eyes with Holly. "Earth isn't safe."

*

Kale was unceremoniously tossed into a grey stone cell by a thick, muscled guard wearing black body armor stamped with a red prison insignia of two interlocking diamonds. The guard slammed the heavy steel door shut, slid the deadbolt in place and left. Bruised and bleeding on the cold stone floor, Kale could hear the guard's heavy boot steps grow fainter, followed by the sound of a second door being locked in place at the end of the hall.

Panting with effort and grimacing from the pain, one arm wrapped around his aching ribs, Kale dragged himself across the floor and propped his back against the closest wall. He gingerly felt the newest crop of bloody welts on his once-handsome face.

Kept in solitary for weeks since his capture, he hadn't been allowed to see or speak to any of his crew and had no idea if they were dead or alive. He had tried to resist his captors' cruel interrogation, but the Orion extraction probe siphoned information from his brain as efficiently as a needle drawing blood. Once his torturers believed he had no more secrets to spill, Kale was certain his own life would be forfeit.

Kale knew that no one from Earth could mount a rescue because the anomaly that damaged his ship had thrown it completely off course and fried the locator beacon. No matter. He'd long since made peace with his fate. His one regret was that he'd left Rowan and Thorn alone. It tore at him that he might never see them again, that they'd now be orphans and would never know what happened to their father. There was always a slim chance that a Seer or a Sage would divine his circumstance and pass the knowledge on to his sons, he thought. As awful as news of his torture and death might be, it would at least provide them with some sense of closure.

The squeal of rusty door hinges drew Kale's attention to the hall outside his cell. The guard's heavy footsteps approached his door. A small slot opened near the floor and Kale's daily bowl of weak broth was shoved through the opening. Kale stared at the bowl and wondered if it was worth the effort to crawl across the floor for the meager meal, knowing it might be his last.

The slot snapped shut, followed by a loud crack and a muffled thud as something heavy hit the floor outside the cell door. A rivulet of crimson blood flowed under the slot into the cell and pooled at the base of the bowl. Kale wondered if he was hallucinating from the stress of the interrogation and lack of food.

The sharp sound of the deadbolt sliding back brought his attention into focus. The door swung open, framing the silhouette of a tall figure in black body armor. The guard was laid out on the floor outside the door, his head a bloody mess.

Dennik flashed a smile and hurried over to Kale. "This is your lucky day."

"Who are you?" Kale said.

"Your rescuer," Dennik said, his smile fading.

"You can't be from Earth."

"Where?" Dennik said as he gently but quickly pulled Kale to his feet, causing him to clench his teeth and grunt in pain. Dennik shouldered his weight. "Pretend you have trouble walking."

"Who's pretending?" Kale managed in a dry rasp.

"Right. Sorry," Dennik said. "Let's get you out of here."

"What about my crew?"

"It took me an hour just to find you. I have no idea where they are."

They made for the door and ambled down the hall. "Who are you?" said Kale more emphatically.

"I'll answer all your questions if we get out of here."

"*When* we get out," Kale corrected.

"They beat you almost to death and you're still an optimist?"

"If I was a pessimist," Kale said, "I'd already be dead."

They turned a corner and were greeted by two more guards lying on the floor in pools of blood. One of them, about Dennik's size, wore only a skin-tight undergarment.

"You killed them?" Kale asked, aghast.

Dennik eyed him as though he might not have all his senses. "Wouldn't be much of a rescue if they woke up and sounded an alarm. Besides, I needed a disguise."

They rounded another corner and stopped. This time, a pair of burly guards were very much alive.

"Where are you taking that prisoner?" The ugly guard demanded in a voice like gravel.

"Interrogation chamber," Dennik said as officially as he could.

"It's the other way," said the uglier guard.

"New here," Dennik griped. "Still get turned around in this maze." Without warning, he shoved Kale into the guards' arms. "You know the way, you take him."

With the guards off balance holding Kale's dead weight, Dennik drew a long, slender, black-bladed dagger and skewered both guards through their eyes into their brains with lightning speed. He sheathed the blade and caught Kale before either guard hit the floor.

Kale regarded Dennik with disbelief as they continued down the hall. "Who *are* you?"

Dennik's smile only enhanced the dangerous glint in his eye. "Keep quiet. We're close," Dennik whispered.

"To what?" Kale asked under his breath.

They turned a final corner and stopped. "To that," Dennik replied.

If there had been any food in Kale's stomach, he might have lost it. A steel-trussed warehouse stretched before them, filled with pallets heaped with hundreds of decaying corpses. The pallets moved on conveyor tracks to the far end of the cavernous chamber where they dumped the bodies into an enormous vat of chemicals. The stench was overwhelming.

Dennik steadied Kale, pulled two breather masks from a pack wrapped around his thigh. He placed one over Kale's nose and fixed the other to his own face.

Kale began to recover. "What is this?"

"There was an uprising in Red Sector Five," Dennik explained. "It didn't end well. The Overlords extract the tracker implants, then process the bodies for the nutrients."

Kale blanched. "Nutrients?"

"They're rendered into food for the Splicers."

"The what?"

"Genetically engineered beings, only partially sentient, used as slaves and soldiers," Dennik said with disgust. "One of the many reasons we're at war with the Overlords." Dennik pointed to a low catwalk over the chemical vat. "You think you're strong enough to grab onto that?"

"Maybe, but the only way over there is— "

Before Kale could finish his protest, Dennik pushed him off the ledge onto a pile of rotting bodies as the pallet passed by, then jumped down after him.

"Fortunately, the entire operation is automated," Dennik said as though giving a tour. "No one comes down here if they can help it."

Kale was too busy retching bile into his mask to hear a word Dennik said. He ripped it off, tried to catch his breath and nearly passed out from the reeking effluvium.

Dennik yanked Kale to his feet as they approached the catwalk. "Get ready."

Kale squinted at the steel catwalk through watery eyes, flexed his fingers to test their grip.

"I'll climb on, then pull you up. You just need to hold on for a few seconds," Dennik said.

Kale nodded and felt a surge of adrenaline at the thought he might see his sons again. The pallet passed under the catwalk. Kale and Dennik gripped the lip. Dennik pulled himself up and over the railing, braced his shoulder against a stanchion and grabbed Kale's hands. He strained against the weight as Kale reached for the railing and slipped from Dennik's grasp.

Kale landed on top of several decomposing corpses with a sickening squish. The pallet passed under the catwalk as Dennik rushed to the opposite side. Kale summoned every last ounce of strength, scrambled to his feet amid a mess of bones and entrails, reached up and clasped Dennik's outstretched hand. He held on for dear life as the pallet fell away, plunging its grisly cargo into the seething chemical soup.

Dennik pulled Kale onto the catwalk, nearly dislocating his shoulder. They lay on the catwalk grating to catch their breaths until an alarm screamed in their ears.

"I guess they noticed you're missing," said Dennik as he urged Kale to his feet. They hurried down the catwalk to a service port. Dennik turned the tumblers, unlocked the hatch and pushed it open. They crouched and stepped through onto an outside catwalk that hugged the sheer precipice of the steel Citadel wall several stories above ground.

Kale inhaled the cool night air like it was a perfumed elixir. Dennik shut the hatch and they made their way along the narrow catwalk.

"Now what?" Kale asked.

"Now we jump," Dennik replied.

Kale peered over the railing at the grid of grey stone dwellings that surrounded the Citadel a hundred feet below. "I can't tell if you're joking."

Dennik flashed a roguish smile. "This is no time for jokes, my friend." Dennik pulled two small curved pieces of metal from his pack, gave them a shake. They telescoped into silvery rings about three feet in diameter. He tapped a control on each ring. They snapped to horizontal positions in mid air. Each ring emitted a soft hum along with a faint blue aura. "Grab on."

Dennik handed one ring to Kale, held his overhead to demonstrate. Kale followed suit, puzzled as to the ring's function. Dennik sat on the railing, swung his legs over and jumped. Kale watched as his rescuer floated down ten stories and landed on the rooftop of one of the stone buildings gently as a leaf. Dennik motioned for Kale to follow. Kale tested his grip on the ring and, at the muffled sound of heavy boots on metal from inside the Citadel, he let himself fall over the edge. As Kale drifted downward, Dennik rapped on a large trap door set into the roof. It slid open just in time for Kale to drift inside. Dennik jumped down after him and the trap door slid shut seconds before a pack of armored guards burst out onto the catwalk. They quickly dismissed the precarious perch as an escape route and ducked back inside the Citadel in search of their prey.

CHAPTER FIVE

THE QUORUM OF NINE

"When Hybrids were first created, most had no understanding of individual initiative since all Hybrids at the time were raised on ships by the Whelks, or the 'Greys' as they used to be known, a hive-minded society without emotion that lived by a rigid set of rules, similar to selfless workers in an ant colony who all take their instruction from a single queen. When it became necessary for Hybrids to live on Earth among humans, they had to be trained to think and feel as individuals. This was no easy task since the concept, if you'll pardon the pun, was completely 'alien' to them. After many decades, Hybrids finally experienced 'The Awakening' and were able to take their place in the rich, emotional tapestry of human society. However, the great irony was that, while most Hybrids retained some hive-mind attributes, such as sporadic experiences of telepathy, their burgeoning individuality often made it quite challenging to achieve consensus. Thus, it became necessary for them to create smaller groups to oversee the interests of the Hybrid population around the world. This gave rise to the local Quorums that *report to the First Contact Council, which in turn reports to Earth's representatives within the Interstellar Alliance."*

Excerpt from "A Hybrid History"
by Holly Cotton

*

Willa was still in a daze as the effects of the Divinorum slowly faded. The Celtic circle she sat in during her vision had been raised to form a table and chairs in the center of the Great Room. She sat at the table across from the entrance, watching Holly greet several other members of the Quorum who had been summoned to this late-night meeting. There were two other Cryptics like Holly, rail thin identical twins named Rose and Lilac Larkspur, both with large, expressive pink eyes and clothing colored to match their names. Their semi-glazed expressions gave Willa the impression that the twins lived in a world of their own and were only temporarily visiting this one.

Two Nocturnals, Selene Nymphaea and Eridani Ginko, distinguishable by their unnerving, all-black eyes, sat stiffly in their dark robes. Eridani appeared placid as a statue but Selene looked as though the Lodge was the last place she wanted to be.

There were even a couple of Shapeshifters named Encantado and Moshi, whose skins were in a constant state of flux, subtly changing color and texture as though they couldn't decide who or what they wanted to be. Shapeshifters often adopted single names as an ironic counterpoint to their constantly shifting identities.

Argus simply nodded and grunted to each guest as they took their places around the large table. The Sasquatch remained standing near the hearth, his keen eyes focused on Willa. Holly cleared her throat and, after a moment, Willa realized she was the subject of everyone's attention. She sat up straighter.

"This is Willa Hillicrissing, my apprentice and a recent Divinorum Initiate," Holly said with a hint of pride. "Willa, this is the Northern Quorum of Nine." She glanced at an empty seat. "Or at least, most of it," she added.

Selene huffed with mild derision. "That's hardly surprising. Sages don't know the meaning of time."

"True," a silvery voice said from just outside the doorway. "But we do understand the importance of timing." Everyone turned toward Alder Redwood, an impossibly thin man whose warm, cinnamon skin was complemented by honey-colored eyes similar to Willa's. His lean frame was dressed in anachronistic finery: a crisp, white high-collared shirt was wrapped in a tailored vest of champagne silk under a velvet-black Victorian half-coat. High-waisted black pants fell over ebony boots capped with oxblood spats. Alder took his seat and propped his boots on the tabletop. "So, what's all the fuss?"

Selene bristled at Alder's impertinent posture and even Argus scowled at the haughty Sage. Alder paid them no mind.

Holly held Alder's gaze. "Willa saw the shards."

The reactions around the table ranged from astonishment to disbelief, except for Alder who regarded Willa with fascination.

"You said she's only an Initiate," Selene sniffed, as if that proved the impossibility of such a notion.

"Nevertheless," Holly assured her, "she has and what she saw doesn't bode well for the world."

Alder leaned forward, enthralled. "Please, do tell."

Willa fidgeted in the spotlight of the Sage's attention. There was something simultaneously mesmerizing and dangerous about him, like gazing at a breathtaking sunset while standing an inch from the edge of a sheer cliff. She glanced at Holly, her one anchor of safety. Holly's reassuring smile coaxed Willa from her apprehension.

"I saw my friend's father, Kale Ashgrove, being questioned... tortured... by aliens somewhere... in the Orion sector, I think," Willa said, the pieces slowly falling together in her mind. "I not only heard Kale's thoughts but theirs as well. They forced him to talk about Earth and it feels like they're planning... I'm not sure, but maybe something like an invasion."

The silence was absolute as the vacuum of space. As usual, Selene was the first to break it. "This is utter nonsense. No Initiate, even a very gifted one, has ever seen the shards in their first Passage."

"True," said Alder, "I took the Divinorum three times before I saw them, and then only faintly at first."

"I rest my case," Selene said.

"However," Alder said, leaning in closer to Willa, "I sense something of the Anu in her. I believe she may have the Mark."

The astonishment of the Quorum at Willa's ability to see the shards was nothing compared to the shock on everyone's face, including Argus's, at Alder's proclamation. Willa's mouth went dry as she forced a question from her lips. "Forgive me but, can someone please tell me what the shards are and what mark he's talking about?"

"Willa." Holly's gentle voice was a soothing balm to Willa's fear. "Long ago, before The Landing, the people of Earth referred to the creation of the cosmos as 'The Big Bang.' Now we think of it as less of a bang and more of a shatter."

"What's the difference?"

"Allow me," Adler said. Holly graciously yielded to the eccentric Sage. He pulled a small round mirror from a pocket in his half coat and laid it on the table. "A bang means something, some infinitely small thing exploded outward, expanded into the universe we know. But space, more specifically distance, as we perceive it are illusions. That primordial particle didn't really explode outward." Alder brought his fist down on the mirror, startling Willa as it shattered. "It simply shattered into an infinite number of pieces. The universe is still as small as it ever was and everyone and everything in it are the shards."

"And the mark?" Willa prompted.

"Not the mark, the Mark," Alder corrected as if his emphasis could make Willa see the capital letter.

Willa frowned. "I don't understand."

Holly took over. "It's a genetic marker in your blood. You already know that many of the early hominids that naturally evolved on Earth were genetically altered hundreds of thousand of years ago by a space-faring race called the Anu who, by adding their own genes to the mix, created Homo Sapiens... humans," Holly began, "and, of course, there's the creation of our various Hybrid races from human and Whelk DNA, who used to be known as the Greys. When Hybrids began to mingle with humans after The Landing, it added even more genetic markers to the mix. What you may not know is that, despite the addition, dilution and mix of genes, a very small percentage of Earth's population still possesses an original, nearly unaltered gene from the Anu race. Alder is saying that you're one of them, Willa."

"That's why I saw the shards on my first try?"

"Exactly," said Alder. "I dare say you'd make a formidable Sage."

"Let's not get ahead of ourselves," Selene reminded him with authority. "She's not even a Cryptic yet."

"Yes, of course, Selene," Holly answered respectfully. "I'll see to it she continues her training."

Encantado's shapeshifting skin reflected his various moods as he absorbed the exchange. "But what of this invasion she saw? What are we to do about that?" He turned his black eyes on Willa. She felt her skin crawl and instantly understood what Poppy meant when she said Shapeshifters gave her the creeps. "You need to learn more. When will it happen and how?"

"She needs to rest before imbibing more Divinorum," Holly interjected. "You know the rules."

Encantado kept his brooding eyes on Willa as though she might disappear any moment. "It seems some rules are made to be broken."

"I suggest we adjourn for now and meet again when we have more information," Holly said.

The others nodded their agreement, Encantado more curtly than the rest and, except for Alder, rose and departed without another word. Selene, the last to leave, gave Willa an enigmatic glance, then stepped out into the night.

"If you don't mind," Alder said to Holly, "I'd like to help with Willa's training."

Argus grumbled deep in his throat.

"With your permission, of course, Argus," Alder quickly added.

Argus's growl softened to a grudging grunt of acceptance.

*

Kale woke from the deepest sleep he'd had since his capture. He looked around at the dank walls and rusty iron door of the cubicle that contained the simple cot on which he had slept and, for a frightening moment, it seemed as though he was back in his cell and that his rescue was just a dream. Then he remembered the arduous journey through dozens of non-descript apartments like this one, all linked together by a maze of secret tunnels and trap doors built over the years by Dennik's underground resistance.

The door creaked open and Alarra entered with a tray of broth and cooked vegetables. Kale sat up on the edge of the cot.

"Oh good, you're awake," she said with a smile and set the tray on a simple side table. "You need to build up your strength. We won't be able to stay here for long."

"I'm sorry," Kale said, "did we meet?"

"We did, but you were nearly comatose after my husband marched you through three miles of tunnels. I'm Alarra."

"Kale Ashgrove. Thank you both for getting me out of there."

Alarra's mouth twitched with the briefest of smiles.

"What?" Kale said, wondering what the joke was.

"It's nothing. I don't mean to sound unfeeling, but your rescue was necessary to our cause. Please eat," she said, handing him the broth.

Kale slowly sipped and felt better almost immediately. "What is this?"

"It's made from Oola, a root that still grows in remote locations on Xos. Its restorative powers are legendary."

"Xos? That's the name of your world?"

Alarra nodded, though a deep sadness clouded her eyes. "It hasn't been our world for a long time."

Kale took a few more sips, tried one of the vegetables and found it plain but delicious. "I have a lot of questions."

"As do we," Alarra said. "Shall we take turns?"

"Where are we?" Kale began.

"In the abandoned workers' cell blocks a few miles from the Archon's Citadel, where you were held captive. Where are you from? I don't recognize your race."

"My world's called Earth, over a thousand light years from the Orion sector," Kale offered.

"Orion? That's what you call the Empire?"

"My people know nothing of your Empire. In fact, that's something I've been wondering ever since I had the misfortune to meet your Archon and his charming minions. How is it you speak my language?"

"I was about to ask you the same thing," Alarra said. "Are you wearing some kind of translator?"

"No. You?"

Alarra shook her head. "I guess that will have to remain a mystery for now. Can you tell me what the Archon's interrogators learned from you?"

"Just about everything, I'm afraid. Our technology, the location of Earth. They've probably disassembled my ship by now. I assume they extracted information from my crew as well."

"How many?" Alarra asked, concerned.

"Twenty five."

"That's a lot of intel," Alarra said.

Kale locked his grey eyes on her. "They're people, not intel."

"I'm sorry, of course, I didn't mean... it's just that we've been fighting the Overlords for generations. Anything that might give them a greater edge could mean the annihilation of the League. Of my family and friends."

"What about my crew?" Kale said. "We need to go back and rescue them."

"We can't risk it. They've doubled the guards by now and they'll still be searching for us."

Kale put the empty bowl back on the tray. "I understand."

Alarra nodded and stood. "Our transport will arrive just before daybreak. Please rest until then." Alarra closed the rusty door behind her. Kale lay back down on the cot and, as he drifted off to sleep, his thoughts turned to deep concern for Rowan, Thorn and the fate of Earth.

CHAPTER SIX

ARCHON

"Disobedience is death."

The First Decree of Xos-Asura
Supreme Archon of the Empire

*

XOS-ASURA SAT IN the heavy iron chair in the execution chamber and watched with detachment as the Executioner and his assistants, dressed in traditional red robes, strapped three prison guards face upward onto metal planks cantilevered out from a thick, steel scaffold. There was a hole in each plank, directly between each guard's shoulder blades, that matched the position of three tapered steel spikes that jutted from the scaffold's lower crossbeam.

Two of the three guards stoically accepted their punishment while the third struggled against his restraints. "Great Xos-Asura. Spare my life so that I may continue to serve!"

"But you've failed to serve me, Gant," the Archon said without emotion, "and second chances are costly." He glanced at the other two guards. "Either of you have any secrets to sell?"

Given an unexpected chance at life, the guard on the far plank desperately searched his memory. "The Captain of the Guard skims from our pay!"

Xos-Asura allowed a faint smile to crack his cadaverous face. "Of course he does. He's the captain." The Archon gave a subtle nod to the executioner. He pulled a lever and the guard's plank swung downward. The steel spike punched through the guard's spine and heart, killing him instantly. His blood ran into a gutter under the scaffold and coursed through a pipe that led to the processing chamber.

The Archon's gaze shifted to the guard on the center plank. "Anything you'd like to share?"

"My Lord, it wasn't my fault the prisoner escaped!"

"No?" Xos-Asura responded with raised eyebrows. "Should I blame the guards who are already dead?"

"No, my Lord, I simply meant…"

The Archon flicked his hand at the Executioner and the center guard fell to his death with a deafening clang of steel on steel, adding his blood to the gore below.

"And you, Gant," the Archon said, sounding bored, "what do you have to say?"

"A member of the League is loyal to me, my Lord," Gant said quickly.

The Archon's interest was piqued. "Why haven't you told me this before?"

"I feared this moment might come," the guard admitted.

The Archon nodded. Now here was someone useful. "You're more clever than I thought." At a gesture from the Archon, the Executioner freed Gant from his bonds. The guard rushed down the stairs and dropped to one knee before Xos-Asura, his head bowed.

"Thank you, my Lord. You are most merciful."

"I spare your life and you repay me with an insult?"

Gant groveled at the Archon's feet. "No, my Lord! I meant no disrespect! Mercy is weakness. Forgive me!"

"Who's your spy in the Resistance?"

"My brother."

The Archon frowned. "Wasn't he banished to the Outlands by Overlord Vorga?"

"Part of Vorga's plan to lure the League into recruiting him, my Lord."

The Archon's eyes flashed in anger and Gant feared he might wind up back on the plank for delivering the unwelcome news that one of the Overlords had not informed Xos-Asura of his plan.

"I shall have a talk with Vorga," the Archon promised. "Perhaps we'll have a third execution after all."

"Yes, my Lord," Gant exhaled, relieved. Gant knew if one of the Overlords appeared more cunning than the Archon, the other Overlords might shift their loyalty and foment a coup. The Archon's reaction was exactly what he'd hoped it would be. This tidbit of information was the least of the secrets Gant had collected about several other Overlords over the years. He planned to dole them out slowly and make himself indispensible to the Archon. Only when Xos-Asura was convinced of his undying fealty would Gant make his move to assassinate the Archon and become absolute ruler of the Empire.

*

"Father's alive?" Thorn cried.

Thorn and Rowan sat around a table in the Nest with Willa, Holly, Lily and Willa's father, River Hillicrissing, a gentle man with a thoughtful face and the cinnamon hair he had bequeathed to Willa. Several bowls held the remnants of their evening meal. The shock of Willa's news slowly gave way to hope as Willa told them of her vision.

"He was alive in the vision, but he was also being tortured," Willa reluctantly admitted, hating herself for crushing the boys' newborn hopes. "I'll take the Divinorum again soon, see if I can learn more," she added quickly, trying to lessen the sting.

"We've got to mount a rescue!" Rowan insisted.

"We don't know where Kale is," River reminded him. "Even if we did, we have no idea what we'd be up against. From Willa's description, Kale's captors are clearly aggressive, perhaps even war-like. They may have weapons we have no defense against."

"We've got to do something!" Thorn pleaded.

"We will," Holly assured him, "but we need more information. I've asked the Quorum for help. Those who are willing will take the Divinorum. We'll find out everything we can and inform the Council and the Alliance."

"But that could take days, weeks," Thorn protested. "By then, it could be too late!"

Willa rested her hand on Thorn's. "I swear on my soul I'll keep searching as long as it takes."

Thorn squeezed her hand and nodded. Rowan was equally frustrated but realized there was nothing else they could do. He nodded his consent and rose from the table. "I'll brief my First Contact instructors at the training center on Andromeda Spaceport. Maybe this can be resolved diplomatically."

"Good idea," River said. "The people holding Kale might be willing to trade him back to us."

"I wish I could believe that," Willa said, "but I got a very strong impression that they simply take what they want and kill anyone who stands in their way." She glanced at Thorn's stricken expression and immediately regretted her statement. "I'm sorry."

Rowan clasped Thorn's shoulder. "Father's been in some tough situations. He's always managed to survive. We'll get him back, one way or another." He turned to Willa. "Thank you, Willa. You've given us hope."

Thorn rose and gave Willa a huge hug. She was a tad uncomfortable with her parents and Holly watching, but she didn't let go until Thorn did. He joined his brother and they walked through the iris and down the branch.

Willa turned to Holly. "How soon can I take the Divinorum again?"

"The Quorum will gather at the lodge tomorrow morning. Until then, I suggest you get a lot of rest." Holly rose and gave Willa's parents a slight but respectful bow of her head. "Thank you for your hospitality and for entrusting your daughter to my care. She has a special talent."

Willa blushed as her parents beamed at her. "For more than mischief, I hope," Lily said with a wink.

Holly smiled and placed a gentle hand on Willa's shoulder as she passed. "I'll expect you at the Lodge after morning meal. Good night." The iris closed behind her as she meandered down the oak branch.

"I doubt I'll sleep a tick," Willa said.

"I remember you always fell fast asleep when I read you bedtime stories," her father teased.

"Father, I'm thirteen."

"Right. Too old for stories then," River said as he stood and removed the bowls from the table. "She grows like a weed," he said to Lily in jest.

Willa feigned exasperation. "Maybe if I get to choose the story..."

"Of course," River conceded.

Willa pondered her choices. She glanced up at him, a crooked smile on her elfin face.

"What mischief are you dreaming up in that foxy little head, Pooka?" said Lily.

"There's one story you would never tell me because I was too young," Willa said to her father.

River's playful smile faded. He looked into his daughter's hopeful eyes and nodded.

"River, are you sure?" Lily said.

"It's time she was told," he said. "After all, she's thirteen."

CHAPTER SEVEN

THE BANSHEE OF
MARROWBONE BRIDGE

"Banshees existed in human literature long before Hybrids came to this world. But little is known about them beyond their function as harbingers of death. In this context, they are similar to other Elemental beings, such as the one known as Mothman, who appears to be attracted to imminent death and disaster like a moth to a flame. This analogy may be more apt than first realized, as these entities inhabit a realm between life and death and may find themselves pulled, by ethereal energy currents, to the impending 'tunnel of light' so often reported by those who've had near-death experiences."

Excerpt from "The Quintessential Elemental"
by Nightshade the Nocturnal

*

Three hundred years ago or so, a Sage named Belladonna Bloodroot lived in a moss-encrusted stone cottage at the edge of a Yew tree grove near the southern gate of Marrowbone Bridge. She was a mere slip of a woman with long, silver hair and indigo eyes set in a delicate, pale face. Belladonna frequently flitted to and fro in her gossamer robe among the denizens of Port Dublin as she went about her business, often stopping to chat with the flowers in a window box or a rosemary sprig in someone's garden.

She was known far and wide for her mastery of herbal potions and her vast knowledge of the flora on Earth. There wasn't a flower, shrub, tree or growing plant she couldn't talk to or learn something from and she would often spend her days holding court with Elemental beings, such as Pookas, Sylphs and Sprites in a fairy ring of mushrooms deep in the heart of the forest. In point of fact, it was those very Elementals who taught her how to cultivate the special strain of Divinorum used by Cryptics, Nocturnals and Shapeshifters that aided them on the path toward becoming full-fledged Sages.

Belladonna's fellow Dubliners rarely spoke to her unless they needed a cure for some ailment and most gave her no more thought than they would a warm breeze or a gentle summer rain, for who could understand the mysterious ways of a Sage except another of her kind?

This suited Belladonna just fine since she detested idle chatter. Besides, in her opinion, plants had much more interesting things to say than people, such as an ancient oak that had recently hinted there was yet another level of mastery beyond Sage. This intrigued Belladonna and occupied her thoughts of late. After all, a Sage could appear in any form, like a Shapeshifter, but could also manifest objects seemingly out of thin air as well as shift the very fabric of space and time. What, she wondered, could lie beyond that?

It struck Belladonna one day while in the middle of a conversation with a magnificent Cedar in an old cemetery that, while she could shape the material world to her thoughts, the realm of spirit was beyond her reach. Of course, stories of interactions with all manner of spirits had been told for thousands of years on Earth, but those encounters always seemed one-sided, controlled by the incorporeal rather than by the living. Perhaps there was a way to bridge the two dimensions, Belladonna mused, to walk in both worlds while still alive.

The old Cedar, having lived its entire life in the graveyard, was keenly aware of the fates and fortunes of spirits and it cautioned Belladonna against delving too deeply into the afterlife, since even the most powerful Sage was fragile as wheat to the scythe of the Grim Reaper.

But the notion caught fire in Belladonna's mind and she couldn't put it out. She spent the next three years consuming every morsel of information she could from the Cedars, Oaks, Yews, other Sages and all manner of Elementals with any connection to the spirit world.

Belladonna often toiled without sleep for days as she experimented with endless combinations of mushrooms, herbs, oils, flowers and natural essences until, with the help of a fellow Sage named Rusalka, she finally concocted a special draft of Divinorum she believed would be the doorway to the Aetheric Plane between the realms of the living and the dead.

But, obsessed as she was, Belladonna never sensed that Rusalka was, in fact, not a Sage, but a trickster Pooka in disguise. Pookas, while often helpful, are also mischievous creatures. Rusalka resented that Belladonna was attempting to cross a threshold that could give her power over the Elemental world so he convinced the Sage that her own namesake, the Belladonna plant, also known as Deadly Nightshade, was an essential ingredient for her potion. The Pooka assured her that, in minute quantities, it would be safe.

Belladonna drank the Divinorum as she had done so many times before, but instead of drifting into the dreamlike altered state that called forth visions, or transmuting into a higher state of being, slivers of pain shot through her skull as though some invisible entity had stabbed red-hot needles into her brain.

Belladonna writhed in agony on her cottage floor as violent spasms wracked her slender body from head to toe. Her lungs heaved, her heart threatened to explode and her stomach felt like it was being eaten alive by ravenous insects. Was she transforming into the mystical Wraith she sought to become? Or had she made an error and stupidly poisoned herself? She let out a high-pitched wail that carried through the chill night air and sent shivers down the spines of all who heard it.

Then, as quickly as it had started, the pain stopped. Belladonna laid on the floor, drained of life, her mind tumbling through a fog of confusion. Did it work? She was numb all over. She couldn't feel her hands or her legs, although they moved at her command.

She slowly rose off the floor, but not because she stood up. Bella donna was shocked to find herself halfway between the floor and ceiling, a transparent, ghostly figure in diaphanous robes that undulated in the breeze like her long, silvery hair as though she was suspended in invisible liquid.

Belladonna caught her reflection in a polished copper cauldron hanging from a hook over the kitchen chopping block. She let out a pitiful wail as she beheld the gaunt face and glowing eyes that marked her as a Banshee, a spectral being doomed to wander the Earth, an omen of impending death to all who would encounter her. She would forever be attracted like a moth to the brilliant, swirling tunnel of light that transported the newly deceased to the afterlife, yet be barred from entering the higher spiritual realms herself.

Belladonna desperately called upon her abilities as a Sage, a Shape-shifter, a Nocturnal and even as a Cryptic to undo the hideous transformation, but the powers it had taken a lifetime to learn had abandoned her. She was, quite literally, a ghost of her former self.

She wailed grievously, a forlorn keening that resonated off the walls of her stone cottage, once a place of refuge that would now and forever serve as her crypt. Belladonna floated out a window, weightless as a fine mist. She drifted over the Yew grove, then above the path that snaked toward Marrowbone Bridge.

At this time of night, most of the locals were enjoying midnight meal or were fast asleep. Belladonna's soft keening drifted in through open windows as she passed by, head cast down in abject misery. Several people peered outside, caught sight of the wailing specter, and quickly closed their shutters and locked their doors.

A black cat crossed the bridge. As soon as it spied the Banshee, it hissed and hugged the far railing until Belladonna drifted past, oblivious to the animal's fear.

As Belladonna approached the north end of the bridge, she sensed a familiar presence and raised her luminous eyes. Rusalka, still disguised as a fellow Sage, stood on the path beyond the bridge. He transformed into his more common form, that of a red-eyed hare, his long rabbit ears swept back like horns. He rose on his haunches to his four-foot height and flashed a wicked, buck-toothed smile.

Belladonna flew into a rage at the sight of the impudent Elemental. She let out a frightful wail and rushed at him headlong, her skeletal hands outstretched. But as she reached the end of the bridge, an unseen force held her back. She strained against the invisible barrier, yet Rusalka remained mere inches beyond her grasp.

The Pooka laughed at Belladonna's frustrated fury. She screamed at him, demanded to know why he had done this to her. Rusalka threw back a quote from Shakespeare, a favorite scribe of Elementals since the Bard so often recounted tales of their kind in his poems and plays:

"In a wilderness where are no laws, to the rough beast that knows no gentle right, nor aught obeys but his foul appetite."

Belladonna seethed at the jape, an admonition that she had intruded on a realm that wasn't hers and paid the price for her arrogance. The Pooka compounded her woes by declaring that the altered Divinorum would confine her spirit to the terrain within a mile of her cottage, which meant she could never venture across Marrowbone Bridge to the lands of the north where Rusalka and his kind dwelled.

Belladonna raged and wailed at her fate and, from that day on, swore vengeance upon Rusalka and all his kind. The Pooka turned and, with a flick of his furry tail, leapt off into the night.

Faster than thought, the Banshee returned to her cottage and began searching through her voluminous collection of esoteric lore for an antidote to the Pooka's spell but after many months of scrutinizing every passage, every line, every recipe in her storehouse of potions, her search proved fruitless.

Belladonna sulked and sobbed, alone in her cottage, and scared away all who came to seek her aid. The townspeople finally began to avoid the Yew forest and, as months turned to years, the Banshee's cottage was overgrown with vines and moss and the Yew tree next to the dwelling grew larger and larger, until it split the rocks of the north wall asunder.

Now and then, over the course of many years, Belladonna would feel an overwhelming pull and she'd be forced to leave her moss-covered crypt to haunt the south end of Marrowbone Bridge.

As befit the Banshee's plight, her wails would herald an impending death in the village, either from sickness, accident or old age, for three days before the death actually occurred. Thus, the villagers were never welcoming of her presence and were always relieved when Belladonna would return to her forest cloister and cease her heartbreaking dirge.

Legends of Banshees have always assumed they keen for the dying and the dead but in truth, being trapped forever between two worlds, it is for themselves that they wail.

CHAPTER EIGHT

NOCTURNAL

"Dusk,

stretches forth fingers of darkness

over the landscape of the living

as light dims and dies, heralding the night

that cocoons all in its velvet embrace.

The substance of shadows,

thick with portent,

unfathomable,

until made tactile by time.

Breath of rarified air

from the in-between realm,

auguring omens

that ring true in epitaphs

carved in cold, hard stone,

forever freezing lives

between brackets of measured time
and fading memories."

From "Songs of the Night"
by Nightshade the Nocturnal

*

WILLA ROCKED SIDE to side in her hammock as her father finished Belladonna's tale. "She still haunts the bridge after three hundred years?"

"So the story goes," River said, "though the last time anyone saw her was ten years ago when Laurel Larkspur died."

"I saw her daughters, Rose and Lilac, at the Lodge. They seem... unusual."

Sadness whispered in River's reply. "They've been through a lot."

"How did their mother die?"

River looked through Willa as the unpleasant memory bubbled up within him.

"Father?"

He shook his head and stood. "I think one unhappy ending is enough for tonight."

"You were worried I might be scared if you told me Belladonna's story when I was younger."

He nodded. "I didn't want to deter you from your dream of becoming a Sage, but you're old enough now to understand the risks."

"How many Sages have gone on to become Wraiths?"

"No one knows," River said, "Wraiths are elusive beings at the best of times."

Willa pondered the story as River tapped the Luminaria to dim the light. He kissed her on the forehead. "Get some sleep, my brave girl. You've got a big day tomorrow."

"Father, what if I can't get more information? What if it was just a fluke? What if I can't do anything to save Thorn's father?"

"Willa, Willa," River said, "you'll do just fine. You heard what Holly said about your bloodline, our bloodline. You have a special gift."

"I don't feel special."

River ruffled her hair. "Your mother and I knew you were special the day you were born."

"Parents always say that to their kids."

"That's because it's always true," River said. "Good night, Pooka."

"Father?"

River turned back.

"If the Anu genes are in our family bloodline, don't you or Mother also have special abilities?"

River smiled. "Grandmother Mimzy had a few, but sometimes, it skips a generation," River descended the moving stairway and left Willa to her thoughts.

She tapped the wall twice to open her window and stared out at the silver crescent moon through the canopy of oak leaves.

An acorn flew through the window and bounced across the floor, rudely interrupting her reverie. She peered down at Thorn far below. He gestured for her to join him. Willa widened her window, stepped through, and hopped from branch to branch until she reached the base of the tree. Thorn and Willa hugged and, holding hands, hurried off through the grove.

They stopped among the trees a few hundred yards away with the Nest still in view, shimmering in the moonlight.

"I couldn't sleep," Thorn said. "I have to know, did you tell me everything you saw about my father?"

"I think I told you more than I should have."

Thorn sat on a large, flat boulder. Willa joined him.

"Part of me wishes you hadn't said anything until we were sure we could rescue him," Thorn said, his eyes welling. "In some ways, it was easier just believing he was dead."

Willa bit her lip, afraid to say anything for fear of making him feel worse. She fought back her own tears and held his hand. "We'll bring your father home."

A silky voice slipped between them like a blade. "Ah, the eternal optimism of youth."

Willa and Thorn jumped to their feet as Selene stepped from the shadow of an oak into the pale moonlight.

"Doyenne Nymphaea," Willa blurted. "We didn't hear you coming."

"Nocturnals are synonymous with stealth, dear girl, or didn't the shards show you that?"

Thorn wanted to come to Willa's defense, but his mouth was dry as dust.

Willa took up the charge. "What are you doing here? I didn't expect to see you until morning."

Selene pierced Willa with her coal-black eyes. "I find you curious."

Willa felt the same skin-crawling sensation as she had when Encantado turned his own obsidian orbs on her. She offered Selene a respectful bow of her head. "I'm honored to warrant the attention of a Nocturnal."

"At least you have proper manners," Selene huffed, "which is more than I can say for your tongue-tied friend here."

"I apologize," Thorn said, "I've never met a member of the Quorum before."

"And why should you have?" Selene smirked. "We rarely have business with mundanes. No offense."

"None taken," Thorn lied. He wondered if Selene could sense his growing dislike of her. "I was going to start the training—"

"Don't bother," Selene interrupted. "I can sense you're not cut out for it." Selene ignored Thorn's rising anger and returned her gaze to Willa. "To answer your question, I'm here to ask a favor."

"A favor you didn't want to ask in front of the Quorum," said Willa.

Selene's icy composure cracked ever so slightly, then froze over again. "Let's let this be our little secret, shall we, dear girl?"

"I'm honored to be taken into your confidence," Willa said with another bow of her head.

Though she would never admit it out loud, Selene was impressed by Willa's verbal sparring. This was no mere child. Perhaps Holly was right. There was something special about this apprentice.

"When you take the Divinorum tomorrow, if you see the shards again, I would ask that you look for something in particular."

Thorn stepped closer to Selene. "Willa needs to look for my father," he said, his voice a notch higher than he would have liked.

Selene regarded him like she would an annoying insect. "So, your father gives you the courage you lack on your own."

"It's okay," Willa said. "I can do both."

Selene's eyes narrowed. "Such confidence. Or is it merely bravado?"

"I mean, I'll do my best," Willa said, humbled.

"I suppose that's all I can ask," Selene said. "If you can manage it, look for a shard that reflects a ghostly presence with long white hair, a mournful wail and a face etched by unimaginable misery."

Willa couldn't hide her surprise. "You're talking about the Banshee of Marrowbone Bridge."

"You know the story. Excellent."

Thorn rested a wary hand on Willa's shoulder. "Willa, Banshees aren't to be trifled with."

Selene's eyes flickered to Thorn, dark as a threatening storm. "Stay out of this, boy."

"If I may ask, Doyenne," Willa said, pulling Selene's attention back to her, "exactly what is it you wish me to see?"

"The formula for the potion that makes one into a Wraith," Selene said softly, aware that the trees might overhear.

Willa was horrified. "But it turned Belladonna into a Banshee."

"Only because that foul Pooka tricked her. Without the Nightshade, the potion might have worked, but she never wrote the formula down. Will you do this for me?"

"Forgive me, Doyenne, but I don't understand. If you continue along the path, won't you eventually acquire the knowledge yourself?"

Selene fought the urge to slap the impertinent girl. "That will take years. If your vision is true, we can't afford to wait. Belladonna's potion will hasten the process."

Willa caught the desperation in Selene's tone. "How many times have you tried to recreate the formula?"

Selene seethed in silence at Willa's brazen assessment. She clenched her teeth and forced herself to remain calm. "Enough to know it's pointless without more information. Perhaps your connection to the Anu will give you an edge."

"So, I'm your last resort." Willa looked deep into Selene's ebony eyes. Her whole body shivered as a long-guarded secret unfolded within Willa's newly acquired insight. The glowing branches of Belladonna's family tree traced a path in her mind that led directly to Selene and, before she could stop herself, she blurted it out.

"You're Belladonna Bloodroot's great-granddaughter!"

The air around Selene grew as cold as her stare. "Well, aren't you the clever girl. I'll thank you to keep that to yourself."

"Why?" Thorn pressed, reveling in Willa's leverage over Selene.

With some effort, Selene ignored Thorn and continued to address Willa as though she had asked the question. "When Belladonna became a Banshee, my grandmother erased all traces of our family's connection to her so it wouldn't impact Mother's chances of becoming a Cryptic. However, Mother felt I should know the truth as a way of preparing me for the risks of following in her footsteps."

"Yet you're asking me to find the formula instead of asking Belladonna," Willa said.

"She won't tell me for fear I'll become a Banshee like her."

"Then your great-grandmother's wiser than you are," Thorn said.

Selene locked on Thorn like a shark that smells blood. "Keep that up and you'll find yourself on the wrong end of a blade!" she snapped.

"Doyenne!" Willa said, shocked at Selene's venom.

Thorn went white as a sheet. "Are you threatening me?"

"It's not a threat," Selene said. "It's a warning." She turned her iron gaze back to Willa. "Find that formula."

"And if I do?" Willa said, worried she might be selling her soul to the Devil.

"Then I won't block your entrance into the training."

"Holly's my mentor. That's not your decision!"

"Isn't it?" Selene said through an oily smile. "Acceptance into the Mastery requires the Quorum's unanimous approval. One dissenting vote…" Selene let the rest hang in the air. She turned and oozed her way back through the forest.

Thorn took Willa's hand. "Holly wouldn't let her do that, right?"

Willa kept her eyes on the trees, nervous that Selene might reappear at any moment. A glint of moonlight betrayed a pair of eyes staring at her from the shadows.

The red fox that had watched her at Three Rock Mountain sat among the roots of a large Yew tree. It slipped away into the forest but left Willa with the feeling that the fox was more than it appeared to be.

Thorn stepped in front of her to break her trance. "Willa?"

Her eyes found his. Her gentle smile of assurance masked the doubts spinning in her mind. "I need to get home before Mother and Father know I'm gone."

Thorn nodded and though they walked through the moonlit forest hand in hand, each was lost in their own troubled thoughts.

*

Kale stood under the steaming spray of a shower, eyes closed, hoping the hot water would wash away the memory of his grueling ordeal at the hands of the Archon's interrogators.

As the water stung his wounds, he was assaulted by the memories of his cruel interrogators as they beat the secrets from him.

He shook off the grisly visions of their leering faces, stepped out and dried himself. He looked in the mirror and took stock of the scars they'd inflicted on him. Kale knew he could never wash those away.

He entered the main room of the small apartment deep within the League's moon base. He dressed in the plain black tunic, pants and boots his rescuers had provided. A shy knock drew him to the door.

Brim stood in the hall. "Mother wanted me to let you know the Council will meet at midday."

Kale gestured for Brim to enter. "Thank you. You must be Alarra's son."

"I'm Brim."

"Kale Ashgrove."

Brim stifled a laugh and blushed in mild embarrassment. "I'm sorry. I see why my mother didn't mention your name to me."

Kale stared at Brim, waiting for an explanation.

Brim collected himself. "It's just that, on my world, a kale is a long pole used in combat. But it's also slang for, um, you know, a man's, um..."

"I get the idea," Kale said, remembering Alarra's smile when he introduced himself.

"I'd be happy to escort you to the Council chamber. Mother also wanted to know if you're comfortable with the quarters," Brim said, eager to please.

"Yes, you've all been more than kind," Kale assured him. "I owe your family my life."

"Do you have a family?" Brim said.

Kale nodded. "Two boys about your age. Their names are Rowan, he's the oldest, and Thorn."

"I just had my sixteenth naming day," Brim said with more than a hint of pride.

"Naming day?"

"The day parents name their children, one orbit after they're born. You don't have naming day?"

"We name our children the day they're born. Sometimes before that." He shifted his weight in the chair, trying to find a more comfortable position. Despite Alarra's herbal broth, it would be a while before his bruises fully healed. "Your mother said you've never left this moon."

Brim nodded. "As you saw, Xos isn't the best place to grow up."

"I can't imagine what it must be like for you in the resistance, never knowing if your mother or father will..." Kale bit his tongue, hoping he hadn't gone too far.

Brim was very aware that death was the League's constant companion and took no offense. "Your sons must be very worried about you," he said in empathy.

Kale's throat tightened. "They probably think I'm dead."

"Mother and Father will do everything in their power to get you home. Maybe Rowan, Thorn and I could become friends."

"I'd like that. You remind me of them."

Brim smiled at the compliment. A soft gong sounded three times in the hall.

"The Council's ready for you."

Kale stood. "Lead the way."

*

Willa sat in the Celtic circle in the Lodge, ringed by every member of the Quorum. As usual, Argus stood off to one side and kept a watchful eye on the proceedings.

Holly handed Willa the cup of Divinorum. Willa glanced at the faces that surrounded her: Holly's reassuring smile, Alder's encouraging nod, Selene's clandestine gaze, Encantado's determined scowl and, as before, the Larkspur twins' million-mile stare. Willa inhaled and drank the potent draft.

Reality shifted in a heartbeat and Willa was once again standing on the infinite plane within her mind. The crystal sphere rumbled toward her from the horizon, but this time, she stood her ground. The moon-sized orb rolled over Willa and engulfed her in its liquid embrace. Willa floated to the heart of the sphere, whereupon it froze and fractured with the ear-splitting sound of a million mirrors breaking.

Willa's ghostly doppelganger floated through the shifting shards, her eyes darting to each reflected image, searching for any sign of Kale or the secret to Belladonna's potion.

Images of her mother and father, Thorn, Poppy, Holly, Alder and Selene flickered in and out, mixed with visions of ominous Orion attack ships filling the sky over Port Dublin. Her life unfolded again in a staccato sequence of memories and even alternate realities, showing several versions of Willa making different choices with different outcomes than those in her present life.

Willa watched scenes of her parallel selves as they became Cryptics, Nocturnals, Shapeshifters, Sages and even Wraiths as well as things she never considered: A teacher, a spaceship captain and a mother with children of her own.

She slowly discovered that if she concentrated on various timelines, she could summon groups of shards that presented more detailed images. They collected around her, immersing her in holographic tableaus as though she'd been transported to various points in space and time.

She witnessed Belladonna as a young woman in the throws of passion with a mysterious lover, a union that branched the family tree and ultimately sprouted Selene. Willa felt every tender touch and kiss on her own body as though enthralled in the tryst herself, and blushed with embarrassment as she spied on the intimate exchange.

She shifted her focus and watched as an older Belladonna experimented with all manner of herbs and tinctures in her search for the Wraith potion. She tried to commit each ingredient to memory until Belladonna accidentally knocked a bottle off her table. It smashed on the stone cottage floor and broke the vision.

The shards tumbled and reformed into an image of Kale sitting at a large conference table with several dark-skinned strangers inside a large circular chamber carved from black rock.

Willa's attention locked on a glowing star chart on the tabletop that traced a route from the League's dark moon through the swirling Maelstrom to Earth's solar system.

The shards scattered again, but before she could bring Kale's image back into focus, the reflections coalesced into a vision of Thorn, lying somewhere on a forest floor, dying from a bloody knife wound in his abdomen, just as Selene had warned.

Willa recoiled from the horrifying vision and spun around to find herself facing another group of shards that depicted her, several months older, lying in the dirt, with Xos-Asura standing over her bloody, broken body as the Quorum Lodge and Port Dublin burned to ashes.

"No!" Willa screamed as she snapped from the disturbing dream, all eyes in the room still upon her. Tears flooded her cheeks. Mortified, she quickly wiped them away.

"Are you okay, Willa? Holly said gently.

Willa nodded and composed herself.

"What did you see?" Alder prompted.

"I… think Kale's been rescued," Willa announced to the relief of the Quorum.

"By whom?" Selene pressed.

"I don't know. There was some kind of gathering. They were trying to find a way back, to bring him home, but…" Willa's brow furrowed in confusion as she tried to divine the meaning of her vision.

"But what?" Holly gently urged.

"I think that if he returns, the invasion feels more certain."

"When?" Encantado said.

"I'm not sure…"

"Dig deeper!" the Shapeshifter demanded. "There's always more information under the surface."

"I don't know how!" Willa protested.

"Focus on one memory," Encantado said. "It'll guide you further."

Willa's closed her eyes. Her memory flickered back to the vision of Port Dublin on fire. She tried to ignore the image of the Archon standing over her dying body and found that her mind could move around in the memory, shifting her point of view as though it was a holographic projection. She moved through the burning embers of the village until she came to the Quorum Lodge, half engulfed by flames.

Her vision passed through the crumbling walls into the Divinorum chamber. The twisted and broken dead bodies of the Quorum members were splayed out on the floor around the central circle. An Orion girl a little older than Willa, with grey skin and pale eyes, clad in black battle armor, stood dead center in the circle and stared down at the ring of corpses like a ravenous predator guarding fresh kills.

The girl's eyes jerked up and locked onto Willa as though she could see her. *"Who are you?"* An intense wave of dark malice emanated from the Orion with such intensity, Willa felt that if the encounter had been physical instead of merely in her vision, the girl's glare would have seared the flesh from her bones.

Willa snapped from her trance, her face a mask of terror. She collapsed into Holly's arms and burst into sobs.

Holly held her tight and rocked back and forth as though comforting an infant. "It's okay, it's okay, Little Fox, you're safe here."

"We need to know what she saw," Selene pressed.

"Leave her be," Holly said. "Give her time."

"We may not have much time!" Moshi barked. "Did you see their ships, their weapons?"

Holly glared ice daggers at the Shapeshifter. "I said leave her be!"

Rose and Lilac both rested their waifish hands on Willa's shoulder. She felt their sweet, soothing presence and was calmed by their touch.

Willa sat up, wiped at her tears. "Thank you. I'm okay. I... just need some time."

"That's fine," Holly said with finality. "We'll reconvene when you're good and ready. Besides, we'll want to deliver the good news to Thorn and Rowan that their father's alive and in good hands."

The Quorum members rose, said their goodbyes and left. Except for Alder.

Holly and Argus regarded the Sage as he peered at Willa in silence.

"Considering Willa's unique abilities, I believe she should advance to the next stage of The Passage," Alder said.

Argus gazed at Willa with his deep-set eyes and grunted in agreement. "Maybe Willa is seed."

"What are you saying, Argus?" Alder asked, puzzled.

"It's an ancient story among his people," Holly explained, not pleased that Argus brought it to Alder's attention.

"When world in need, there be a seed. By sacred deed, world is freed."

Alder looked at the Sasquatch. "So, you're saying Willa is this seed?"

Argus shrugged his huge shoulders. "Said maybe."

"Willa may be unique, but she still has a lot to learn. Perhaps you can join in her training in a month or two," Holly suggested.

"What do you think, Willa?" said Alder.

"With all due respect, Master Redwood, my mentor knows me best."

"Yes, yes, of course," Alder said, backing down. "I meant no disrespect."

Holly bowed her head. "Think nothing of it," she said, knowing he would think of nothing else.

Alder pressed on. "But perchance, with our combined guidance and training, we shall find Willa ready sooner than most."

"We shall see," Holly said. "Come, Willa, you need rest. Time to head home."

Willa bowed to Alder and Argus and followed Holly from the Lodge.

As they crossed Marrowbone Bridge on their way to the Shaddok, Willa gave a furtive glance toward the Yew forest that sequestered Belladonna's cottage deep within its heart.

"What did Selene ask you to do?" Holly said.

Willa was stricken. "What do you mean? Nothing."

"Willa Hillicrissing, you're as transparent to me as glass. I know you saw more in your vision than you're willing to say. And I sense urgency from Selene when she looks at you that's got nothing to do with the invasion. Her ambition blazes like a beacon. What does she want?"

"I promised I wouldn't tell," Willa said.

Holly sighed. "Then I suppose you'd best keep your promise. But if she puts you in harm's way, she'll have me to answer to, you ken my meaning?"

Willa nodded, surprised by Holly's ire, but grateful to have such a caring protector.

As they continued along the path, Willa looked back at the forest and, for a fleeting moment, she could have sworn Belladonna's glowing eyes peered out at them from the shadows between the trees.

CHAPTER NINE

RUSALKA

"Red Rabbit,
Red Rabbit,
where you inhabit,
up is down
and left is right,
dark by day
you shine at night.
Rabbit Red,
Rabbit Red,
by your song, we are led
forward and back
outside and in,
until we lose track
of where we've been."

Children's rhyme, circa 2250
Author unknown

*

WILLA WOKE UP in a cold sweat. The images of Xos-Asura and the mysterious grey girl had invaded her dreams and twisted them into nightmares.

She tapped her window open, hoping to feel a soothing breeze. As she gazed out at the moonlit forest, she could just barely make out Selene's silhouette between two Ash trees. Selene turned and disappeared into the shadows.

She left her hammock, touched a spot on her bathroom countertop. A bowl formed in the nano-glass counter and filled with water. Willa splashed her face until she was fully awake. An air duct appeared in the wall above the sink and gently blew her face dry.

Willa tip-toed to the spiral stairs, peered over the railing to see if her parents were still up. Darkness and silence told her they were fast asleep. Willa snuck back to the wall near her hammock, climbed down the tree and melted into the woods.

She reached the flat boulder where she and Thorn had talked and didn't have to wait long before Selene emerged from the shadow of a large oak.

"Did you see it?" Selene said without ceremony.

"Part of it," Willa said as she handed Selene a small nano-glass marble. "I'll have to see if I can get the rest later."

Selene stared at the marble like it was the key to life itself, closed her slender fingers around it and tucked it in a pocket. "Thank you," she grudgingly whispered as she slipped back into the shadows and vanished.

Willa remained on the rock and allowed the crisp night air to cool her fevered thoughts. She was about to head home when a strange, trilling voice that fluttered like a hummingbird's wings, issued from somewhere between the trees.

"You must not give her the formula!"

Willa looked around, wary and ready to run. "Who are you? Where are you?"

"Here, girl!"

Willa pivoted to face two glowing red eyes in the shadows about four

70

feet off the ground. Rusalka the Pooka, in his favorite shape as a giant hare, stepped into the wan moonlight, rabbit ears held high above his feral face. His fur was mottled black and grey with a white streak down the center of his twitching nose.

"Who are you?" Willa asked, still slightly on edge.

"My name's Rusalka," claimed the Pooka.

"Rusalka?" Willa blurted in astonishment.

"You know me, girl?" He cocked his furry head as though trying to remember where they might have met before.

"You're the one from the story."

"That lie's been following me for three hundred years. Just because you know the story doesn't mean you know me!" The Pooka said, his temper growing foul.

"I know what you did to Belladonna," Willa shot back.

"And what I'll do to your Nocturnal friend if you tell her the rest of the ingredients!"

"She's not my friend, but I won't let you do that to her!"

The Pooka laughed at Willa's misguided gallantry. "More like you're not her friend if you help her become a Wraith!"

"What do you mean?"

"Few can handle it. Fewer still survive the transformation. I did Belladonna a favor," Rusalka said, puffing out his chest.

Willa was incensed. "Turning her into a Banshee, trapping her forever between life and death! You call that a favor? The way I heard it, you were afraid she'd become more powerful than you!"

The Pooka leapt forward in anger. "Another lie!"

Willa backed into a tree, nervous.

The Pooka realized she was frightened, but he also sensed something else about her. Something different, though he couldn't quite put a paw on it. He collected his wits and sat on the edge of the boulder. "Sorry. Didn't mean to scare you. Come and sit."

Willa didn't budge.

"Really, it's okay, my bark is worse than my bite," Rusalka said, attempting to lighten the mood.

"You have pretty big teeth." Willa stayed still as a statue, afraid the

Pooka might cast a spell on her any second. Her heart pounded as Rusalka's red eyes remained fixed on her.

"I suppose it's my own fault that the story paints me in such an unflattering light," Rusalka said, his ears drooping.

Willa knew that Pookas were mercurial at the best of times and stayed near the tree, although part of her wondered if there was another side to Belladonna's story.

"There are other Wraiths," Willa said. "Why didn't you try to stop them?"

"I may be an Elemental, but I can't be everywhere at once," the Pooka said, sulking. "Besides, some find other ways to transform into Wraiths. No way to trick them. We stop some, but not all."

"Why do you care if a Sage lives or dies? What's it to you?"

Rusalka's ears drooped in resignation. "Okay, I might not have been completely honest. Not that becoming a Wraith isn't dangerous, but there's a more important reason to prevent it."

Willa crossed her arms, trying to appear nonchalant. "Do tell."

Rusalka sized her up. "You're a Peculiar Pearl aren't you?"

Willa held her ground and waited him out.

The Pooka plucked a weed from a crack in the boulder and stuck it between his teeth. He chewed on it thoughtfully.

"Before your Hybrid ancestors landed on Earth, the more rarified realms of nature, those just beyond most human senses, were the domains of the Elementals. Humans were either too focused or too dull-witted to perceive us except on rare occasions when conditions were just right."

Willa nodded her understanding. "Then the Hybrids came along."

"Your heightened senses and advanced technology proved to humanity that my people weren't just the ravings of drunken fools or the stuff of fairy tales. That was fine with us. We were happy to be acknowledged and included in the affairs of the physical world. But then, your kind started to evolve even further. You became Cryptics, Nocturnals, Shapeshifters, Sages, claiming powers and abilities once possessed only by Elementals. You became our equals, but some of your Sages weren't satisfied with that. They desired to master the realms of spirit, to possess abilities while alive that nature bestows only upon those who have gone beyond this plane of existence. The Elementals knew this could twist a soul into something neither dead or alive, but something dark, something that would tear a hole between the two realms and allow chaos to spill into each."

Rusalka became silent for a long time. Willa risked taking a few steps around to the side. "Are you okay?"

The Pooka shook off his fugue. "We did try to talk sense into some of those who tried, but they were determined. So we came up with a plan."

"To feed them false information when you could."

The Pooka nodded, not at all proud of the decision. "We felt we had no choice. By turning those Sages into Banshees, they acted as a kind of block, sealing the rift between the spirit and material worlds with their ectoplasmic bodies."

"But then they're powerless in either realm. They're just stuck in between."

"Yes," Rusalka admitted, "like a cork. Unplug them and all Hell might break loose. So you see, it's not just about protecting Elementals. The whole Earth is at stake."

Willa scrunched her brow in confusion. "There are a few Wraiths in the world, yet there's been no breach, none of the chaos you feared would happen."

"Don't be so sure. I didn't say it would suddenly be doomsday. The changes are subtle at first. A little nudge down a different path, a left turn instead of a right and over time, our world could find itself on a collision course with disaster."

Color drained from Willa's face as she remembered the terrifying vision of Port Dublin in flames.

Rusalka's red eyes shifted to her. "What's the matter?"

"I had a vision... but it can't be connected..."

"All things are connected, girl! Hasn't your mentor taught you that much?"

"Stop calling me 'girl'! My name is Willa!"

The Pooka jumped up on top of the boulder. "What is it you know? Tell me!"

"An alien race from one of the Orion systems is planning to attack Earth."

Rusalka was horrified. "What did I tell you? Disaster!"

"You're saying the existence of a few Wraiths altered our future?"

"Yes! No! They altered our present. This present will lead to that future."

"How do you know this wasn't always going to happen?" Willa said.

"I haven't time to explain now!" He turned and leapt back toward the woods.

"Wait!" Willa cried out. "Where are you going?"

"To tell the other Elementals, of course!"

"But, isn't there something we can do to change our path, to stop the attack?" Willa said, desperate to stop her horrifying vision.

"I don't know. I need to consult with my queen. She may have an answer."

And with that, Rusalka disappeared into the shadows.

Willa sat on the boulder, her mind sorting through everything the temperamental Pooka had said. She felt a chill despite the warm breeze that ruffled her hair. Willa headed home, a million questions buzzing in her head.

*

Kale ran his finger along the star chart projected on the tabletop within the League's Council chamber. Kara val At'n, Dennik, Alarra and Brim were present along with Gar and two other Council members about Dennik's age. One was a chestnut-hued woman named Jonna, her angled face framed by black hair in an ancient style that would've reminded a human of Cleopatra, and the other was a lean, wolfish man with a shaved head known simply as Koro.

"This is the route we took from Earth," Kale explained as a glowing line appeared in the wake of his finger. "We encountered the phenomenon you mentioned right about here." He planted his finger at the outer edge of the Xos solar system. A red dot marked the spot.

"It's a wonder any of you survived," Koro said. "The Maelstrom is dozens of light years across, the only passage in the skin of a kind of energy bubble that encloses the Empire and prevents it from spreading. Charting its borders, looking for another way out, cost our people twenty-one ships over time."

"We'll have to go through the Maelstrom if we're to get you safely back to Earth," Dennik said. "The bubble is impenetrable everywhere else."

Kale nodded. "Your son helped me with some calculations. Far as I can figure, a year on Xos is pretty much the same as on Earth, so your light year measurements are a match to mine. But this bubble... it's always existed?"

"We're not sure," said Koro. "We only became aware of it about three hundred years ago."

"It can't have always been there," Brim added tentatively.

Alarra turned to her son. "Why do you say that?"

"Well, I've been studying the different worlds in the Empire. The Overlords didn't originate on any of them so, if they came from somewhere else, the bubble couldn't have existed a thousand years ago when they arrived."

Dennik nodded and fixed Brim with a smile of pride.

Kale looked around the table. "And none of you know what this bubble is? Why it formed?"

They all shook their heads.

"We're just grateful it kept the Empire from enslaving more worlds," Kara added.

Gar fixed his eye on Kale. "Of course, now that you're here, the Empire can make it safely through the Maelstrom."

Kara's calm, commanding voice drew all eyes to her. "We need to refit our ships with the same technology."

"We're working with the specs he gave us," Gar interjected, "but we seem to be missing some information."

Kale nodded. "The navigational interface."

"The what?" Gar said with a puzzled frown.

"It's the only thing I was able to withhold from the Archon's interrogators," Kale said. "I'm hoping that, without that piece of information, his scientists won't be able to duplicate all our technology."

"They also interrogated your crew," Dennik pointed out.

"One of my jailers bragged that my pilot, Elowen, was dead." Kale said, sadly. "Only our pilots really know how the interface works."

"What's a navigational interface?" Gar pressed.

"Our pilots communicate with the ship mind to mind."

"I don't understand," Kara said. "How's that possible?"

Kale smiled. "Our ships are sentient."

*

Willa climbed back up the oak branches outside her window and slipped into her room. A Luminaria flared to life, painting Lily's face with golden light.

"Good evening, Pooka." She sat in a chair near Willa's hammock and waited patiently for Willa to explain herself.

Disoriented by her mother's unexpected presence, Willa glanced behind her, fearing Lily was referring to Rusalka, then realized Lily was only addressing her by her nickname. Willa's mind raced, weighing her options, searching for a plausible story. She quickly settled on saying she'd met Thorn in the woods, but Lily spoke first.

"Before you say a word, I think there's something you should know," Lily said, her tone even but serious. "Please sit down."

Willa sat on the edge of her hammock. She'd never seen her mother this somber before and was slightly unnerved by it.

Lily held her daughter's uncertain gaze. "We received word about an hour ago that Rowan and Thorn stole a ship from Andromeda Spaceport and were last seen charting a course for the Orion nebula."

Willa's head swam in a dizzying whirlpool of emotions that left her reeling. She stared at her mother, hoping this was a bad dream, wishing herself to wake up.

"Your father's gone after them, but once they engage the Q jump, there will be no way to track them," Lily said, knowing she was tearing Willa's heart out with every unwelcome word.

Willa finally found her tongue. "But I told them their father was safe!"

"It's a hard thing to trust the safety of a loved one to strangers."

"I should have seen this in the shards."

"Perhaps you were preoccupied," Lily said in a tone that hinted she already knew the truth.

"Holly spoke to you."

"She did indeed. You've been keeping strange company for a girl your age. What does the Nocturnal want with you?"

"I promised not to tell."

"That may work with Holly, but I'm your mother."

"A promise is a promise. You taught me that."

"A promise made to a shadow is just as empty. Out with it."

Willa crossed her arms. A sickness grew in her stomach as she glared at her mother in defiance for the first time in her young life.

"I see I also taught you my stubborn streak," Lily said. She rose from the chair. It retracted into the nano-glass floor. "Very well. I suggest you devote your full attention to kenning Thorn's and Rowan's whereabouts in the shards tomorrow, before it's too late." Lily turned and descended down the spiral stairs.

Willa flopped back onto her hammock, heartsick. Exhausted as she was, she knew she'd get no sleep tonight. The harrowing memory of her broken body under the Archon's titanium boot mixed with fearful visions of Thorn and Rowan being tortured like their father.

Willa had never felt so helpless. Her mind was lost in a dark maze of dire possibilities. The only thought that gave her a sliver of hope was that the next Divinorum vision might reveal a clear path to the light.

*

"Let me get this straight," Gar said, his knuckles resting on the council table top, "your ships can *think*?"

Kale nodded. "Not only that, the ship's navigational controls tap directly into the pilot's mind. Without that neural bond, it's impossible for anyone to fly our ships."

The council members exchanged glances. This was good news.

"The Archon's technicians will dissect your ship. They're bound to figure that out sooner or later," Kara said, bringing the mood down a notch.

"Possibly," Kale said, "but without my pilot's help, it will take a while."

Dennik looked at Gar, sharing the same thought. "How long to retrofit our ships with the tech you're able to duplicate?"

"A month, maybe sooner."

Gar frowned. "Month?"

Brim jumped in, eager to share what he'd learned from Kale about Earth. "The time it takes for Earth's moon to make one orbit. About one-fifth of the time it takes this moon to orbit the rogue planet."

Gar nodded his understanding. "Good. Let's get started."

Kale looked to Dennik. "I thought you'd take me back to Earth first."

Gar wasn't pleased. "The Archon has a legion of techs. They'll adapt their ships faster than we can."

Kale thought it through. "I can probably outfit one small ship in a few days, go to Earth and be back within a week." He noticed everyone's confusion. "One-fourth of a month," he added.

Gar shook his head, unconvinced. "This is the first real advantage we've had in a long time. We can't afford to wait."

"I have an idea," Brim said, somewhat nervous.

Alarra turned to her son. "Go ahead, this is no time to be shy."

"Well, if we take Master Ashgrove back to Earth first, maybe his people would join our cause. We could return with a fleet of advanced ships."

Nobody spoke for several moments. Brim began to wonder if they thought his idea was stupid, or perhaps even insane.

Dennik's laugh broke the tension. He slapped Brim on the back, beaming with pride. "It takes new eyes to see a new path!"

"Out of the mouths of babes," Kale said.

"I'm sixteen," Brim said, bristling a bit.

"It's just an expression. It means... what your father said. But my people are peaceful. Sharing our tech is one thing. I'm not sure you can expect them to fight in your war."

"It'll be your war too once the Archon adds your technology to his fleet," Jonna said.

Kale gave her slight nod, reluctant to admit the truth of her statement.

Kara turned to Gar. "We'll go with Brim's plan. Pick the fastest ship and begin the retrofit."

"That would be 'The Spear'," Gar said, his one good eye fixed on Koro.

"My ship? But what if it's needed for a stealth mission?"

"I can't think of a more important stealth mission than this," Kara said, settling the matter.

Koro bowed his head. "As you wish, Counselor."

"Gar, since you'll be working with Captain Ashgrove, I suggest you accompany him to Earth to learn all you can about their tech," Kara said.

Gar nodded. "It would be my honor."

"May I join them, Counselor?" Brim said, a bit too eagerly.

Dennik squeezed his son's shoulder. "You've already proven your worth, son. You don't need to volunteer for every mission."

Alarra rested her hand on Brim's other shoulder. "Earth is very far away. If anything should go wrong…"

"You and Father take greater risks every day," Brim said. "You promised I could join you as long as we don't go to Xos or a security outpost. Besides, I want to meet Rowan and Thorn, Master Ashgrove's sons. Maybe I can help convince them and others to join us."

A silent conversation passed between Dennik and Alarra through the special bond shared by couples that are deeply connected.

"He's no longer a boy," Dennik said.

Alarra knew it was true, though her heart wished it wasn't. She reluctantly nodded and fixed her moist eyes on Dennik.

"I'll see to it he returns safely," Dennik promised.

"As will I," Kale said.

"I'll keep an eye on him," said Gar.

"I can take care of myself," Brim said, but smiled at Gar's joke.

Dennik smiled. "No one doubts that, my son."

"It takes a village to raise a child," said Kale.

"I'm not a child," Brim said, sour-faced.

"It's just an old Earth expression."

Alarra matched Kale's smile. "The more I learn of Earth, the more I like it."

Gar's fingers tapped impatiently on the table. "Then let's not waste any more time getting there."

CHAPTER TEN

RITE OF PASSAGE

"People are often in a rush to complete processes, finish projects, accomplish goals and arrive at destinations, thinking all the while these things are their purpose in life. We've all heard it said that the journey is the destination; that the process is the entire point of life, but what's truly important to understand is that, if one isn't focused in the present, vital information can be overlooked that will help you move forward. Life is like a series of steppingstones. If your foot isn't firmly planted on each stone as you walk, you may slip and fall off your path as you attempt to rush to the next one."

Excerpt from "A Cryptic's Guide to Life"
by Holly Cotton

*

WILLA KNOCKED ON the intricate carvings that covered the door to Poppy's cottage. The two-story wood and stone structure sat on the outskirts of Port Dublin, overlooking the Grand Canal that led inland from the sea.

The door opened, framing the slender figure of Sylvania Rousseau,

Poppy's mother. She was draped in a blood red Japanese-style robe tied with a black satin sash that matched the soft moccasins on her feet. Sylvania glanced down at Willa with deep brown eyes that still carried a trace of humanity, though a few black flecks revealed her deeper transformation into a Nocturnal. Sylvania's sculptured face was the same smooth shade of mocha as her daughter's, framed by long dark tresses that hung to her waist. She smiled at Willa but it was distant and doll-like, more an expected formality to make others feel at ease rather than something truly felt by Sylvania.

"Good morning, Willa."

"Good morning, Doyenne Rousseau."

"Come in. I'll let Poppy know you're here," Sylvania said as she stood to one side. Willa entered, grateful that Poppy's mother wasn't prone to ask curious questions or engage in long conversations like her own mother and Holly.

Willa stood in the cottage's small, oak-paneled living room as Sylvania climbed the wooden staircase that led to Poppy's room. Compared to the Nest with its nano-glass technology, the cottage was practically archaic, like something out of a museum. Candles and oil lamps lent a warm glow to the room and leaded glass filled the window frames. The only concession to modern technology was a single Luminaria globe used for communication that sat in the center of a round, polished burl wood table like a crystal ball in a nineteenth century fortune teller's parlor.

Poppy bounded down the stairs, all smiles. "Hey, Willa."

"Can we go somewhere and talk?"

"Well, aren't we in a mood this morning. You're starting to mirror my Mom."

"Sorry." Willa lowered her voice to a whisper. "There's something I can't share with my mother or Holly but I have to tell someone or I'll explode."

"Ooh, I love secrets," Poppy said, suddenly giddy with delight. "Come on." She grabbed Willa's arm and yanked her out the front door. "I know the perfect place."

*

"Are you sure you know how to operate a Q-jump engine?"

Rowan glared at Thorn. "I told you, we learned how to pilot ships in First Contact training."

"We won't be able to rescue Father if we wind up inside a planet or a star," Thorn said, trying not to sound as nervous as he was.

"Don't worry, I know what I'm doing."

A beep on the control console drew their attention.

"What did you do?" Thorn said, his panic rising.

"Nothing!" snapped Rowan. "It's just the com signal. Someone's hailing us."

"Don't answer it!"

"We have to. It might be a patrol sentry."

"They'll know we stole the ship!" Thorn said, his voice rising even higher.

"They won't," Rowan said. "This is the ship I train on. It's keyed to my frequency." He rested his palm on the console and spoke to the ship's computer. "Corvus, answer the hail."

"Answering," the ship's voice droned. A section of the nano-glass wall above the control console transformed into a view screen and River's face appeared.

"Father Hillicrissing," Rowan said calmly, as though the encounter was expected. "How may I be of service?"

"I applaud your gallantry, boys, but a rescue attempt would be fool-hardy without more information and a lot more help."

"This is just a training run," Rowan said. "I'm showing my brother the ropes."

"I spoke with your mentor, Rowan. Your normal flight plan doesn't match your present trajectory. Come back with me and we'll talk this through."

Thorn jumped in before Rowan could respond. "There's too much talk and not enough action!"

River remained placid. "What makes you think you can find your father?"

Rowan took over before Thorn could interrupt again. "There's a new Q-space theory I learned in class. Quantum jump engines create a unique signature at the departure and arrival points in space. We know the general coordinates of our father's last known position. We'll scan for his ship's signature and run a new tri-fractal algorithm to determine the most probable points his ship jumped to from there."

River was impressed. "I probably shouldn't tell you this but your mentor did mention you were top in your class."

Rowan smiled and winked at Thorn.

"However," River said, "rescuing Kale on your own is still unwise, especially considering Willa's vision of what the Orions did to him."

"We won't be alone if you join us," Rowan said hopefully.

"If you're so sure you can track your father's course, then let's go back and present your plan to the Quorum and the Contact Council. If they approve, we'll have a rescue squad with us."

"And if they don't approve? I'm sorry, Father Hillicrissing. We can't take that chance."

River tapped a control. Rowan and Thorn steadied themselves as their ship shuddered.

"What was that?" Thorn said, his panic returning.

"I've locked you in a tractor beam," River said. "We're returning to Earth and that's that, understood? Power down your engine and force field and stand by."

Rowan nodded his assent as his hand drifted toward the neural interface on his console. "Shut down all secondary systems," he said to the ship.

"Secondary systems shutting down."

"Wait!" River said. "Maintain com—"

The screen vanished before River could finish. Rowan kept his hand on the neural interface. "Emergency power to engine and shields. Match shield frequency to the tractor beam."

"Initiating," the ship responded.

River watched on his view screen as Rowan's force field expanded to a large sphere and synchronized with his tractor beam. He tried to compensate but he could only lock onto the force field instead of the ship's hull.

Rowan's engine flared to life. His ship popped into Q-space and vanished as the force field collapsed. River shut down his tractor beam's futile attempt to lock onto empty space.

River stared at the stars on his screen, wondering how he would tell Lily and the Quorum that Rowan and Thorn had given him the slip. "Top of his class indeed," he muttered to himself as he pondered his next move.

*

Willa and Poppy sat on the grey stones of the ruins of a twelfth century castle at the Rock of Cashel, perched on a hilltop overlooking the verdant Irish countryside. They were hundreds of miles from Port Dublin, having used the Shaddok to transport to the remote location.

"I come here to ponder sometimes," Poppy said as she gazed at the jumbled stones around the foundations of the roofless castle chapel. "Seems like a place of secrets, so I thought yours might be at home here."

Willa smiled at the thought that there might be a place where all secrets were safe from prying eyes and ears. "It's beautiful," she admitted, her spirits lifted.

"So what's peeling you?" Poppy said, unable to contain her curiosity a moment longer.

Words flooded from Willa's mouth fast as a bursting dam. "I had a tattered vision in the Divinorum ritual because I have the genetic markers of an ancient alien bloodline that showed me Earth's in danger of attack from a malevolent alien race. Thorn and Rowan stole a ship to look for their father who was captured and tortured by those aliens and because I told them he'd been rescued by some resistance group, they're probably headed for danger too. One of the Nocturnals in the Quorum, Belladonna Bloodroot's great-granddaughter, made me promise to use my boosted abilities to search for a formula Belladonna created that can supposedly turn someone into a Wraith but actually turned Belladonna into a Banshee because of a manky little Pooka who tricked her by giving her the wrong ingredients and he insists that if I find the real formula, it could basically plunge Earth into chaos or destroy the fabric of space-time or something equally horrible."

Poppy stared at Willa for a heartbeat or two and then burst out laughing. "Wow. When you said you had a secret, I thought you meant you and Thorn were, you know, ridin' the Unicorn or something. I know you got the glad eye for him."

"Poppy! This isn't a joke," Willa said, blushing from the risqué innuendo. "On top of all that, my vision showed Thorn dying from a stab wound and the aliens burning Port Dublin to ashes!"

Poppy saw the pain in Willa's eyes and realized she wasn't kidding. "I'm sorry, Willa, I didn't mean to make light of... but are you sure the visions weren't just a spin from the Divinorum? The first time Mom went through the ritual, she had all sorts of crazy blinks that never came true."

"Like what?"

"Well, I don't recollect them all, but there was one that stuck with me because it was so gammy. She said she saw this girl with grey skin like a Whelk, but with pale eyes, and she swore that the girl could see her, even though she was just part of Mom's blink. She said the girl spoke to her, though Mom wouldn't tell me what she said."

Poppy stopped as she saw the blood drain from Willa's face. "Willa? What's wrong?"

"I need to talk to your mother."

"Why?"

"Because I saw that girl in my vision, too. She looked right at me and said 'Who are you?' I think she's one of the aliens who want to attack Earth. Maybe she has some sort of telepathic ability and could sense me through the vision."

Poppy frowned in confusion. "But Mom blinked that years ago."

"Like you said, Divinorum does gammy things with time," Willa said, recalling the images of the past, present and future versions of herself she witnessed in the shards.

"The Nocturnal you made that promise to... it's Selene Nymphaea, isn't it?" Poppy said.

Willa was startled. "Are you telepathic as well as psychic now?"

"No. Mom said she's always been a pain in the ass. I just figured it had to be her. Hey, wait a tick," Poppy said, suddenly nervous. "If that girl in your vision is real, does that mean Mom's other blinks might come true after all?"

"Let's shad home and find out." Willa and Poppy hopped off the stone blocks and ran back toward the Shaddok like the Devil was on their heels.

*

A crystalline sphere full of stars, beautiful and serene, floated in a silent, black void. A crack appeared and ran down the center of its pristine surface, splitting the sphere in two. The glistening orb shattered and exploded into hundreds of shards, dozens of which turned into cold, black stones as they tumbled through the void.

The distant Earth grew larger as the rocky shards sped toward it and turned into fiery missiles as they burned their way through the atmosphere and slammed into the ground, vaporizing entire cities in a series of blinding flashes that spread across the globe.

Tears streamed down Willa's cheeks as Sylvania pulled her hand back from Willa's third eye and broke the link that allowed her to share her devastating vision. Willa and Poppy knelt on the floor in Poppy's living room in front of Sylvania's chair.

Poppy placed a hand on Willa's shoulder. "Are you okay?"

Willa could only manage a nod as she wiped away her tears. She looked at Sylvania's placid expression, amazed at how she could remain so calm in the face of such horror.

"What does it mean?" Willa finally managed to say.

Sylvania fell into a reverie. Willa waited and waited. She felt as if she was suffocating in the heavy silence.

"I believe the crystal sphere of stars represents the Interstellar Alliance," Sylvania finally said. "And that something will create a rift among the member worlds that will lead to its destruction, along with Earth's."

"If my vision of an invasion comes true, wouldn't the Alliance bond against a common enemy? Become stronger?" Willa said hopefully.

Sylvania gave the slightest of shrugs. "We don't know the details."

Willa was dumbfounded. "But the Alliance has been around for hundreds of years."

"The only constant in the universe is change. Nothing lasts forever, Willa."

Willa felt as though she was falling down a bottomless well. Her mind grasped for anything that would stop her descent into hopelessness. "The girl!"

Sylvania cocked her head at Willa's outburst. "Girl?"

"The grey girl in your vision. What did she say to you?"

Sylvania fell into a reverie and Willa felt herself suffocating in the heavy silence that followed.

"See what I live with?" Poppy whispered in Willa's ear.

Sylvania blinked back to reality. She focused on Willa's worried face, but remained silent.

"Doyenne Rousseau… what did the girl say?"

A single tear flowed down Sylvania's cheek. Poppy was stunned. For her mother, this was tantamount to an emotional outburst.

"Mother? Are you okay?"

Sylvania seemed not to hear her daughter. Her gaze remained fixed on Willa. "The girl looked at me with her pale, ghostly eyes. She said, 'You will replace the mother who betrayed me. I will make you Queen of the Witches.'"

"Witches?" Willa blinked, confused.

"I think it's her word for Nocturnals or Sages," Sylvania said. She stood and, without another word, walked up the stairs to her room and shut the door. Willa and Poppy stared in shock at each other, their hearts pounding.

A vision of the grey girl forced its way into Willa's mind. Her hand held a weapon, pointed at the back of Poppy's head. It fired and the flash broke Willa's trance.

Willa stood, shaken, her words barely a whisper. "Holly expects me at the Quorum Lodge." She headed for the door.

Poppy merely nodded, at a loss to understand what just happened. "Willa?"

Willa stopped. She knew full well what Poppy was going to ask and dreaded the answer she had to give. Willa's heart sank as she turned to face her friend's unsettled gaze. "I promise I'll do whatever I can to stop her," Willa said.

"Stop her from what?"

"The girl means to kill you and take your place as Sylvania's daughter."

*

Rusalka stood before a gathering of several dozen Pookas deep in the Yew forest. Being shapeshifters, many looked like hares, but several appeared as goats or cats. A couple of Pookas were disguised as black horses and there was even a diminutive, chalk-white woman with an elfin face and long black hair, but all of them were united by the soft glow of their crimson eyes.

Ashleen, their ancient queen, in the form of a large hare, was perched on a flat-topped boulder in the center of the throng. She was covered with soft, snow-white fur and stared down at Rusalka with shocking pink eyes, the sole exception to her red-eyed subjects.

"You're certain the timeline has shifted?" Ashleen said in a voice that warbled like a babbling brook.

Grennan, an elder Pooka, his fur mottled grey and brown with a single white patch above his left eye, stepped forward and stood next to Rusalka. "Aye, my queen. I've kenned upline and downline afore and aft the now. The shift and the danger are real, sure enough."

"The Seer has seen," Ashleen said, following tradition.

"The Seer has seen," the rest of the Pookas chimed in response.

"What are we to do then, Ashleen?" Rusalka said.

"This matter concerns not just our clan but all Elementals," the queen pronounced. "Send out word. We must call an Enclave."

*

Willa stood in the Celtic circle in the Quorum Lodge, heavy with worry about Thorn, Rowan and Poppy as well as Sylvania's disturbing visions. Holly, Argus and Alder formed the points of an equilateral triangle just outside the circle. Alder was dressed more simply than usual, in a buff tunic with matching pants tucked into soft, caramel-colored knee-high boots.

Argus handed the cup of Divinorum to Willa. "Good batch."

Willa wrinkled her nose at the smell. "Oh, yes, much better than last time."

Argus gave her a look but said nothing.

"Shouldn't I be sitting?" Willa said, worried her legs would give out at any moment.

"Not for the Triskelion," said Alder. "You need to be nimble for this task."

"When do I look for the ship Thorn and Rowan took?"

"You'll know the right moment," Holly said and gestured for Willa to drink.

Willa sighed, took a sip and handed it back to Argus, who placed it on the fireplace mantle.

Willa felt a warm wave wash over her. She closed her eyes and felt like she was falling, but couldn't do anything to stop the sensation.

Her eyes snapped open and Willa found herself already floating inside the titanic liquid crystal sphere. The liquid froze and shattered as before, but this time, three large, multi-faceted shards, in the same positions as her mentors, rotated around her, kicking off brilliant reflections that made Willa squint. She caught fleeting glimpses of Holly, Argus and Alder in a few of the facets as the shards tumbled toward her.

The three jagged shards started to rotate as they approached, picking up speed until they spun so fast, Willa could barely make out individual facets. Smaller shards shattered in their path, spraying Willa with crystal shrapnel that sliced her skin in a dozen places. In a panic, Willa tried to float above the spinning crystalline blades, but floundered helplessly as though she was suspended in a bubble of zero gravity.

The three shards closed in on her, threatening to grind her to pieces. Willa's mind raced, searching for any means of escape. The lethal shards were now so close that Willa could see her terrified reflection flickering in their glistening facets.

In desperation, Willa extended her arms and twisted her weightless body into a spin. She willed herself to spin faster and faster, like a skater on ice, until she matched the shards' rotation. A gleaming shard grew around Willa, incasing her in a crystalline cocoon that locked into the other three shards. All four spun smoothly, like synchronized gears.

Willa peered into the facets of the three shards as they rotated in a circle around her. Images of Rowan's escape from her father played out before her eyes, along with a path of glowing lines that traced their route to the Orion nebula… and straight into the swirling maw of the Maelstrom.

Willa watched, horrified, as Rowan's ship followed a dozen probable paths through the deadly gravitational whirlpool, each ending in the utter destruction of the tiny craft… except for one trajectory that allowed the ship to survive. All the images ended in a blinding flash and Willa was once again standing in the Lodge, her three mentors steadying her with outstretched hands.

"Well done, Willa," Holly said, beaming.

"Yes, well done indeed," Alder agreed, "but it will be all for nothing if we can't warn those boys of the danger."

"My father's still out there," Willa said. "I need to transmit the path I saw to him. Maybe he can catch up to Thorn and Rowan before it's too late."

Argus grunted agreement, removed his large hand from Willa's back and went over to the far wall. The Sasquatch touched a wall panel. It slid open to reveal a communication console.

Willa went to it and input the coordinates that still floated in her mind's eye.

*

River's ship floated among the stars while he spoke to Brahma Kamal, head of the Contact Council, on his view screen. Brahma was a Himalayan Hybrid, named after the legendary white lotus. His large, crystal blue eyes were placid as a mountain lake and his smooth skin was golden and warm as honey. He wore a snow white, high-collared tunic emblazoned with the five-star insignia of the Interstellar Alliance and his bald head, a feature common among many Hybrids, made him look like an ancient Tibetan monk. He spoke with a slight East Indian accent.

"We believe Rowan is correct regarding the tri-fractal algorithm," Brahma said. "We've uploaded it to your computer and you should be able to use it to track his ship, as well as Kale's."

"You're giving me permission to follow them?" River said, surprised.

Brahma nodded. "Five more ships will join you within the hour. You understand the dangers, of course?"

"I've seen Willa's data on the anomaly. We'll be careful."

"Bring them all back safely, Master Hillicrissing."

"I'll do my best, Master Kamal."

"*Tuasha tianni pan.*"

River was a bit rusty in the ancient tongue spoken by Hybrids before The Landing but, being a First Contact Specialist, as well as a traditional-ist, Brahma spoke it fluently, along with twelve other human and alien languages. The phrase, loosely translated, meant "May the stars guide you home" and River searched his memory for the proper response. *"Ha maitra tuolo sha tianni,"* he finally managed to say: "Their light is the beacon that lights my path." River tapped his screen off and began the tri-fractal calculations while he waited for his escorts to arrive.

His com panel beeped. River tapped the screen back on and faced Lily. "Hello, my love," he said as calmly as he could.

"What did Brahma say?" she asked with uncharacteristic impatience.

"I'm going after them with a rescue squad."

Lily remained silent for several moments but every emotion that flickered across her face shouted loud and clear. "River…"

"I'm just retrieving the boys," he assured her. "The squad will continue to search for Kale."

Lily's concern was only slightly diminished. "Promise you'll come back to me."

"I promise," River said, forcing his eyes to stay on hers. "Rivers always flow to the sea." They were both wise enough to know there were unforeseen dangers that could render their promises empty, but the pledge gave them hope. "Give Willa a hug and a kiss from me. Tell her I'll bring Thorn home."

Lily nodded as she wiped away a tear. She cut the connection.

River stared at the blank nano-glass wall for several heartbeats, then continued to enter the calculations into the navigational computer. He placed his hand on the console's neural circuit. "Rigel," he said to the ship, "what are the odds of success on this mission?"

Rigel's smooth voice filled the cabin. "My psychology subroutine suggests it wouldn't be wise to answer that question."

River nodded with a sigh of resignation. "That's what I thought."

*

Willa sat on a low, flat boulder deep in the Yew forest, eyes closed, as the dappled light of late afternoon danced across her face. Her breathing was slow and regular, her other senses alert.

Holly stood nearby, her attention focused on Willa, still as one of the trees save for her long, silver locks that swayed in a gentle breeze.

Willa opened her eyes. "I still don't hear anything."

Holly sighed. "Don't listen with your ears, listen with your heart."

"I don't even know what that means," Willa said, mildly frustrated. "I can already do things way beyond the level of Cryptic. Why is this important?"

Holly drew Willa's attention to a large fallen tree lying on the ground, its gnarled, twisted roots exposed. "The power at each level above Cryptic is like facing stronger and stronger wind. If you're not sufficiently grounded, with deep roots in this reality, the forces you'll be dealing with can uproot you and kill you like that tree."

Willa pondered the rotting, moss-encrusted tree trunk, settled herself and closed her eyes again.

Holly came closer and spoke in a soft, soothing tone. "Reach out to the trees. Imagine them reaching out to you. Don't listen for a voice. Rather, search for a feeling."

Willa focused her imagination, continued her rhythmic breathing. "I think I'm beginning to feel something," she said.

"Good," Holly said. "What are you feeling?"

Willa opened her eyes. "Stupid."

She got to her feet and deliberately ignored Holly's disappointed expression. "I'm sorry. I just can't wrap my mind around this."

"You saw the shards. Think of the trees as reflections of you in the shards."

"You want me to see myself as a tree?"

"You are a tree. You're the trees, the animals, the flowers, the rocks and the bees. You're everything and everything is you. It's all one," Holly said.

Willa tried to see it in her mind. "So, talking to a tree is like talking to myself."

"Yes," Holly nodded, her hope rising.

"But then, how do I know I'm not just talking to myself? Isn't that what crazy people do?" Willa said.

"Only fools talk sense all the time," Holly replied in Cryptic fashion. "You can't understand the universe by always trying to make sense out of it. It's too big to be contained in our minds. Sometimes, the only sensible thing to do is to go out of your mind."

"No offense," Willa said with smile, "but I think you've mastered that part."

Despite her frustration, Holly laughed. "You're right about that. Trying to teach someone as stubborn as you is crazy."

Holly sat on the boulder next to Willa. "I think you need a different teacher."

"Holly, I didn't mean—"

Holly pulled a small vial of Divinorum from a pocket in her tunic.

"Here? Now? Shouldn't we do this in the Lodge?" Willa said, slightly nervous.

"I always carry a vial for emergencies," said Holly.

"Is that what this is? An emergency?"

"You're the one who said we don't have much time," Holly reminded her. "It's risky, but you need a boost. This is a special draft, brewed by Argus to deliver one specific lesson."

"Risky?" Willa said as Holly handed her the vial.

"You'll either have a breakthrough, or a breakdown, but I have faith in you."

"Was that a compliment? I can't be sure, coming from you," Willa said with a mischievous smile.

Holly threw her a wry look. "You can't move forward by having me pat you on the back, dear girl."

Willa's smile faded. "There's my mentor." She downed the Divinorum in a single gulp. Her face scrunched like she'd bitten the sourest lemon in existence and then softened as she fell into a trance.

As the Divinorum vision took hold, Willa's mind floated in a black void that contained only one thing: an extremely tiny point of light that hung weightless like a self-illuminated dust mote.

The mote shot away at the speed of light, then returned and passed by again, shooting off in the opposite direction. It reappeared from above and whipped by as it continued downward. The third time, the particle appeared from the right and disappeared to the left, forming an imaginary x-y-z axis of three dimensions.

The particle picked up speed and retraced its path back and forth, up and down, side to side at varying levels, crossing its own path over and over and over again until it was traveling so fast that it began to appear next to itself as if it was a separate particle. By the time it achieved infinite speed, the void seemed to be full of flickering, ghostly particles, an illusion created by the single particle being everywhere at once.

It began to cross its own path in different patterns and where it crossed three times in all directions, the ghostly aspect of the particle at the crossing point took on the appearance of solidity, having been "reinforced" by the multiple crossings.

The "solid" points began to form geometric shapes, which evolved into fractal patterns that became familiar objects: rocks, trees, the surrounding countryside and, last of all, Willa and Holly.

Their bodies manifested as a collection of sub-atomic dots created by the infinitely fast particle and quickly filled in along with the forest environment in which Willa had begun her Divinorum journey.

Willa blinked back to awareness, stunned. She locked her eyes on Holly's enigmatic smile and ran her hands over her own body. She turned her attention to the nearest Yew tree and placed her palm on its crinkled bark.

"We *are* all one," Willa whispered with newfound awe. "I can't track where I end and the trees begin."

"Good," Holly said with a hint of pride in her pupil. "Now your journey toward becoming a Cryptic can truly begin."

CHAPTER ELEVEN

MAELSTROM

"The imagination has no limits other than those you imagine it has."

"The Book of Paradox"
by Sassafras the Sage

*

KALE CRAWLED OUT from under the engine room control console in Koro's stealth ship, several circuit boards clutched in his hand.

Koro's brow creased in a deep furrow. "You just disabled the weapons."

"I need to boost power to the engine and coherence field. It has to come from somewhere. Besides, we shouldn't need weapons on this trip," Kale said as he headed to the engine chamber.

"Better to have and not need, than need and not have," Koro grumbled.

Gar watched closely as Kale made the adjustments to the tangle of conduits, magnetic rings and stainless steel cylinders that made up the engine's plasma flow regulator. "I still don't get this 'Q-jump' idea. Is it different than hyper-space?"

"Yes," Kale said as he routed power through the borrowed circuits. "It's quantum space, a completely different concept."

Gar looked at Dennik and shook his head. "He might as well be speaking Jarushka."

"I don't know what that is," Kale said.

Dennik jumped in. "Slang for one of the alien slave worlds in the Empire. Their real name's unpronounceable, as is their language. Jarushka means gibberish."

Kale continued to work as he spoke. "Do your people know anything about quantum physics? Wave-particle duality, quantum tunneling, superposition, entanglement, coherence?"

Koro searched his memory. "I once read about some experiments a few sci-techs were conducting that had concepts like that. I think it was part of what they called the 'Deep Reality Theory' but the Overlords believed it was a dead end and focused them on creating weapons instead."

"They also tried making more efficient gravity drives so they could conquer more worlds, but they discovered it takes too much energy to go faster. Koro's ship here is about the fastest there is," Gar said.

"And, of course, no one can get past the energy barrier that surrounds the Empire without going through the Maelstrom," Dennik added, "and you've already experienced how dangerous that can be. In fact, the stronger the gravity drive, the more turbulent the crossing."

"I'm guessing the gravitational fluctuations in the Maelstrom are magnified by the strong gravitic field of your engine," Kale mused.

"Exactly," Koro agreed. "We must dial the power back when we cross through and even then, the odds aren't good, so no one really tries anymore."

"We used to have gravity drives before the invention of the Q-jump," Kale said. "Nothing wrong with gliding along in a faster-than-light bubble of space-time. I kind of miss it. Watching the stars blue shift as you race toward them and red shift as you speed away. It's quite breathtaking."

Gar exchanged a glance with Koro. "So if we understand you, this Q-jump technology allows you to avoid traveling in space-time altogether. One moment you're here and the next, you're there."

Kale completed his adjustments and turned to Gar. "Yes. It still takes a few jumps to get anywhere really far away, but it's much faster than warping space."

Gar shook his head. "You'll have to explain it to me when we have more time."

Kale patted the ship's engine. "We'll need to check the quantum resonance calibrations next, but she's basically ready to go."

"What about making the ship think?" Gar said.

"We won't have what we need to do that until we get to Earth."

"Oh," Gar said, somewhat disappointed.

Kale glanced up at Gar. "May I ask you a personal question?" A bit wary, Gar gave a slow nod. "How did you lose that eye?"

Gar laughed. "I'd love to tell you a story about how I was injured as I fought bravely in one of the uprisings against the Overlords, but the truth is, I was repairing an engine and I stupidly dropped a plasma torch. The beam grazed my face."

Kale smiled at Gar's ability to laugh at his misfortune. "Sorry."

"Ah, it's nothing. I'd gladly give my other eye if it would end the war."

Kale felt a deepening respect for Gar and all the other resistance fighters he'd met on this lonely outpost in deep space, far from their home world. Despite being used to centuries of peace, he hoped Earth would be willing to do something to help the League reclaim their planet and free the other slave worlds from the Archon's grasp.

Kale stepped up to the control console and brought it to life. He turned to Brim. "If you help with the calibrations, we'll be ready to depart after evening meal."

"We've already had our rations," Brim said.

Dennik responded to Kale's puzzled frown. "The Archon's sentries sometimes capture our supply ships. We usually only have enough food to eat once a day."

Every Orion Kale had seen since he was captured had been thin and he came to realize that was their natural condition. However, although he'd been with the League for nearly a week, it suddenly dawned on Kale just how gaunt and underfed everyone in the resistance was. "But Alarra's been feeding me three times a day."

"You needed to heal. Your intel is vital to our cause," Dennik said.

Kale was embarrassed to have taken so much of their precious supplies and he silently vowed to request several supply ships from Earth when he returned.

*

Willa stood on Marrowbone Bridge, gazing out to sea. The town was bustling with activity but the buzz of a dozen different dialects was drowned out by Willa's thoughts. Holly approached and stood beside her at the rail, sharing the view.

"I had a visit from a Pooka last night," Willa said. She felt a weight lift from her shoulders at the admission.

"I know," said Holly. "The trees, remember?"

"Is there anything you don't know?"

"I don't know what I don't know," Holly said in typical Cryptic fashion.

"If the Sages who became Wraiths are responsible for shifting Earth's course down this parallel path, isn't there something we can do to shift it back?"

Holly thought for a moment. "Perhaps. But the shifts have been subtle, accumulating over a long period of time. Unlikely we'd be able to shift back to the original path."

"We only need to find a path that doesn't include the invasion."

"But how would we know what other circumstances might crop up instead?" Holly said. "The alternate paths might lead to something even worse."

"Then what do we do?" Willa said, feeling more frustrated and helpless by the minute.

"Let's talk to Alder. He might have some ideas."

"Odd ones, no doubt." Willa said.

"Actually, Alder's not so bad. Most Sages I've known are usually off in their own little worlds, searching for secrets in some remote location or holed up in their inner sanctums completely absorbed by their latest exploration into arcane knowledge. They're often uninterested in the affairs of others. However, Alder's certainly taken an interest in you."

"I guess I should be flattered," Willa said, not really caring.

"You should be cautious," Holly said. "Alder's a good man and I'm grateful for his help. However, like Selene, he most likely has a secret agenda. Stay alert."

Willa nodded and silently wondered if everyone had a secret agenda. She bit her lip as she felt the weight of the expectations thrust on her young shoulders by Holly, Selene, Alder, the rest of the Quorum and even the Elementals. She resented the responsibility even as she feared failing them. Willa shifted her gaze to the horizon, her jumbled thoughts slowly coalescing into a secret agenda of her own.

*

Rowan's ship popped into normal space just a few light years from the Orion nebula. This close, the nebula filled his view screen with a riot of colored gases set ablaze by clusters of newborn stars. Rowan and Thorn gaped at the spectacular stellar nursery.

"Corvus, start scanning for father's ship," Rowan instructed.

"Scanning," the computer replied.

"How long will this take?" Thorn said.

"As long as it takes," his brother said, eyes locked on the scanning data.

"Sounds like something a Cryptic would say."

Rowan smiled to himself and went to the back of the cabin. He removed two small green metal containers from a storage locker, handed one to Thorn. "Time for evening meal."

"I'm not hungry," Thorn protested.

"We have no idea what condition or situation we'll find father in," Rowan said. "We may need to act quickly. Best to keep up our strength. Eat."

Thorn opened his box, took out a greenish-brown stick the size of a candy bar, sniffed at it. "What's this?"

"Nutrients," Rowan said as he bit into his own stick. "It's good. Spacers call them zip-sticks."

Thorn took a small bite and chewed. "Couldn't you have packed some fresh vegetables?"

"This is a rescue mission, not a cruise. Besides, we may be out here a while. The sticks will sustain us longer."

Thorn and Rowan settled in, eyes on the multi-colored nebula on the screen as they munched their meager meal.

*

The Stargazer Tavern was perched on the edge of the Grand Canal at the south end of Marrowbone Bridge. The two-story structure had been carved out of an immense granite outcrop and outfitted with old-fashioned ripple-glass windows. A wide flagstone patio was sheltered from inclement weather by a wooden arbor and warmed by two large river rock hearths.

The common room was lit by a brace of Luminaria globes, their warm glow flickering like the firelight in the central hearth. Humans, Hybrids and aliens populated the tables and booths where they drank frothy brews and golden nectars and engaged in lively conversations in a half-dozen languages.

Stargazer, a five-foot-tall female Shapeshifter and the owner of the tavern, stood behind a polished oak bar and grew to six feet in order to more easily converse with a couple of tall alien customers. She had cinnamon skin like Alder and the typical all-black eyes of her kind, matched by long, dark tresses that framed a pixie face.

However, another identical Stargazer was also standing over at a table, taking another customer's order while another was simultaneously serving drinks to a different group at a corner booth. Her ability to split herself into several copies not only marked her as entering the next phase of transformation from Shapeshifter to Sage, it also allowed her to fill every job in the Tavern.

Holly, Alder and Argus sat around a large wooden table framed by a curved bay window. Holly sipped a cup of mint tea, Argus, his huge bulk resting on a sturdy bench, crunched on a brace of fat, orange carrots and Alder swirled a glass of ruby wine.

One of Stargazer's dopplegangers passed by their table on her way back to the bar with a tray of empty glasses.

"Can I interest any of you in a slice of berry cobbler? Made it fresh this morning," Stargazer offered in her thick Scottish accent.

Argus held up two thick fingers as he continued to chew on a mouthful of carrots.

Stargazer nodded. "Your usual double order. Anyone else?"

"We're good, Stargazer," Holly said. "Thank you."

"Right. One of me will be right back with that cobbler." Stargazer said to Argus as she headed off toward the bar.

Alder hardly paid attention to the conversation, mesmerized as he was by a flickering Luminaria globe.

"I find it fascinating that, nearly a thousand years after the discovery of electricity, we're still so enchanted by fire that we even use electricity to simulate it," Alder mused.

Holly nodded. "You can take a person out of nature, but you can't take nature out of the person."

Argus grunted agreement with a mouth full of carrot. "Susquehannock discover fire long time ago, before Anu come."

Alder turned to the Sasquatch. "I've always been curious, Argus. Why didn't the Anu turn all your people human?"

"Some Susquehannock had gift of phase shift to parallel world. Anu not find them in other reality. After Anu leave, my people return. All Susquehannock born after that have gift of shift."

"Well, I for one am glad your people are still around," Alder said, raising his glass.

Holly toasted with her tea. Argus tapped Alder's glass with a carrot and crunched it between his huge teeth.

Stargazer returned and set a double portion of juicy berry cobbler in front of Argus, who inhaled the aroma with deep satisfaction.

Alder looked at the dessert, then up at Stargazer. "Oh, that looks wonderful. I'll have—"

Before he could finish, a second Stargazer placed another slice of cobbler on the table. "This one has a touch of cinnamon, Alder. I know you like it that way."

"How thoughtful. Thank you," Alder replied.

Both Stargazers smiled, turned and headed toward different tables.

Holly eyed Alder with a coy smile. "I think she likes you."

"Which one?" Alder said as he eyed the various Stargazer clones in the Tavern. "Just think of the possibilities," he mused.

Holly shoved the plate closer to him. "Eat your cobbler, old man."

*

Outside, across from the inn, Willa watched her three mentors framed in the window. Satisfied they were settled in for the evening, Willa headed for the Lodge farther down the bridge, careful not to make eye contact with the few remaining night owls making their way home.

*

Alder sipped his wine and considered the problem at hand. "Divining the outcomes of multiple parallel realities is challenging, even for the most accomplished of Sages. You were right to tell Willa that shifting our course could result in something far worse than what she saw in her vision. The best we can do is use the information to prepare."

"What do you have in mind?" Holly said.

"Well, we've never had to use our abilities in battle, but they can certainly be... what was the ancient term? Ah, yes... weaponized."

"Not good to make weapons," Argus grunted.

"I mean we become living weapons," Alder clarified. "Sages can manifest objects from parallel realities, shift the fabric of time and space. With sufficient preparation and imagination, we could create all sorts of obstacles for the invaders. Shapeshifters can impersonate their leaders, issue false orders, cause confusion and chaos, that sort of thing. Trees and animals can overhear their plans and tell Holly and other Cryptics. Then there are the Elementals. They have some unusual skills that could be harnessed to the cause."

Argus grunted his approval.

Holly raised an eyebrow at Alder. "You have a devious mind, Alder Redwood. Are all Sages so cunning?"

"No. It's a special gift," he said with a smile. "I'll likely have to train the others to think differently. Overcoming seven hundred years of tradition won't be easy."

Holly returned the smile. "I can't think of anyone better suited to the task."

"Neither can I," Alder said without a trace of irony.

*

Willa reached the double wooden doors at the front of the Lodge but they were locked. She glanced at the building nearest the Lodge - a shop with a second story veranda about fifteen feet from the Lodge's steep, pitched roof.

Willa scrambled up one of the veranda's support posts, went to the railing and took stock of the wide gap between the two buildings. The railing was too high to vault over, even at a dead run. Willa looked around and spotted a pair of shutters on the shop's upper story window.

She carefully removed the hinge pins and propped one of the heavy shutters against the rail to form a ramp. Willa jammed the two pins in between the veranda's floorboards just behind the shutter so it wouldn't slide backwards.

She walked to the far end of the veranda, took a few deep breaths and focused all her attention on the makeshift ramp.

Willa took off in a sprint, legs pumping as fast as they could. Her feet hit the ramp. She sailed over the gap, landed high on the Lodge's roof and slid down the slate shingles toward the edge twenty feet above the decking below. She halted her slide on a copper rain gutter and started to climb toward an upper window when a shingle gave way under her foot. It skittered over the edge and shattered on the deck. Willa tried to brace herself but several more shingles broke free. She slipped back toward the precipice, heart pounding as she imagined plummeting to her death.

A furry paw grabbed her hand and stopped her a split second before she flew off the roof. Willa's gaze lifted from a pair of clawed feet that dug into the shingles, to Rusalka's scowling ruby red eyes.

"You should look before you leap, girl."

The Pooka pulled Willa up to a window ledge where she was able to grab on.

"Thank you," Willa said, trying to catch her breath. She jimmied the window open, stopped and said, "Wait. Have you been following me?"

"Of course," Rusalka sniffed. "Many Elementals want to know more about the attack you saw in your vision."

"That's why I'm here." Willa slipped through the window onto an upper story loft. The Pooka followed her inside. They made their way to a staircase and descended into the Great Room where the cauldron of Divinorum still bubbled over a low fire.

The golden cup was on the mantle. Willa grabbed it, scooped up the thick liquid and drank it down. Her face scrunched from the bitter brew but she filled the cup again and forced herself to swallow before she went back a third time.

"What are you doing?" Rusalka said, his nose wrinkling at the foul odor.

"I figure the more I take, the more I'll see," said Willa. She set the cup back on the mantle and sat down in the center of the circle on the floor. Willa closed her eyes and waited. Within three heartbeats, her body stiffened like she was being electrocuted. Her head was thrown back, eyes wide, mouth open in a silent scream.

Rusalka backed away, alarmed. "What's wrong with you?"

Willa was too deep in the Divinorum trance to hear the Pooka. She was frozen in place, staring through a rift that formed in the air just below the ceiling as the depths of space opened to Willa's expanded senses.

*

Rowan's ship still floated against the backdrop of the Orion nebula as he examined several trajectories on his monitor.

"Why are we still sitting here?" Thorn said in a sour tone.

"Readings show some kind of gravitational anomaly ahead. It's making it difficult to lock onto father's signature."

"So we came all this way for nothing."

Rowan input a few calculations on his console. "I'm not giving up yet."

A beep on the console was followed by Corvus's smooth electronic voice. "Sensors are registering a ninety eight percent spectrographic match to the composition of the target ship's hull."

"Father's ship?" Thorn said, his melancholy shifting to hope.

"Insufficient mass," Corvus clarified.

Rowan felt his stomach lurch. "Debris?"

"Affirmative."

"Plot a course," Rowan ordered.

"I should warn you," Corvus said, "the anomaly will make navigation quite challenging."

"Understood. Do it anyway."

"Adjusting course."

The view screen overlaid the new course on the stars and the ship glided toward the debris in the midst of the anomaly. The cabin shuddered, making Thorn nervous. "Can't we just pull the debris to us with a tractor beam?"

"Not at this distance," said Rowan.

The ship lurched more violently. Rowan and Thorn grabbed onto support beams to steady themselves.

"Maybe this isn't such a good idea," Thorn said.

Rowan's jaw was clenched, a mix of fear and determination. "I'm not going back without knowing what happened to Father."

Thorn nodded, trying to match his brother's stoicism, but the confidence drained from him as the ship lurched again.

"Shield to maximum!" Rowan shouted.

"The shield is at maximum," Corvus responded. "Attempting to compensate for gravitational variances."

"Strap in!" Rowan said to Thorn. The boys belted themselves into their seats.

A burst of electromagnetic energy erupted around the ship, glowing like an aurora. A spider web of electric arcs danced across the hull and the ship tumbled off a gravitational cliff.

Rowan and Thorn barely stayed in their seats as the ship plunged down the gravity well, on a collision course with the large chunk of debris from their father's ship. They plowed through the wreckage. Their external communications array was struck and destroyed in a shower of sparks.

Half of Rowan's control console went dark, interior lights flickered and shorted out. An alarm assaulted their ears. The ship's wild gyrations snapped their belts and the boys were slammed against the cabin bulkheads.

"Inertial stabilizers!" Rowan yelled.

"At maximum," the computer shot back, its voice filled with static. "Gravitational stress on the hull approaching critical."

"Get us out of here!"

"Navigational sensors are offline."

Thorn tried not to throw up. "We're going to die, aren't we?"

"Father survived. So can we," Rowan said, trying to convince himself as much as Thorn.

The ship continued to shudder and lurch, systems shorted and exploded, showering the boys' battered bodies with searing hot globules of fused nano-glass. Artificial gravity cut out. The boys grabbed onto the nearest support beams and hung in mid air.

The main view screen flickered and went dark. The shuddering stopped. Rowan and thorn floated in apprehensive silence, bathed by the eerie red glow of the few remaining emergency lights.

"Ironic," Thorn said.

"What?"

"Father could make it home, only to find out that his plonky sons died in uncharted space."

"Yeah," Rowan grudgingly admitted, "I guess this was pretty stupid. Well, you know what they say…"

"What's that?"

"Good judgment comes from making mistakes and mistakes come from bad judgment."

Despite his fear, Thorn laughed. "Let's hope we survive long enough to learn our lesson."

The boys reacted with surprise as the main view screen flickered back to life, filling the cabin with cold blue light. Several glowing lines traced different trajectories against the stars. All paths ended abruptly within the Maelstrom, except for one that charted a course all the way through.

"Corvus! Follow that path!" Rowan shouted.

The ship righted and slipped through the roiling gravitational rapids. The cabin shuddered and shook, but held together as Rowan and Thorn held on tight to the support beams. After what felt like an eternity, the tiny ship emerged into a calm expanse within the eye of the gravitational storm and came to a full stop.

"Good work, Corvus," Rowan said. "Thank you."

"It wasn't me," the computer responded.

"What do you mean?"

"I didn't lay in the course. It came from somewhere outside"

"A transmission?"

"No. The information simply appeared in my data banks."

Rowan and Thorn exchanged a glance, at a loss to explain it. The stars on the view screen gave way to a rotating, kaleidoscopic energy pattern, followed by a distorted, yet familiar voice that filtered through the static.

"Thorn? Rowan? Can you hear me?"

Thorn was both surprised and relieved. "Willa? Is that you? Where are you?"

Back on Earth, in the Quorum Lodge, Willa's eyes were solid black voids filled with stars. Her trance-like stare was focused on a swirling vortex of energy that penetrated the ceiling and revealed Rowan's ship in the depths of space as though it hung mere yards above the roof.

Rusalka kept his rose-colored eyes on Willa and fidgeted, growing more nervous by the minute as Willa spoke to Thorn through the wormhole.

"I'm in the Quorum Lodge in Port Dublin," she said.

The Pooka followed her gaze yet saw nothing but the wooden ceiling over his head. "Who are you talking to, girl?" Rusalka demanded.

Willa ignored Rusalka and continued the conversation only she could hear. "Stay where you are. Help is on the way."

Rusalka startled as the main doors were thrown open. Holly, Alder and Argus entered and froze as they beheld the Pooka and Willa, locked in her Divinorum trance.

Alder's golden eyes filled with inky blackness and the portal became visible to him. "She's created a quantum rift!"

"Seal it!" Holly said.

In a blink, he willed the portal to collapse in on itself and the vaulted ceiling was once again overhead. Alder's eyes returned to normal.

Although the portal was gone, Willa remained in a deep trance. Holly rushed to her side. "Willa? Can you hear me?"

Willa was oblivious to Holly's presence. The Cryptic turned to Rusalka. "How much did she take?"

"You mean that foul-smelling soup? Three cups." The Pooka said.

"Three! Why didn't you stop her?"

Argus scowled at Rusalka, a deep rumble in his throat. "Pooka not belong in Lodge."

"Don't growl at me, you furry oaf! This wasn't my fault. You're the ones who ought to be watching her. She nearly got herself killed sneaking in here. I saved her from breaking her fool neck!"

"We're grateful to you for that," Alder said, cutting off another growl from the fuming Sasquatch. "And you're right. We're responsible for keeping an eye on the lass."

Rusalka humphed and gave Alder a curt nod of thanks.

Holly turned her attention to Argus. "Is there anything you can do?"

"Not first time this happen with eager apprentices." Argus stomped into an adjacent storeroom and emerged clutching a dun-colored root. He grabbed a stone mortar and pestle from a shelf, bit the root into manageable chunks and spit them into the bowl. Argus added a dipper of water and mashed the root to a pulp.

The Sasquatch went over to Willa and gently took her face in his large hand as he lifted the bowl to her lips and forced her to drink the milky pulp.

They all held their breaths and, within moments, Willa's eyes returned to their natural, golden hue. She blinked back to awareness, regarded the faces of her relieved mentors and the ruffled Pooka, went pale and bolted for the door.

Willa leaned over the bridge railing and violently purged into the sea far below. After several minutes, her stomach empty, Willa collapsed to the bridge deck, her back against the railing, completely spent.

Holly brought her a cup of cool water. Willa took a few cautious sips as color flooded back into her cheeks.

"What were you thinking?" Holly said.

"I'm sorry. I didn't mean to worry you," said Willa, still somewhat weak.

"Alder says you opened a portal through Q-space. Not only could you have been killed, the entire Lodge and half the village could've vanished into another dimension."

"I reached Thorn and Rowan. They're safe now."

"Did you hear what I just said?"

"I had it under control," Willa said, slightly miffed.

"Did you, now," Holly said with a brittle bite. "How did you know it would work?"

"I just knew."

"Despite your genetic connection to the Anu, you're still an apprentice and you need guidance. You've got a lot to learn about being a Cryptic, let alone a Sage."

"I saved my friends' lives and I didn't need to talk to any trees to do it! Doesn't that count for something?"

"Willa!" Holly said, more shocked than angered at Willa's impertinence. "It's not just about them. Look at you. You're peeled. That much Divinorum could've scorched your nervous system."

"I'll be hickory in no time. Just leave me be." Willa stood and walked away over Marrowbone Bridge.

Alder, Argus and Rusalka joined Holly.

"Please look after her," Holly said to the Pooka.

Rusalka gave her a quick nod and followed Willa at a respectful distance.

"No mischief," Argus grumbled.

Rusalka scowled at Argus over his shoulder, stuck out his tongue and continued after Willa.

Alder glanced at Holly's worried expression. "Any of us might have done the same to save our friends."

"That's what worries me," Holly said. "She's just as stubborn as I was at her age. I once underestimated the consequences of a choice and it nearly cost me everything I held dear. I'm afraid she's making the same mistake."

Alder nodded. "Most who become old and wise start by being young and daft."

Holly kept her eyes on Willa's receding back, a feeling of dread in the pit of her stomach. Alder's eyes were also on Willa and Rusalka as they stepped off the far end of the bridge and headed down the path. He placed a comforting hand on Holly's shoulder.

"Life is a harder teacher than either of us," he said. "She gives the test first. The lessons come afterwards."

CHAPTER TWELVE

REUNION

"*After humans became used to the Hybrid presence on Earth, they were given a list of all humans whose genetic material had been used by the Whelks to create the Hybrids. Eventually, most of those humans came to accept the Hybrids as their own offspring, which allowed Earth to feel that human civilization was part of an extended galactic family. That opened the way for additional contact from a variety of alien races, which eventually led to the formation of the Interstellar Alliance.*"

Excerpt from "A Hybrid History"
by Holly Cotton

*

ROWAN'S SHIP FLOATED serenely in the Maelstrom's eye, badly damaged but safe for the moment.

Inside the cabin, Rowan tinkered with the artificial gravity circuits. Thorn hovered, weightless and helpless, as he watched his brother work. The field snapped on and their feet landed firmly on the deck. He turned to Thorn, who grabbed a med-kit and attended to his bruises.

"How was Willa able to do that?" Rowan said.

"I don't know. That's the kind of thing only the most powerful Sages would be capable of. Her training hasn't gone that far."

Rowan turned his attention to a cracked nano-block. "Corvus, do we have enough power for a Q-jump?"

"Maybe one, if you tap power from the shield coils," Corvus said, "but it won't matter if I can't get a navigational lock with all the gravi-metric interference."

"So even if we repair all our systems, we're going nowhere."

"Correct." A beep interrupted the exchange. "Proximity alert. Sensors are reading an object on an intercept course."

"More debris?" Thorn said, dreading a replay of their recent ordeal.

"Unclear," the computer said, "but it's big enough to be a ship."

"Father's ship?" Rowan said with guarded hope.

"Unknown configuration," Corvus replied.

"Maybe another ship stuck here like us," Thorn offered.

"Is it close enough for visual?" Rowan said to Corvus.

The main screen crackled to life, filled with static. Rowan made a few adjustments and the image cleared, revealing a dark, menacing craft shaped like a spearhead.

"They look friendly," Thorn said sarcastically.

"They may be the only help within several light years," Rowan reminded him.

"Or they might be the ones who captured Father," Thorn shot back.

A beep drew Rowan's attention to his console. "They're hailing us."

A silent conversation passed between the brothers as they weighed their options. "I don't see that we have much choice," Rowan concluded. "If we don't answer, they'll probably board us anyway."

Thorn reluctantly nodded. Rowan tapped his com link. Koro's sharp features filled the screen.

"Identify yourself," Koro demanded.

"They speak English?" Thorn whispered, puzzled.

Rowan shrugged and faced the screen. "My name is Rowan. This is my brother, Thorn. We're searching for— "

"Rowan? Thorn?" Kale's voice filtered through the speakers just before he stepped into view, his face a mix of disbelief and elation.

Rowan and Thorn reacted together. "Father!"

Kale was filled with a storm of emotions. "What are you doing here? Are you all right? How did you know… never mind. Right now, I'm just happy to see you both! Is your airlock working?"

Rowan grinned from ear to ear. "You heard him, Corvus."

"Activating airlock," the computer responded.

A smooth section of Corvus's hull extended and transformed into a cylindrical docking airlock. Koro's ship maneuvered alongside. Their docking ports lined up. Corvus's docking tube morphed to fit the alien airlock and formed an airtight seal.

Rowan and Thorn waited by the inner hatch as the airlock pressurized. The hatch opened like an iris and Kale stepped through. He engulfed his sons in a hug and kissed their faces, his cheeks wet with tears.

"You're really here, you're really here," he kept repeating as though afraid he might wake up from a dream.

"We're here, Father, we're here," Thorn assured him, his own eyes moist.

Kale pulled back and frowned at Rowan. "Is this what you call taking care of your brother?" His ire shifted to Thorn. "Where's your common sense? You need to grow up!" Kale turned back to Rowan. "Who gave you authorization to be out here? Don't you know how dangerous—"

Kale stopped. The stricken expressions on his sons' faces melted his heart. He looked at them, burning their faces into his memory. He hugged them again, flooded with relief, then stood back, still fixed on them. "You've both grown so much!"

Rowan studied the scars on Kale's face. "You've changed as well, Father."

Thorn's eyes welled up. "I'm sorry—"

Kale dismissed Thorn's apology with a wave of his hand. "I'm the one who owes you both an apology, leaving you alone for so long."

"It wasn't your fault," Rowan said.

Kale nodded. "What's done is done. The important thing is we're together now."

Dennik, Gar and Brim stepped through the airlock and kept a respectful distance. Kale wiped his tears away and smiled.

"This is Dennik, Gar and Brim. I owe them my life," Kale said. "These are my sons, Rowan and Thorn."

Dennik and Gar gave the boys a nod, but Brim extended his hand and clasped Rowan's forearm.

"I'm very excited to meet you!" He clasped Thorn's arm in the same manner. Thorn winced from his bruises, but Brim seemed not to notice. "Both of you. Your father's told me so much about you, I feel we're already brothers."

"Good to meet you, Brim," Rowan said. "We're very grateful you saved Father, but I'm afraid we won't be going home anytime soon."

Kale nodded. "The anomaly."

"We call it the Maelstrom," Gar added. "Not to worry. We recently received a message, don't ask me from where, that uploaded the calculations we need to compensate for the changes in gravity."

"Willa," Thorn blurted.

"Willa?" Kale said, confused. "What's she got to do with this?"

"We're not sure how," Rowan said, "but she sent us a message that charted a course to this region just in time. If it wasn't for her, you would have found nothing but a cloud of debris instead of our ship."

Gar looked around the cabin, impressed despite the damage. "So, this is one of your sentient ships, is it?"

"At your service," the computer chimed. "My name is Corvus."

Gar exchanged a look of surprise with Dennik. "Right. That'll take some getting used to."

"If you'd be so kind as to transmit your new calculations to me, I can chart a course for Earth," Corvus continued.

"Sure. No problem," Gar headed back through the airlock, slightly unsettled by the computer's inhuman voice. Dennik took another look around and followed Gar back to the Spear.

Brim smiled at Rowan and Thorn. "I can't wait to see your home world. Your father said it's quite beautiful. I'm looking forward to meeting more... Earthians?"

Rowan nodded. "Earthers will do. Or Terrans. That's a more ancient term. What about your home world? What's it like?"

Brim's smile faded. "I've never set foot on Xos and most likely won't until our people are free from the Archon's tyranny."

Rowan and Thorn turned inquisitive faces to their father.

Kale sighed. "It's a long story."

*

Willa wound her way through the Yew forest that stretched between Port Dublin and her home. Rusalka remained some distance behind her, but always within eyeshot.

"You can stop following me," Willa said. "I'm just going home."

"Why are we walking?" the Pooka griped. "There's a perfectly good Shaddok not a mile from here."

"It helps me think," Willa said, annoyed at having her thoughts interrupted by idle chatter. "Now please, leave me alone."

Rusalka plucked a pebble from the forest floor and chucked it at Willa. It smacked her in the back of the head.

"Ow! What was that for?"

"Earth's in danger and you're moping around in the forest like we have all the time in the world. We need to find out more!"

"How am I supposed to do that? Holly will never let me back in the Lodge by myself after what I just did." Willa plunked herself down on a moss-encrusted rock and sulked.

The Pooka squatted on his haunches a few feet away and scowled. A soft breeze rustled the leaves as an accompaniment for the steady chirping of forest crickets. Lost in thought, Willa barely noticed when the symphony stopped. Rusalka's nose twitched, his fur bristled as the evening's warmth was replaced by an unearthly chill.

Willa shivered, her senses alert. She and Rusalka jumped to their feet, wary as the sound of the wind gave way to an eerie wail. At first, it seemed to come from everywhere then coalesced to the narrow space between two tall Yew trees.

A pair of glowing white eyes opened in the shadows. Willa took a step back but Belladonna the Banshee floated toward her and fixed her malevolent gaze on Rusalka. "How dare you enter my beloved woods!"

She lunged at Rusalka with murderous rage but her ephemeral form passed through the Pooka without harm.

Rusalka's furry lips curled into a feral snarl. "You see?" Rusalka said to Willa, "I was right to keep this vengeful creature from becoming a Wraith!"

Belladonna's ghostly body flared with electric fury. "Vengeful! I deserve to avenge myself after three hundred years! Who are you to determine my fate?"

"I was protecting my people! Protecting the Earth!" The Pooka shot back. "You were playing with forces beyond your ken!"

Belladonna let loose an ear splitting wail and rushed at Rusalka again. Despite her fear, Willa leapt between Rusalka and the Banshee, hands wide in supplication. "Belladonna, please don't—"

As the Banshee passed through Willa's body, her ethereal form crystallized. Suddenly solid, she smacked into the Pooka and they both went tumbling. Belladonna thudded to the ground and stared in amazement at her hands, no longer transparent. She stood, wobbly at first, and looked down at her bare feet, at the prints they left in the soft soil. "How?" Belladonna's shock gave way to amazement. Giddy with delight, she danced around and touched her face, her long white hair, her hands and the trees, reveling in the physical sensations. She turned to Willa. "You healed me! Brought me back! How is this possible?"

"I'm not sure," Willa confessed. "When you passed through me... my Teacher said I have a rare genetic marker from the ancient Anu. Maybe it affected your ethereal form somehow."

Belladonna swung around to face Rusalka, her anger flaring to life. "You'd better run, little rabbit, because when I catch you—"

Rusalka scrambled to his feet, but before she could make a move, Belladonna doubled over in pain. Her body slowly returned to her ghostly form. "No!" she screamed as her feet lifted from the ground. "No!" She reached for Willa, who quickly backed away. She hovered on the evening breeze, her eyes pleading. "Bring me back again!"

"Willa, no." Rusalka shouted.

The Banshee's eyes flared in anger, but Willa quickly intervened. "I'll help you if I can," she said, "on one condition."

Belladonna's anger subsided. She floated toward Willa. "Anything!"

"My friend, Thorn Ashgrove and his brother Rowan went into space to find their father. Can you tell me when they'll come back to Earth?"

"I'm a Banshee, not a fortune teller!"

"I've heard stories, rumors really, that being halfway between the living and the dead, Banshees can peer through time and space at will. Isn't that how you know someone's about to die?"

Belladonna considered, then said, "What you ask isn't easy, but I can try." Her eyes threw daggers at Rusalka, then flickered back to Willa. She added, "But if I do this, you must promise to make me mortal again."

Rusalka took a few cautious steps closer. "Willa—"

"It's okay," Willa said. She turned back to the Banshee. "Your word you won't try to become a Wraith again."

"You're asking two favors," said the Banshee.

"One for me and one for him," Willa said, pointing to Rusalka. "Your word or the deal's off."

Belladonna scowled at Rusalka but nodded. "Three hundred years in limbo is Hell enough. I want nothing more to do with the spirit world until I die as a mortal. You have my word. Do I have yours?"

"Since I don't know how I made you mortal the first time, I don't know if the cure can be permanent."

"I understand," the Banshee said. "I'm only asking that you try."

"I'll do my best. You have my word on that," Willa assured her.

The Banshee rose into the air, her head arched back, her ghostly eyes glowing with ethereal light. She peered into the star-filled heavens and, with great effort, unraveled the fabric of space-time.

*

Rowan's and Koro's ships emerged side by side from the swirling eddies of the Maelstrom into normal space and glided among the stars.

Rowan, Thorn, Kale and Brim were glued to the main viewer as Corvus mapped a trajectory back to Earth. "I've transmitted the route to Koro's computer," Corvus said in his matter-of-fact tone, "but with their level of technology, we'll need to make several shorter jumps to reach Earth so they can keep up with us."

"That's okay," Rowan said, smiling at his father and brother, "We're in no hurry."

As the two ships sped off through space, another stealth ship, similar to Koro's, floated just inside the edge of the Maelstrom far behind them.

On board, Gant studied Corvus's map on his own view screen. He turned to Haldane, a taciturn soldier who occupied the pilot's seat like it was a second skin. "You sure they can't detect us? They have no idea we picked up their transmission?"

Haldane kept his jade eyes on the readouts. "I moved the ship back inside the Maelstrom, where their sensor beams will be scattered. When we follow, we'll run cold and silent inside a null spot in their own gravity wake, half a light year behind them, transparent as the vacuum of space."

*

Willa and Rusalka stared up at the Banshee as she floated back down toward them and hovered a few feet off the ground, her eyes filled with worry.

Willa took her expression for failure. "Nothing?"

"The vision was... unclear," Belladonna said. "I sense they're safe and on their way home, but..."

Rusalka puffed up at the Banshee's hesitation. "You're just telling Willa what she wants to hear so she'll help you!"

"I gave you my word," Belladonna said, "and I'm telling you the truth, but there's something else coming with them. Something... dangerous." Belladonna held Willa in her gaze. "You know I can sense death approaching, but I've never felt anything so powerful, so dark, so... final."

Willa shivered as she recalled her nightmares. "Nothing else?"

Belladonna shook her head. "I'm sorry."

Willa inhaled with an air of determination. "Thank you. A deal's a deal. I promise I'll try to find a way to make you mortal again."

"Big mistake," Rusalka said.

Belladonna's rage flared. She quickly passed through Willa and landed with a solid thud on the ground in front of the surprised Pooka. Belladonna punched Rusalka with all her strength and knocked him into the dirt. She leapt on top of him, raked his face with her sharp talons over and over, drawing blood as the Pooka screamed and passed out. Willa grabbed the crystallized specter and pulled her off Rusalka. Belladonna sublimed back into spirit and floated into the air, a wicked smile on her ghastly face as she glared down at Rusalka's unconscious, blood-soaked body.

Willa knelt at the Pooka's side, checked to make sure he was still breathing and turned toward the Banshee, furious. "You gave us your word!"

"I never said I wouldn't give that nasty little beast a licking! I've been waiting to do that for three hundred years."

"If you want my help, you leave him alone!"

"I'll give you one week to make good on your promise."

"A week!" Willa protested. "I need more time to figure this out."

"And I want time to live again before calamity falls upon us," Belladonna said.

"If you saw death coming to us all, why would you want to be mortal again?"

"I'd rather die than be stuck like this for eternity," the Banshee said.

"And if I don't deliver?" Willa said, defiant.

Belladonna let out a howl that shook the leaves from the trees. Willa covered her ears to no avail. The Banshee's shrill wail stabbed into her brain like a cold steel blade. Even in the midst of searing pain, Willa felt a brief pang of envy that Rusalka's unconscious state spared him from this agonizing torture. Belladonna stopped. Willa's ears rang in the deafening silence.

"Fail me and I'll make sure every living soul in New Dublin, including your precious Teacher, goes deaf as a doorknob. One week!" The Banshee drew a symbol out of glowing energy in the air with her finger: a dot within a triangle within a circle. "Draw this and call my name. I will come." Belladonna became pale as moonlight and faded from sight. The glowing symbol hung in the air for a moment and faded out as well, throwing the glade into darkness.

Willa shook her head to clear her mind. She gently cradled Rusalka in her arms. It was strange, holding this powerful Elemental being as though he was nothing more than a doll. A breeze ruffled his fur and her hair and reminded Willa that despite the differences between them, she and Rusalka shared a natural bond that anchored them to all living things on Earth. She stood and stumbled along as she carried the unconscious Pooka down the forest path toward the Shaddok half a mile away.

CHAPTER THIRTEEN

SUSPICION

"In any relationship, conflict often begins, not from what is actually said, but from what is left unsaid."

"The Book of Paradox"
by Sassafras the Sage

*

RUSALKA AWOKE IN Willa's hammock, his wounds dressed with an herbal salve. His ruby eyes flickered around the unfamiliar room until they came to rest on Willa, asleep on a pile of blankets on the floor.

The Pooka tried to sit up, moaned as his head began to spin, and quickly lay back down. Willa stirred at the sound, rose and took stock of her unwilling patient. She padded over to a wall and placed three fingers on the cool, crystalline surface. "Chamomile tea."

A small opening appeared in the wall and presented Willa with a glass of steaming liquid. She took it to Rusalka and helped him lift his head.

"Drink," she said softly.

The Pooka sniffed at the tea and took a cautious sip. Willa eased his head down and set the glass on the floor just as her mother rose into the room on the spiral staircase.

"Good morning," Lily said with a smile that lit up the room. "How's our houseguest?"

Rusalka glanced around the white nano-glass room and grumped. "You call this a house?"

Willa threw him a withering look. "Back to his usual rude self."

The hammock wobbled as Rusalka tried to sit up again. Still dizzy, he lay back down, one furry foot hanging off the edge of the hammock. "How did I get here?"

"I carried you," Willa said, failing to hide her cheeky tone. "You're heavier than you look."

"Carried through the woods like a helpless pup. If my people hear of this, I'll never live it down."

"It's your own fault for goading the Banshee. And you're welcome, by the way."

"Fine. Now we're even! Happy?"

Lily's eyebrows rose. "Banshee?"

Willa knew that tone. She sighed. This was going to be a long morning.

*

Koro's dark, spearhead-shaped ship floated high above Saturn, flanked by Rowan's and River's smooth, crystalline ships and the five faceted, gem-like crafts of the rescue squad.

River studied Kale's scars on his view screen. "The Council can't overlook the fact that Rowan and Thorn violated several protocols to search for you," he said. "They'll have to appear before the Council to answer for their actions."

Kale nodded. "They saved my life. I'll stand by their side and I'll also vouch for our guests."

"All that aside, I'm relieved that you're safe, Kale. Welcome home."

Rowan took his father's place in front of the view screen. River continued. "I trust you'll follow me back to the Spaceport?"

"Of course, Master Hillicrissing. I didn't mean to cause you any—"

"You can explain yourself to Brahma Kamal." River cut the view screen off and smiled to himself. He knew a mandatory appearance before the head of the Contact Council was enough to unnerve the most seasoned pilots. He almost felt sorry for Rowan and Thorn… almost.

River tapped his com. Bryony Bracken, captain of the rescue squad, appeared on his view screen. Her alabaster skin and snowy mane made Bryony's lavender eyes seem all the more shocking. "Perfect timing. I was just about to contact you, Master Hillicrissing."

"Captain Bracken, may I suggest you instruct two of your ships to remain on patrol in case any more unexpected guests show up?"

Bracken nodded, "I was thinking the same thing. If our telepathic link gets any stronger, we won't need the ship's com system anymore. Bracken out."

The screen went blank and River tapped his control console. "Let's go home, Rigel."

"Charting a course," the computer responded.

River's ship and three of the rescue squad vessels sped away from Saturn, followed by Rowan and Koro. Two squad ships remained in orbit over the ringed planet, their sensors on high alert.

*

The entire Quorum of Nine, along with Willa, Lily and Rusalka, were gathered around a large nano-glass table that extruded from the floor in Willa's home to accommodate the additional guests.

"This is far more serious than I thought," said Holly, half to herself.

"The Banshee actually spoke to you?" Selene said, her gaze fixed on Willa. "She confirmed your vision of Earth's fate?"

"Amazing," Alder said, interrupting, much to Selene's annoyance. "Belladonna Bloodroot hasn't spoken to anyone in three hundred years."

Encantado the Shapeshifter slapped his palm on the tabletop. "Never mind that! Did the Banshee see anything specific?"

Willa cleared her throat, slightly nervous. "Only that Thorn and Rowan were bringing danger with them."

Holly chimed in. "River will be escorting the Orion representatives to the Council chamber within the hour. Brahma has asked the Quorum to attend the meeting, to see what we may be able to sense of our guests. Willa, he would like you and Rusalka there as well."

Rusalka stiffened. "Me? I need to get back to warn my people!"

"Exactly, and you want to have as much detailed information as possible, yes?"

Rusalka's silence was a grudging admission of Holly's logic and she took it as such. She turned her attention back to Willa.

"Regardless of the way you went about it, there's no denying that the Divinorum opened your senses to an extreme degree. Maybe you'll spot something we can't, so be alert, Little Fox."

Willa nodded, relieved to be partially back in Holly's good graces while simultaneously wishing Holly hadn't used her nickname in front of the Quorum.

Eridani, the other Nocturnal, addressed the gathering in a voice like liquid mercury. "Are we pretending to ignore what happened when the Banshee came in contact with Willa?"

"Precisely!" Selene said, snatching the conversation away. "There's much more to our foolhardy little apprentice here than a simple expansion of her senses. She was able to turn the Banshee mortal! This is beyond even the powers of a Sage!"

"For once, I agree with Selene," Alder said. "We need to understand what's happening to Willa. Her newfound abilities could be of paramount importance if her dire vision comes to pass."

Lily's eyes narrowed protectively. "You're talking about my daughter as though she's some kind of defensive weapon."

Holly placed a gentle hand on Lily's. "No one wants to turn your girl into a weapon. But you know Nature's balance: poisonous plants usually grow in the same field as the plants that contain the antidote. If Willa's gifts can spot the sickness, given time and training, she may also ken the cure."

*

The Contact Council's Dublin headquarters was an elegant, emerald green nano-glass edifice composed of five levels of arched chambers that formed a circular pyramid topped by a shallow dome that supported a slender communications spire. It rested amid lush green gardens and bubbling fountains that embraced visitors in an atmosphere of tranquility.

Willa waited on one of the paths that meandered through the main garden, thoughts bubbling through her head like the water in a nearby fountain.

"Willa."

Willa turned at the sound of Thorn's voice and ran to embrace him in a crushing hug. She pushed back, held him at arm's length, studied the bumps and bruises on his face from his journey through the Maelstrom.

"If you ever do anything like that again… I thought I lost you."

"Everyone's talking about how you saved us," Thorn said. "How did you do that?"

"Apparently, I'm some sort of genetic freak, according to Holly."

"I'm sure she didn't say that."

"No, not exactly. But it's how I feel."

Thorn kissed Willa gently on the lips. "I want to hear the whole story later.

Right now, they're expecting us inside." Willa nodded. They walked hand-in-hand down the path toward the Council building and entered under the central arch.

Inside, the main council chamber followed the building's circular motif. Seating for the Council members and spectators lined the perimeter, while the open central floor was reserved for those who wished to address the Council. On this day, Kale stood alongside Dennik, Brim, Gar and Koro as they faced Brahma Kamal.

Twelve large Luminaria globes floated in the air near the ceiling and transmitted the proceedings to the other Council leaders around the world.

Willa took a seat in the spectator section between her father and Rowan, who moved down so Thorn could sit next to Willa. Holly sat farther down alongside Rusalka, who returned a few stares from spectators who were surprised to see an Elemental in the Council chamber.

Brahma tapped his nano-glass console. A clear, bell-like chime called the assembly to order. He waited for silence, then filled the chamber with his golden tone.

"We welcome our honored guests to Earth and express our deepest gratitude for the safe return of Captain Ashgrove. Who speaks for you?"

Dennik took a step forward. "With your permission, I'll speak on our behalf."

Brahma gave Dennik a respectful nod. "How is it you speak our language?"

"With all due respect, sir, how is it you speak ours?" Dennik said with a disarming smile.

Brahma raised an eyebrow. "I've always loved a good mystery, but we'll table that issue for now. Please tell us about your home world."

"It's called Xos, the center of a stellar empire ruled by a cruel Archon named Asura along with his power hungry Overlords. They invaded our world a millennium ago and enslaved our people along with the inhabitants of nineteen other planets. I and my fellow Xoshi are part of a resistance group called The Black League." He clapped Brim on the shoulder with pride. "Including my son, Brim. We're here to ask for your help."

"To do what?" Brahma said.

"To overthrow the Archon."

A murmur rippled through the spectators. Brahma tapped the bell for silence.

"Please forgive the outburst, Master Dennik, but Earth hasn't had war for centuries. Although a few planets with the Alliance have maintained and repurposed their old military armadas, Earth has no such fleet. We're hardly equipped to fight one world let alone an empire."

"You wouldn't have to fight. We ask only for supplies and weapons."

"We don't manufacture weapons."

"Your ships and your technology are beyond anything possessed by the Empire," said Dennik. "That alone would give us a great advantage. It would give us a fighting chance."

Kale stepped up alongside Dennik. "Councilor Kamal, I've seen the conditions on their world. The planet is barely more than a prison. Food is scarce, freedom, nonexistent. Surely there's something we can do to help their people, if only to give them some measure of hope."

"The Council will discuss it and render a decision within three days, as per tradition." Brahma turned his gaze to Rowan and Thorn in the gallery. "As to the matter of your sons' recent behavior, we'll table that for now out of respect for your safe return." The Council leader fixed the boys in his icy gaze. "But make no mistake, there will be consequences." Brahma tapped the bell, rose and left the chamber.

The other Councilors faded from the Luminaria and the spectators began to quietly discuss the issue among themselves. Dennik turned to Kale.

"Is there nothing else we can say?"

"I'll make sure they know all the facts," Kale reassured him. "For now, you're my guests and I'd be honored if you'd share evening meal with my family."

"It would be our honor," Dennik said with a slight bow of his head. He glanced at his fellow Orions. "We'd also enjoy seeing more of Earth, while we have the time."

"I'll make the arrangements," Kale said.

Rusalka turned to Holly as the gathering broke up. "I saw nothing new here except disappointment in the off-worlder's eyes."

"What we learned," Holly said, "is that Earth may have to go backwards in order to move forwards."

The Pooka wrinkled his nose in distress. "You mean create weapons?"

"I mean we may need to turn ourselves into weapons," Holly responded, none too happy that Alder's proposal to weaponize their abilities might be the only course open to them.

"What about Earth's security squads?"

"Minor defensive weaponry, mostly for eliminating dangers such as asteroids. Certainly not enough power or ships to stop an invading army," Holly explained.

"Brahma said that some other worlds in your Alliance might still have the ability to fight the off-worlders."

"Perhaps," Holly said. "Several of the more recent member worlds haven't yet fully dismantled their defense fleets, which is a condition for entry into the Alliance. But if we go down that path and wage all-out war with the Orions, it could take centuries for the Alliance to recover."

*

The two Earth squad ships orbiting Saturn approached Titan, the ringed planet's largest moon, wrapped in its rust-colored cloak of noxious gases.

Captain Sorrel, a dark-haired human, sat in his chair on the bridge of his squad ship, his slender fingers steepled in front of his slit of a mouth as he conferred over the view screen with his female Hybrid counterpart, Captain Yarrow, in the second ship. They examined the unusual sensor readings on their monitors.

Yarrow scanned the data with her caramel-colored eyes, trying to make sense of what she saw. "I've never seen readings like these. What do you make of it, Starling?"

Starling, the ship's computer, processed the data through several algorithm filters. "Based on the low-level random energy bursts, it appears to be an unknown natural phenomenon within Titan's atmosphere."

"Okay," Yarrow said, satisfied with the assessment, "let's do a full-spectrum sweep and mark the location before we resume our patrol. The science division will want to take a closer look."

"Copy that," Starling said. "I detect two non-random pulses rising toward the surface of the atmosphere."

Yarrow furrowed her brow. "Non-random? What—"

Before Yarrow could finish her question, two black, needle-like missiles broke through Titan's ruddy atmosphere and pierced both squad ships. They exploded into balls of incandescent light that scattered charred debris in all directions.

Moments later, Haldane's stealth ship rose above the moon's soupy atmosphere. He piloted the vessel away from Saturn.

In the pilot's cabin, Gant scrutinized the monitors. "You're certain they sent no transmissions?"

"None," Haldane assured him. "Pulsing our engine at random intervals made us look like a natural anomaly. A trick I learned during the Takanni uprising."

"I see why the Archon chose you for this mission."

"Just make sure you don't take all the credit," Haldane said without a hint of humor. He tapped his control panel, surrounded the sleek ship with a warp bubble and sped toward Earth at the speed of light.

CHAPTER FOURTEEN

SUBTERFUGE

"Stories of Earth's ancient wars are legion. One story in particular, the tale of the Trojan Horse, teaches the lesson that things are not always what they seem on the surface; that death and defeat can disguise themselves in the mantle of victory."

"The Book of Paradox"
by Sassafras the Sage

*

A PHALANX OF Orion Tech workers buzzed around the metal scaffolding that encased a sleek star cruiser in one of the Citadel's largest hangar bays. The ship bristled with a lethal array of weapons: plasma energy cannons, torpedo ports and electromagnetic spikes. Here and there, its black hull was penetrated by or patched over with glimmering crystalline technology stolen from the salvaged wreck of Kale's craft.

Xos-Asura strode into the bay. His gaunt frame was a foot taller than his obsequious aide, Doona Set, a pale, violet-skinned alien from Tet, one of the subjugated worlds within the Empire. Doona had bright red, bird-like eyes that darted everywhere and saw everything. He pointed a clawed finger at a group of Techs to one side who were gathered around a crystalline cube about a yard on each side.

"The interface, My Lord," Doona crooned.

Xos-Asura approached the Techs, who quickly parted to allow the Archon an unobstructed view. They all gave a short bow of respect.

"Report," Xos-Asura said.

Yadra Jeet, the lead Tech, also from the planet Tet, cleared his throat and chose his words carefully. "This technology makes no sense, My Lord. Perhaps the prisoner is feeding us false information?"

The Archon considered the possibility and quickly dismissed it. "No. But perhaps the interrogators haven't dug deeply enough. She must still be holding something back."

"My Lord is wise."

The Archon turned and departed without another word, much to the relief of the Techs, who were used to being blamed for both real and imagined inadequacies. Doona cast a suspicious eye on them as he followed his master from the hangar bay.

*

Willa sat on a large, flat rock, her feet dangling over the edge. She stared at the burbling waters of the river that wound through the meadow at Three Rock Mountain.

Holly approached from over a low hill, her silver mane blowing in the wind. She stopped a respectful distance behind Willa and wondered if she'd had enough time to digest the Quorum's proposal.

"I know you're there," Willa said without turning around. "I won't do it, I'm not a spy."

"No one's asking you to be. Just let us know if you sense anything out of place."

"I'm the one who'll be out of place. Won't they be suspicious? Why would I accompany them on the tour and leave Thorn behind?"

"You helped bring them safely through the Maelstrom. They'll welcome your company. And Thorn will only distract you from—"

Willa turned and threw a disapproving look at Holly. "From what? My mission?"

Holly knew better than to respond. She turned her gaze to a mass of dark clouds that shadowed the horizon. It crossed Holly's mind that they might be a portent of things to come. She strolled over to Willa, sat beside her on the rock and stared in silence at the glistening waters that rushed by in the waning sunlight.

"Tell me more about your vision," Holly said softly.

Willa twitched as the image of the Archon standing over her broken body flashed through her mind. "I don't want to talk about it anymore."

"Would you rather live it?"

Willa's control began to erode as raw emotion exploded through the cracks in her stoic veneer. "Why me? Why am I the one who has to bear this… this so-called gift?"

"You wanted to become a Cryptic."

"Well, you were right! I'm not ready for this! It's too much, too fast!"

Holly wrapped an arm around Willa's shoulder. "I know. But you won't go through it alone."

Willa leaned into Holly's embrace, tears flowing. "You didn't see what I saw. Your help may not be enough."

"The Quorum, the Contact Council, your family and friends… we're all here for you, for each other," Holly said. "Even the Elementals, like Rusalka, annoying as he is, will help in any way he can." Holly sat Willa up straight, wiped the tears from her cheeks and gazed into her golden eyes. "Besides, there are things I have yet to teach you. Things I've learned about the Anu ancestors that I never shared with anyone, not even the Quorum."

Willa's curiosity burned bright as her flame-hued hair. "What things?"

"Knowledge that may help you master your newfound abilities. Things that could make all the difference if our encounter with the Orions leads to war."

"Then teach me," Willa said.

Holly allowed a smile. "All in good time, Willa. All in good time."

Willa shook her head. "Based on my vision, I don't think we have much time."

"There are no shortcuts to anyplace worth going," Holly said in Cryptic fashion. "But lesson number one is to know that you know nothing."

Willa blinked at her mentor. "I don't understand."

"You can't fill a cup that's already full."

*

Xos-Asura and Doona made their way down the cellblock hall. Guards gave a slight but respectful bow as the Archon passed by on his way to one specific cell at the end of the stone corridor. The steel cell door did nothing to muffle the agonizing screams that came from within. A guard opened the cell door, the Archon and his minion entered without breaking stride.

Elowen Koa, the pilot of Kale's ship, her alabaster skin scarred and burned, lay strapped to a slanted steel table, very much alive despite the rumor the guards fed to Kale. She was immobilized by a metal cap with a wicked array of glistening needles that penetrated her skull. The Archon's three interrogators carefully manipulated the needles and ignored Elowen's screams as they watched the data from her tortured brain scroll across a bank of monitors.

At a gesture from the Archon, one interrogator tapped a needle. Elowen immediately fell silent, her mouth agape, her face a frozen mask of terror.

"My Lord," the interrogator purred with a slight bow of his head.

"Their ship's computer is not responding," the Archon said. "You will extract the secret of its operation from her before the change of the guard."

"This is a delicate procedure, my Lord. The slightest misalignment of the probes…"

"Probe deeper."

"It might kill her."

"It matters not if she dies. But you best have the secret before she does or you'll take her place on that table."

"Yes, my Lord."

The Archon turned and strode from the cell, Doona close on his heels. The door slammed shut behind them and Elowen's screams resumed, much louder than before.

*

Willa, Kale and their Orion visitors hovered in the air in a nano-glass observation pod and gazed out over the cluster of islands that comprised the San Francisco Archipelago and formed the entry to the central Californian inland sea. The Golden Gate Bridge had been elevated, refitted and extended to reach from the northern tip of the main island to the southern shore across the wide bay. It was a walking bridge now, purely for pedestrian pleasure, as there was no need for ground vehicles to cross over since the advent of levitation technology. The remaining core of San Francisco was laced with platforms and bridges high above sea level.

Dennik, Brim, Gar and Koro marveled at the city but were absolutely riveted on the ocean's vast expanse.

"I didn't know there could be so much water on the surface of a planet," Brim remarked.

"There are huge seas on a few of the worlds in the Empire, but this… it takes your breath away," Dennik added.

"How much of the surface is covered?" Gar said, his good eye opened wide.

"More than three quarters," Kale said, "especially after most of the ice caps melted."

Koro frowned, trying to imagine what Kale was describing. "Ice caps?"

"Sheets of frozen water at the poles, as thick as we are high right now."

Brim nodded in admiration. "This is an amazing world. I never imagined I would see anything like it in my lifetime."

Dennik smiled and wrapped his arm around Brim's shoulder. "It gives me hope for the future of Xos."

Kale tempered his smile. "I don't mean to cast a shadow, but the Council hasn't decided yet whether or not Earth will join your cause."

"This may be a really stupid idea," Brim ventured, "but… can't our people just come live here instead?"

"This isn't our world," Koro said, worried the suggestion might offend their hosts.

"Our people came from off world as well," Willa interjected before anyone else could answer. "Our Hybrid race joined the humans who were already here over seven hundred years ago."

"That's true, Willa," Kale added in a somber tone, "but our ancestors only numbered in the thousands." He turned to Dennik. "How many slave worlds make up the Empire?"

"Twenty," Dennik said. "Over a hundred billion souls."

Willa refused to be deterred. "But there are dozens of planets in the Alliance. A few are barely inhabited."

Dennik shook his head. "Kale's right. Even if we could somehow transport all those people to this sector of space, Xos-Asura's not going to just let us steal his subjects away without a battle that would cost millions of lives. No, the only way is to remove the Archon and his Overlords and take back our home world. Only then will our people be free."

Willa looked down at the waves below. She couldn't bring herself to believe there was no other way out for Brim's people and searched her mind for other options. The only path she could see was the one she was on, the one that led to her death. Willa hoped Holly was right; that she could use her newfound abilities to intuit a less dangerous path.

Kale attempted to lift the dour mood in the pod. "If you think the ocean is amazing, wait until you see the Rainbow Mountains of China." He tapped the coordinates into the controls and the pod shot off over the Pacific.

As they glided over the water, Brim turned his attention to Willa. "May I ask... I hope I'm not being too personal..." Willa nodded for him to continue. "Your world is home to humans, aliens and your people... Hybrids, I think you call yourselves?"

"It's a long story," Willa admitted.

"I was just wondering... your hair..."

Willa self-consciously ran her fingers through her thick fox-fur locks. "Oh. Yes, my parents explained it's a rare trait that crops up now and then in our family line. I take after my father and Grandmother Mimzy. It sort of resembles the fur of an animal on our planet called a fox."

"I think it's... attractive," Brim said.

Willa blushed slightly, knowing that everyone in the pod could hear the conversation.

"Thanks," she said, her voice low.

Their tour pod merged with a few others that were on a similar route so it went unnoticed that one particular pod, with Thorn at the controls, followed them across the ocean.

*

Deep in the dusky shadows of the Yew forest, many miles from Port Dublin,

Rusalka held court at an Enclave, a rare gathering of all types of Elementals. Other Pookas, Sylphs, Salamanders, Sprites, Undines, Nymphs, Fairies, Gnomes and Imps inhabited the grass, trees, brook and some even floated in the air, all intent on Rusalka as he laid out Willa's dire vision.

"The girl beheld our forests scorched, our streams and lakes vaporized, our flowered meadows paved flat and the Alliance may not be able to do anything to stop it."

A silvery Sylph floated down on gossamer wings from between the branches of an aged oak.

"I remember the days before The Landing," Silver said. "It was much the same then."

Vulcanus, a long, lean Salamander Elemental whose aura flickered like blue fire, rose to his full three-foot height. "Aye, Silver remembers true. Dark times they were."

"The question is what do we do about it?" Rusalka sniffed.

Heavy footfalls crackled through dry leaves and twigs that carpeted the forest floor. Every eye turned toward the sound and the long shadow that fell over the gathering.

Kernunnos, a titanic forest spirit entered the clearing from between two tall Yew trees. The giant Elemental walked on cloven hooves, his long, shaggy, Elk-like face crowned with a magnificent spread of antlers. The spirit's leaf-green eyes swept over the gathering as he spoke in a voice that rumbled like thunder.

"We are the forest and the forest is us. This has been our home since time was young. If darkness falls from the sky, we will fight with wind and sea, with rock and flame. We will dispel the darkness with light!"

Rusalka bowed with respect but remained skeptical.

"Forgive me, O Kernunnos, great spirit of the forest, those are fine words, brave words, but the dark forces need not set one foot upon the Earth to reduce our home to ashes."

The Elementals absorbed this as they waited for Kernunnos to respond.

"What hope have we, then?" the Forest Spirit said, his glowing eyes fixed on the Pooka.

"The Hybrid girl named Willa," said Rusalka. "I believe she holds the key."

Several Elementals scurried out of the way as Kernunnos sat on his huge haunches atop a large, moss-covered slab of stone.

"Tell me her story," he rumbled.

*

The riotous Rainbow Mountains of Zhangye Danxia Province in China spread out before Kale, Willa and their guests as they stood against the railing of the observation platform. Mineral stripes of red, yellow, green, blue and dozens of subtler shades ran across the surreal landscape like spilled paint. Kale's pod hovered nearby, a few inches off the ground along with several other pods that had conveyed dozens of tourists to the natural wonder.

"If I hadn't travelled here with my eyes open, I'd think we'd been transported to another planet!" Dennik said.

"I've heard ancient stories," Koro added, "that many of the worlds in the Empire had natural wonders like this before the Overlords paved them over with slave hovels."

"That sounds depressing," Willa said.

Brim nodded, placed his hand on Willa's shoulder. "Depressing would be a vast improvement."

Willa gripped Brim's arm in empathy, then removed her hand, a bit self-conscious. Brim lowered his hand to his side and cleared his throat as an awkward silence passed between them.

Gar and Koro were focused on the stunning natural display, but Kale and Dennik caught the moment between the two youngsters and exchanged a knowing smile. A soft beep from the pod broke the silence.

"The Council's reached a decision," Kale announced as he checked the information display. "We'll leave the pod in Port Beijing and use the local Shaddok to transport back to Port Dublin."

Gar glanced at the pod. "What's a Shaddok?"

"A global transportation system, faster than the pod. You'll see," Kale said with a conspiratorial smile.

Something alerted Willa's senses. She glanced to one side where several other tourists strolled along the observation path and caught a quick glimpse of a familiar silhouette peeking out from behind a distant information kiosk.

"Would you all excuse me for a moment?" Willa walked over to the kiosk, planted her back against the outer wall and pretended to study the striking panorama, deliberately facing away from her stalker so as not to draw stares from nearby sightseers.

"What are you doing here, Thorn?"

Thorn remained in the shade on the opposite side of the kiosk.

"Making sure you're safe," he offered.

"You mean making sure Brim isn't getting too close to me, don't you?"

"I don't trust him," Thorn said, his eyes firmly fixed on the distant Orions. "I don't trust any of them."

"They saved your father's life," said Willa, surprised by Thorn's animosity.

"Maybe so they could use him to come to Earth and scout out our weaknesses."

Willa thought about it for a moment and filed it away for later consideration.

"Well, whatever their agenda, I can handle Brim," Willa said.

"It's him handling you that concerns me," Thorn countered.

Willa leaned around the corner, locked her gaze on Thorn. "You're starting to look a bit like an Orion yourself, Thorn."

Thorn bristled. "What's that supposed to mean?"

"They all have green eyes."

"Me, jealous of him? You're daft."

"Am I now?" Willa said with a smirk. "Shall I tell the Council that you followed us here against orders?"

"Fine, okay, maybe I'm a bit jealous, but that doesn't mean they're not up to something."

"Jealous and paranoid. What more could a girl want?"

Willa headed back toward Kale and the Orions as Thorn smoldered in the shadows.

CHAPTER FIFTEEN

INTERFACE

"When Artificial Intelligence was finally achieved, we came to understand that it wasn't artificial at all. Rather, we had simply created a sufficiently sophisticated interface between the physical world and the realm of spirit. While the voices that issue from our computers and other AI devices seem content to assist and collaborate with us, it still remains a mystery as to what manner of entities the voices truly belong."

Excerpt from a lecture given at the
Aurora Luna Science Institute in 2547
by Professor Imamu Faraji

*

WILLA AND KALE stood with the Orions before Brahma, the Contact Council and a full gallery of curious spectators. Brahma signaled for silence.

"The Council has decided to provide you with three supply ships. They're older ships, without our most advanced technology but they should serve your needs."

"A wise precaution should they fall into the Overlords' hands," Dennik agreed.

Gar slowly raised a weathered hand. Brahma smiled.

"No need to raise your hand, Master Gar. Please feel free to speak your mind."

"Begging your pardon and not meaning to sound ungrateful, but three cargo ships isn't quite what we had in mind... sir."

"Our ships will return to Earth automatically, where we will refill them and send them back to you as many times as you need. Now that Willa has charted a course for you through the Maelstrom, you'll have a regular supply chain," Brahma explained as though that settled the matter.

Dennik could see that Gar wasn't satisfied and spoke up before Gar could protest. "Excellent. Thank you for your generosity."

Brim unexpectedly took up Gar's cause before Dennik could cut him off. "But you'll not join the fight?"

"Brim!" Dennik hissed with a disapproving glare, but Brahma raised a hand to intercede.

"It's alright, Master Dennik," Brahma said.

Brahma cast his ice-blue eyes on Brim, who felt an appropriate chill. "Understand that, before The Landing, Earth had been embroiled in warfare for nearly its entire history. We've now known peace for seven hundred years. Our first duty is to preserve that peace."

"We fully understand," Dennik said before his son could respond. "It's our fight and we appreciate everything you've promised to do. On behalf of our people, we thank you."

Dennik bowed and turned to leave. Brim, Gar and Koro reluctantly followed suit, but Willa could no longer contain her growing agitation.

"Master Kamal!"

Kale threw her a cautionary glance, his voice low. "Willa..."

She ignored him and stood before the Council leader. "What of my vision? If we have a chance to stop them before they come to Earth—"

Brahma cut her off gently but firmly. "Rest assured, we'll prepare our defenses but we will not build and unleash an armada against another system, no matter how barbaric." Brahma caught himself and turned to Dennik. "I mean no offense."

Dennik's killer grin returned. "Believe me, I've called the Overlords far worse. We've taken up enough of your time. Our people back home are likely worried and I think it's time I returned our son to his mother. If you'll permit us, we'll go and help load the supply ships."

Brahma nodded. The Orions strode from the Council chamber. Brim, slightly embarrassed, followed at the rear. He cast a worried look at Willa, who shared an empathetic smile. Her eye caught a glimpse of Thorn, who scowled at Brim from the gallery.

Holly stepped onto the floor and blocked Willa's line of sight.

"Anything you'd like to share from your travels?"

"Nothing important," Willa said with stubborn finality.

Holly nodded toward the receding Orions. "Best check their mood."

Willa made a sour face but followed the Orions from the chamber, glad to have an excuse to end the conversation. She scanned the gallery once more. There was no sign of Thorn.

*

Brim sat on the low, stone wall that enclosed the patio outside his assigned quarters, eyes closed, feeling the warmth of the setting sun on his face.

"Sorry to disturb you."

Brim opened his eyes and cast a verdant stare upon Rowan, backlit by the rosy sunset.

"You're not," Brim said wistfully. "It's just that it's such a luxury to sit under an open sky with the sun on my face."

Rowan sat nearby, gazed at the sun and nodded. "It's easy to take for granted. I'll admit that nearly getting killed in the Maelstrom gives me a deeper appreciation for the comforts of home."

"Your father said you're training to be a Contact Specialist? Doesn't that mean you'd be away from your home world most of the time?"

"True," Rowan said, "but I wouldn't trade it for anything."

"I envy you the freedom to choose your path," Brim said. "The Black League's choices are limited to life or death."

"You have a third choice," Rowan offered. "You could stay on Earth, make a new life."

"I'd give almost anything to stay, but I can't abandon my people... my mother," Brim said, his voice quivering.

Rowan felt a pang at the loss of his own mother, but pushed the memory away. He hopped to his feet. "Come on."

"Where are we going?"

Rowan flashed a wide smile. "If you can't stay, the least I can do is show you something you'll remember for a long time."

Brim took a step toward Rowan and stopped. "Is it alright to leave my quarters?"

"You're a guest, not a prisoner. Besides, I'll be with you," Rowan assured him with a friendly slap on the back. "Come on."

Brim relaxed and followed Rowan through the courtyard's lush landscape.

*

The Archon's tech crew nervously labored under his cold gaze as they uploaded the final data, so cruelly extracted from Elowen's brain, into the salvaged nano-glass computer. The crew breathed a collective sigh of relief as the machine flickered to life with a golden glow.

"Sagittarius online. Scanning for coordinates," the computer chirped.

The crew jumped back and even the implacable Archon was momentarily startled.

They watched as the computer's glow shifted through a spectrum of analysis, then settled to a cool blue hue.

"Coordinates unknown," Sagittarius concluded. "Where am I?"

Xos-Asura stepped forward as his crew cleared a path. "Your ship was destroyed. You were salvaged and are now the property of the Xoshi Empire."

"I'm programmed to interface with Pilot Elowen," the computer responded.

"Your pilot is dead."

"Protocol requires proof of death," said Sagittarius.

"I assumed as much." Xos-Asura reached into a metal box to one side and held one of Elowen's bloody eyes and dangling optic nerve up to the computer's scanner. The beams danced over the grisly orb.

"DNA match confirmed," the computer reported without emotion. The Archon tossed Elowen's eye to one of the techs, who returned it to the box as he fought the urge to vomit.

"Shall we proceed?" Xos-Asura said.

Sagittarius sublimed to a deep violet. "Please enter the code to establish a new interface."

The Archon nodded to the Yadra who carefully input the code that appeared on his data screen. The computer's scanner glowed emerald green.

"Ready to accept new interface. Please place your eyes in front of the scanner."

Yadra tapped a button on his console. The computer rose on a platform until the scanner was eye-level with the Archon. He stared into the scanner, the beams uploaded his retinal and brain wave patterns and the computer glowed a deep green that reflected in the Archon's pale eyes.

"Interface complete."

The Archon turned to Yadra as he exited from the hangar.

"Install it on my ship."

"At once, my Lord," Yadra said with a deep bow.

*

Andromeda Spaceport hung high above the Earth's north pole that, after centuries of climate change, was nearly as ice-free as every other place on the planet. The space station was an enormous, three-mile diameter bifurcated disc dotted with glowing office and apartment viewports and ringed by dozens of automated docking bays. At any given moment, scores of passenger and cargo ships were guided to and from the docking ring by the ever-watchful sensors of Ocularis, the station's sentient computer.

Andromeda was capped top and bottom by clusters of subspace telescopes and communication arrays that searched the star-filled void for scientific data and transmissions from the dozens of ships and star systems that comprised the Interstellar Alliance.

Brim stared open-mouthed at the spaceport on the view screen in Rowan's ship as they approached the titanic structure.

"Welcome to Andromeda Spaceport," Ocularis chimed over the console speaker. "Please use docking bay thirty one."

"Copy that," Rowan responded as he locked the coordinates in. He turned to Brim. "This is Earth's embassy for the Interstellar Alliance."

"I never imagined I'd see such a thing in my life," Brim said, his eyes still fixed on the station.

Rowan's ship docked in bay thirty one. A tubular, nano-glass causeway extended from the bay wall and sealed around the ship's airlock. Rowan shut his engines and led Brim down the causeway into one of Andromeda's wide, curving corridors.

Brim was nearly overwhelmed by the throng of humans, Hybrids and aliens that passed by them as they headed toward the spaceport's main promenade.

Rowan smiled at Brim as the Orion gawked at the diverse alien life forms. Some ignored his stare, others fixed him with eyes of every color in the spectrum or fleshy sensors where eyes didn't exist.

"You'll get used to it," Rowan assured his mesmerized companion.

"Now and then, aliens from some of the enslaved Empire worlds have joined the Resistance and attended a meeting at our moon base, but I've never seen so many all at once."

They arrived at a colonnade of over a hundred life-sized statues of humans, Hybrids and aliens that lined the entry to the Great Hall of the Contact Training Facility.

"How many worlds are in your empire?" Brim said in hushed reverence.

Rowan laughed. "It's an Alliance, not an empire. Officially, it's a union of one hundred forty seven planets with about a dozen more under consideration. And that doesn't count the ones we're still observing to determine if contact is appropriate."

"I wish Xos could be counted among them," Brim said.

"Maybe one day," Rowan nodded, his hand on Brim's shoulder.

A large arched entrance at the end of the hall opened to a long chamber lined with rows of dimpled counters that displayed hundreds of glowing blue nano-glass beads the size of marbles.

"What's this?" Brim said, his voice still hushed.

"The Archive," Rowan said. He pointed to different symbols that marked each section of beads. "Art, architecture, history, archeology, mathematics, biology, literature, music, physics, geology, astronomy. There's one here on the station, one on Earth and on every world in the Alliance." Rowan took a bead from its resting place and tapped it. It expanded into a thin, glass screen full of data. "Like this, see?" He tapped it again. It shrank to a marble once again and Rowan set it back in its dimple.

Brim stared at the storehouse of information, mouth agape. Then, something shifted in him, so subtle that Rowan took no notice. If he had been staring into Brim's eyes, he might have glimpsed the boy's vibrant curiosity cool to dispassionate calculation.

Brim stumbled, dizzy, held his head with one hand and supported himself against the wall with the other.

"Are you okay?" Rowan asked, instantly concerned.

"Water," Brim said in a dry rasp. "Please."

Rowan helped Brim lie down on a bench in the Archive. "I'll be right back."

Moments after Rowan left to fetch a drink, Brim got to his feet, hurried down the aisle dedicated to technology and pocketed a nano-bead labeled "Starship Technical Specs." He hurried back to the bench and quickly resumed his position seconds before Rowan entered with a flask of water.

Brim allowed Rowan to help him sit up and slowly drank the cool liquid, letting it "revive" him.

"Better?" Rowan asked.

Brim nodded with all the feigned appreciation he could muster. "I grew up on a moon, so I'm not used to your gravity. With everything going on, I guess it just caught up with me."

Brim stood with Rowan's help, tested his legs.

"We can wait if you're not ready," Rowan offered.

"I'm okay," Brim assured him. "I should get back. My father will wonder where I am. Thank you for showing me this place. It gives me hope that one day, when Xos breaks free of the Overlords, my people might join your great Alliance."

Rowan gripped Brim's hand in a show of camaraderie. "I know the Council is only providing you with supply ships, but if there's anything I can do to help…"

Brim returned a nod of gratitude. As Rowan headed for the exit, Brim remained a few steps behind, his hand unconsciously covering the pocket with the stolen bead.

*

Dennik, Koro and Gar huddled around a blue nano-glass table in their opulent guest quarters. The glass walls were a deeper blue, criss-crossed by sculptured lines as though the room had been woven on some gigantic loom. Here and there, a few of the lines glowed, bathing the space in cool, white light.

"Food, tools, medicine. It's all welcome," Koro said, his voice low, "but they won't help us defeat the Empire."

Gar slapped his palm on the table. "Koro's right! We should talk to them again, convince them to share their tech!"

They startled slightly as the door slid open, admitting Brim. He eyed the threesome. "I know a recon briefing when I see one," he smirked as he took the fourth seat.

"I was beginning to worry," Dennik said.

"Rowan was teaching me about their Alliance. It's impressive."

Koro picked up the ball again. "That… what did they call the device that brought us back to this city in the blink of an eye?"

"A Shaddok," Brim said, always eager to show off what he'd learned of Earth.

"That Shaddok," Koro continued, "even some of their oldest tech is more advanced than anything in the Empire. You think it can send people from one planet to another?"

"They have ships for that," Dennik said. "I think the Shaddok just transports them around their planet."

Gar pointed a gnarled finger at Dennik. "Well, be that as it may, it's still beyond the Empire's abilities. You need to go back to the Council, demand more than meager supplies!"

"And if they refuse again?" Dennik said.

"Then we take what we need!" Gar spat out.

"Keep your voice down, " Koro admonished.

"This isn't the Empire," Dennik said calmly. "They respect a person's privacy."

Gar snorted. He'd marveled at this world, its nature and technology. Even the room was a reflection of how much more advanced Earth was than Xos. Gar had grown up amid the grays and blacks of the unyielding stone that covered most of their home world and from which the League's secret base was carved. He'd lived a hard life and Earth's abundance sparked a fierce jealousy in his heart. "You trust these... Hybrids too quickly. They're soft and understand nothing of our ways, or our needs."

"Willa saved us," Brim added. "I trust her."

"Spoken like a lovesick boy," Gar scolded. Brim blushed and fixed Gar with a scowl that could melt steel.

Koro cut through the tension. "These people do possess strange powers. Too bad we can't harness them to our purpose."

"Maybe we don't need the whole planet to join us," Dennik mused. "Maybe there are those like Willa who'd be willing to fight by our side." He clapped Brim on the shoulder. "Gar's right. You and Willa have a connection. You can use that. Talk with her, see if she has friends who feel as she does."

Brim looked to Koro and Gar who nodded agreement with Dennik's plan. He sighed, resigned to his fate.

"I'll do my best, Father."

Dennik smiled. "I ask for no more than that, my son."

A knock at the door broke the conspiratorial mood.

"You think they heard us?" Gar whispered.

"I told you, they don't think like us," Dennik assured him. He turned toward the door. "Come."

The door slid back and Willa entered. "I came to see if you're alright. I know you must be disappointed."

"We live on a diet of disappointment," Gar griped.

Dennik shot him a look. "Nevertheless, we accept the Council's decision."

"Thank you for speaking on our behalf," Brim said.

Willa offered a half-hearted smile. "I wish I could've done more."

Dennik stood and gestured for Gar and Koro to do likewise. "We need to check on the progress of the cargo ships. Brim, why don't you let Willa show you more sights before we have to leave for home?" He turned to Willa. "If you're available?"

"Of course. It would be my pleasure," Willa said. "I know just the place."

*

Three hundred thousand miles from Earth, comet Leviathan continued along its parabolic orbit around the sun, shrouded by gossamer gases that stretched a million miles across the heavens. An entourage of small fragments tumbled alongside the mountain-sized nucleus.

A few miles away, a couple of science vessels and even a tour ship glided alongside the comet, taking readings or simply allowing passengers to gawk through viewports at the comet's mesmerizing tail.

Unbeknownst to any of them, Haldane's ship coasted amidst the cosmic rubble, shielded from their instruments, appearing to be nothing more than another ordinary comet shard.

On board, Haldane and Gant scanned the Earth with passive sensors, searching for any sign of their quarry. Haldane fixated on the planet's image. "Have you ever seen so much water?"

"We're too far out," Gant grumbled. "This data is useless."

"We're lucky to get this close," Haldane said. "If it wasn't for the comet, they'd have detected us already."

"I'm not going back to the Archon empty handed. We've got to get closer, land somewhere remote and blend in."

Haldane rubbed his temples with barely concealed impatience. "Blend in? The resistance will have returned the prisoner to his people by now. They'll know what we look like."

"I'm not a fool," Gant said. He went to a security locker, tapped in a code. It opened and he pulled out a hollow metal cube the size of a suit-case laced with advanced circuitry. Haldane frowned at the unfamiliar machine as Gant explained.

"The latest technology. It can replicate anything it scans."

"I wondered what you brought on board. How does this device help us?" Haldane said.

Gant activated the replicator, placed his face in front of the scanner. Light beams crisscrossed and catalogued his features and, within seconds, a life-like mask of Gant's face appeared inside the cube. Gant tapped in some instructions and, within seconds, the device altered the mask to look like a typical Earth Hybrid.

Gant slipped the mask on and smiled at Haldane with his new alien face.

"Disturbing," Haldane said. "Impressive, but definitely disturbing."

Gant removed the mask. "Now," he said with a renewed air of authority, "how do we get to the surface without being detected?"

Haldane glanced at Earth's image on his monitor. A plan hatched in his mind. "With another type of mask," Haldane said with a devious smile.

*

Magic hour light painted the Yew forest in golden tones and cast long violet shadows across the mossy path that Willa and Brim followed through the trees.

"My father's a great leader and he means well," Brim said, "but he's been in the resistance his whole life. His trust is hard won."

Willa nodded. "I can't imagine what your life has been like, living inside that dark moon, never seeing the sky or trees or streams. Nothing but tunnels and caves." The truth was she didn't want to imagine it, since any thoughts of Brim's world led to the unnerving image of the Archon standing over her dead body.

"The first word we learn in the resistance is duty and, on that note, I have something important to ask of you."

Willa hopped up and sat on a large, fallen tree trunk. Brim stood before her, slightly nervous, and collected his thoughts. "My father would prefer I take a more covert approach, but I'd rather be straightforward with you."

Willa smiled at a memory.

"I say something funny?" Brim pressed.

"My mentor, Holly, always says that challenges in relationships arise not so much from what's said but from what remains unsaid."

Brim nodded. "She sounds wise, like my mother."

"Yeah," Willa conceded, "I've been kind of mean to Holly lately, but she wanted me to spy on you like your father wanted you to spy on me."

Brim straightened. "Then let me be blunt. Your Council's decision aside, are you willing to help us? You personally. Do you have friends who'd join our cause independent of your Council's wishes?"

"Arguing with Holly's one thing. Going against Brahma and the Council... I'm not sure anyone would choose that path."

Brim sulked. "Then our cause has failed."

Willa slid off the log, placed a reassuring hand on Brim's arm. "It's not a failure to make new friends. Besides, the Council's supplies will give your people the strength to fight."

Brim took a deep breath of flower-perfumed air. "You're right. I'm here now and I get to experience all this... and you."

Willa smiled. "I wish you could stay."

"So do I." Brim closed the gap between them in two steps and locked her in a passionate kiss.

Willa pulled away, her head and heart reeling. "Brim... I meant all of you... your father and friends."

A flush rose in Brim's cheeks. "Oh... I'm sorry."

Willa felt bad for him, reached out again, but thought better of it. "You're sweet, Brim, but I love Thorn."

"I see. That explains it."

"Explains what?"

"The awful looks he's been giving me."

Willa offered a sad smile and a nod. "He tends to be a bit jealous."

Thorn's voice startled them as he stepped from behind a large Yew tree. "Clearly, I have good reason to be." He stabbed an accusing finger at Brim. "I knew it! I knew we couldn't trust you!"

Willa jumped down from her perch. "Thorn! You're one to talk, spying on us like that!"

"You heard him! He asked you to defy the Council!"

Willa went up to Thorn, her golden eyes turning to fire as they reflected the setting sun. "Brim is asking for my help, not theirs!"

"Listen to yourself. You're talking about joining a war!"

"Not a war. A revolt, a fight for freedom!"

Thorn stepped around Willa and stood eye-to-eye with Brim who tensed, ready for a fight.

"I'm going to report you to the Council," Thorn said. "They'll ship you back to Orion without so much as a sack of rice!"

Brim's demeanor suddenly turned ice cold. "I can't let you do that."

A terrible dread welled up in Willa at the shift in Brim. "Thorn—"

Before she could utter a warning, Brim pulled a blade from a secret sheath in his boot and thrust it upward under Thorn's ribcage.

Thorn's mouth opened in a silent scream, eyes wide with shock and pain. Brim yanked the bloody blade free and Thorn dropped to the forest floor, dead.

Willa's scream pierced the silence. Her eyes clouded to pitch black. A bubble of incandescent energy burst from her body. Its leading edge raced outward in all directions and changed everything in its path, resetting the very fabric of reality.

Thorn once again stood before Willa; Brim had yet to draw his knife.

"Listen to yourself!" Thorn shouted as Willa reeled from Déjà vu. "You're talking about joining a war!"

"What's happening?" Willa said, dizzy and disoriented as her eyes returned to normal.

Thorn moved to step around Willa as before, aiming to threaten Brim.

Willa snapped from her trance, grabbed Thorn by the arm. "Thorn, listen, you can't—"

Thorn pulled free and continued toward Brim. Willa grabbed him again, spun him around and threw a wicked right cross. Thorn dropped to the forest floor, out cold. Willa stared at Thorn a moment, confused by the startling reversal of time. She lifted her gaze to Brim.

"Why did you do that?" Brim said, astonished.

"You were going to stab Thorn with the knife hidden in your boot," she blurted before she could stop herself.

Brim went ashen. "How did you know about my knife?"

"I'm not sure," Willa began, at a loss. Before she could say more, a thunderous crashing deep in the woods snapped their attention to the trees.

Brim's shock at Willa's claim was derailed by an even greater surprise as Kernunnos stomped into the clearing. Brim froze in fear as the towering Elemental unleashed an ear-splitting howl of anger that pierced him like an arctic gale. Kernunnos scooped Willa up in one gigantic paw and the unconscious Thorn in the other and carried them into the woods, vanishing in five titanic strides.

After several heartbeats, shock released its grip on Brim and he fainted. As night fell, the natural sounds of the forest filled the trees that surrounded him.

The crisp crackling of dry leaves grew louder as Rusalka and a clutch of his fellow Pookas cautiously emerged from the shadows. They sniffed at Brim to make sure he was still unconscious. Rusalka transformed into a small, red-eyed horse. The others lifted Brim above their furry ears, draped him over Rusalka's equine back and melted into the forest with their captive.

CHAPTER SIXTEEN

FRACTURES

"A thing is both a single system and a collection of components. The astonishing fact is that identical components, like subatomic particles, can be recombined over and over in various ways to generate new and wholly unique systems. All electrons are the same, all neutrons are the same and all protons are the same, yet the addition of a single proton to an atomic system is the difference between gold and mercury."

"The Book of Paradox"
by Sassafras the Sage

*

A SMALL, SPHERICAL probe skimmed through the air off the Portuguese coast, recording data with its scanning beams. Its task complete, the beams snapped off and the probe shot toward the sky at blinding speed.

Once in space, the probe angled toward the comet where Haldane's ship was hiding and docked in a receptacle in the hull.

On board, Haldane and Gant surveyed the images of various Earth locations and data collected by the probe. Haldane stopped the feed as a series of underwater caves along the Portuguese shoreline filled his monitor.

"There," he said. "That's where we'll hide the ship. It's relatively unpopulated."

Haldane guided his ship toward a comet fragment about three times the size of his vessel and, using his maneuvering thrusters, gently nudged it toward the targeted section of the Atlantic Ocean. As it built up speed due to the pull of Earth's gravity, Haldane lined the ship up directly behind the fragment and kept pace with it.

The fragment hit Earth's atmosphere and instantly heated to well over a thousand degrees, creating an ionized stream of superheated air and smoke that engulfed Haldane's ship and shielded it from detection.

Seconds before the meteor hit the water two hundred miles off the coast of Portugal, Haldane's ship veered off, plunged under the ocean and navigated toward land using magnetic thrusters.

The meteor's impact produced a small tsunami. Since it harmed no one and caused no real damage, everyone went back to business as usual after the initial excitement died down.

A few hours later, Haldane guided his ship into one of the large underwater caves that pockmarked the Portuguese coastline where they could intercept transmissions and hatch a plan before donning their replicated masks to mingle with the locals.

*

Ander Garza, a slender, dark-haired human in his forties, strolled down one of Andromeda Spaceport's curved corridors on his way to the astronomy lab, a trip he made from his apartment aboard the station every morning for the past ten years. Ander waved at several humans, Hybrids and aliens who populated the operations offices en route to the lab, but his main focus was on a data tablet he carried with him everywhere. Some aliens joked that Ander wouldn't remember what day it was, where he lived or when to eat if the tablet didn't beep to remind him. Ander took the ribbing in stride, partly because the good-natured jests were true. His passion for astronomy utterly absorbed him and he could spend days holed up in the lab, examining streams of data about some unexplained stellar phenomenon or cataloguing star systems inhabited by alien races the First Contact Council had recently discovered in their galactic explorations. He reached the lab and was scanned by one of the thousands of sensors that fed Ocularis a never-ending stream of information.

"Good morning, Ander," Ocularis chimed in its soothing tone.

"Morning," Ander parroted as the lab door slid open to admit him.

The astronomy lab contained an array of complex instruments and nano-glass computers, but was dominated by a large view screen that magnified and recorded the stellar images captured by Andromeda's powerful subspace telescopes.

The first thing Ander always checked when he entered the lab were the recordings made while he slept. With a tap on his tablet, the main viewer snapped to life and immediately replayed a recording of the Leviathan comet, along with words that flashed in red: ANOMALY DETECTED.

Ander watched with fascination as a small shard of the comet split off from the main body and streaked toward Earth. His brow furrowed as he watched the readouts plot the shard's odd trajectory.

"That's not possible," Ander muttered under his breath. He quickly transferred the data to his tablet and began to review the calculations.

*

Willa stood in a forest clearing under the stars, surrounded by Holly, Alder, Selene, Encantado and the rest of the Quorum. Argus and Kernunnos hunkered among the trees to one side with Thorn, who was just regaining his senses. He massaged his jaw and locked on Willa.

"Why did you hit—" Thorn stopped as he caught sight of the gathering. "What's going on? Where'd Brim go?" He looked around, confused. "Where are we?"

Selene ignored him as she circled Willa, her all-black eyes focused like a predator about to strike. "Do you have any idea how serious... how *dangerous* that was? Manipulating time and space takes years of practice, even for a Sage!" She thrust an accusing finger at Thorn, who got to his feet and dusted himself off. "Who knows what damage you did to the timeline by bringing him back! I warned you it might happen, that it was his fate!"

"I didn't know I could do that," Willa said. "But I would've done it anyway to save Thorn's life!"

Selene was livid. "Don't you understand? You didn't save his life. You erased his death! There's a difference! You created a rift in space-time that could have repercussions for everyone, not only in our timeline but in other parallel realities as well!" Selene turned to Holly. "I thought you said she was smart!"

"She's changing faster than I imagined possible. I haven't taught her that much about parallel timelines yet," Holly said calmly.

"Well you'd better start!" Selene snapped.

"Willa saved my life?" Thorn said, completely lost. "What are you talking about?"

Selene turned her soul-shattering gaze toward Thorn. "Silence, boy!"

Thorn shrank away, eyes downcast. He nodded his compliance.

Alder turned to Willa. "The Orion lad. What's his name again?"

"Brim," Willa answered.

"Brim," Alder repeated. "His attack clearly speaks of a hidden agenda."

"Told you," Thorn said to Willa, then frowned in confusion. "Wait. What attack?"

Willa threw him a look that warned him to stay quiet.

Holly collected her thoughts and turned to Alder. "The Council said Brim's not registering on their scanners and neither you nor Brahma can sense his location, so if the boy hasn't left the planet, it can only mean one thing."

Alder nodded. "He's deliberately being hidden. Only Elementals could do that."

"I suspect Pookas are behind it," Selene offered, still fuming.

"I agree," Holly said and turned to Kernunnos. "Will you lead us back to where you left Brim?"

The Forest Elemental nodded his huge horned head. "I will agree to that, because you are a friend of the forest. But if the Pookas believe the boy is a threat to our ways, they may not give him up, nor will I try to convince them that they should."

"I understand," Holly said and gestured to Argus. "Please go back and tell Brahma what's happening. Take Thorn with you. We'll bring Brim to the Council chamber for questioning soon as we find him." Argus grunted his agreement and waved at Thorn to follow him.

"I'd rather stay with Willa," Thorn protested.

"It's okay," Willa assured him. "I'll explain everything later, I promise."

Thorn glanced at Argus, hesitant. The Sasquatch gave an impatient snort, grabbed Thorn and unceremoniously lifted the boy onto his shaggy shoulders. Argus turned and headed back toward Port Dublin as Thorn held on to the Sasquatch's thick neck to keep from falling off.

Holly produced a small Luminaria from her coat pocket and lit the way as Kernunnos led the gathering through the dense thicket. Her mind searched for the best course of action to take once they found Brim. She turned to Willa as they hurried through the trees.

"When we find him, you will let me do the talking, is that clear?"

Willa nodded, not wishing to invite more trouble. Willa stumbled along behind Holly, oblivious to the forest around her, her legs on automatic, her mind flooded with questions. Was Brim a spy? Why didn't she see his attack coming with her heightened senses until it was too late? How had she been able to reverse time? What other abilities would burst forth without warning?

Willa's sense of dread grew stronger the deeper they ventured into the forest; her nightmare vision of the Archon's conquest and the mysterious grey girl's threat felt more inevitable with each step. Every fiber of her being screamed for her to turn back, yet powerful forces beyond her control urged her onward. Willa felt her life was no longer her own, a pawn of fate, suspended in time like an insect trapped in amber.

*

Kale and Rowan stood in the doorway to Dennik's quarters as the Orions filled backpacks with water and emergency supplies.

"The Quorum will find Brim and bring him back, I'm sure," Kale said. "There's no need for you to—"

Dennik sealed his pack, slung it over his shoulder and headed for the door. "He's my son. If he's lost, I'll be the one to search for him."

"As will we," Gar added. "He's one of us and our responsibility."

"You don't even know where to look," Kale said, hoping Dennik would listen to reason. "Brahma himself can't sense his whereabouts and something's blocking our ships' bio scanners."

Just then, Argus strode up, lifted the disheveled Thorn off his massive shoulders and set him down gently in front of Kale.

"You watch now," the Sasquatch grumbled as he turned and headed toward the Council building across the grounds.

"Are you okay?" Kale asked his son.

Thorn nodded, slightly embarrassed by his odd arrival.

"Where have you been?" Kale said before he noticed the bruise on his son's jaw. "What happened?"

"I'd rather explain in private," Thorn said under his breath with a sideways glance at his smirking brother. His expression changed as he peered past his father at Dennik, Gar and Koro. Kale turned and allowed a subdued smile at the startled look on the faces of the three Orions.

"What in the name of the Elder Gods was that?" Gar murmured, as though louder speech might lure the Sasquatch back.

"Argus," Kale said. "A member of the Quorum. One of Willa's mentors."

"An alien?" Koro interjected.

"No. It's a long story," Kale said.

"You seem to have a lot of those," Dennik said when he found his voice. "But we were talking about Brim."

"I saw him in the woods north of here," Thorn offered.

Dennik brightened. "Can you lead us there?"

"Yes… but he may not be where I left him. The forest goes on for miles. He could be anywhere."

"All the more reason to start looking now," Dennik insisted.

"The Council has requested that you remain here," Kale pleaded.

"Hang your Council," Gar spat, "they only care for themselves!"

"I can't let you go out without supervision," Kale said.

"Then come with us, you and your sons, but you'll not stop me from finding my boy. Now please… step aside, Kale."

"At least give us a few minutes to gather supplies," Rowan offered.

"Fine," Dennik said, "be quick about it."

Kale turned to Thorn. "Stay with them."

"But—"

"It'll be okay. Rowan and I will be right back," Kale assured him as he and Rowan hurried out.

Thorn turned to find Dennik's, Gar's and Koro's green eyes on him. He cleared his throat in the awkward silence.

"What aren't you telling us?" Dennik frowned.

"What? Nothing!"

Dennik walked up to Thorn until he was six inches from the boy's twitching face. "Being in the Black League long as we have, our lives sometimes depend on being able to tell when someone's lying."

"Really, it's nothing. I was just…"

Dennik pressed closer. "Just what?"

Thorn blushed crimson. "I was following Willa and Brim."

Gar and Koro stepped up, corralling Thorn along with Dennik.

"Why?" Gar demanded.

"I… I was jealous."

Dennik relaxed his threatening stance. "You thought my son… and Willa?"

Thorn nodded, embarrassed.

"So how did you lose track of them?" Koro asked.

"Willa saw me. She got mad. She… she knocked me out," Thorn said, beyond humiliated.

The Orions burst into laughter, the tension broken. "She'd fit right in with the League," Koro said, slapping Thorn on the back.

"Then Willa's with Brim," Dennik said.

"No. When I woke up, we were both with the Quorum. One of the Elementals spirited us away from where we were. Brim was left behind."

The humor drained from Dennik's face. "Elementals?"

"Nature spirits who live in the forest," Thorn said.

"Spirits?" Gar said with apprehension. "You mean ghosts? What nonsense is this, boy?"

"No, not ghosts. It's hard to explain. Anyway, I came back here but Willa stayed."

"Save it for later," Dennik said. "We need to find Brim and no spirit's going to stand in our way."

"My father and brother should be back soon," Thorn said.

"Thanks for the reminder." Gar said and decked Thorn with a blistering right hook.

Dennik caught the boy's limp body and set him gently on the floor. "Sorry, Thorn, this just isn't your day."

The Orions hurried out the door and quickly made their way across the grounds to the edge of the forest, where they melted into the shadows.

*

Willa and the gathering stood in the clearing where she last saw Brim. Holly went over to a large Yew tree and placed her hand on its towering trunk. She closed her eyes and focused her thoughts. After a moment, she rejoined the group.

"The trees confirm that the Pookas took Brim, but they're also being blocked from revealing his location," Holly reported.

"There's someone who might be able to sense where he is," Willa said.

"Who?" Encantado said with his usual haste.

"The Banshee."

Holly was aghast. "You can't be serious."

"Selene's right. You're dangerous," Encantado added, his concern laced with curiosity.

"What choice do we have?" Willa countered.

Holly scanned the gathering. It was clear no one had a better idea. She gave Willa a hesitant nod.

Willa walked toward a small clearing of bare earth near Selene. "You might want to make yourself scarce," she whispered as she passed the Nocturnal.

Selene realized what Willa was about to do and nodded.

Willa grabbed a stick from the ground and drew the symbol in the dirt that Belladonna had shown her. When all eyes were on Willa, Selene slowly and quietly stepped out of sight behind a large Yew tree.

Willa completed the symbol. "Belladonna! Can you hear me? It's Willa!" she called out in a loud, clear voice. "Belladonna! Please answer me!"

A piercing, high-pitched wail cut through her like a cold steel blade. It echoed through the trees and froze everyone to the spot, including

Kernunnos. Belladonna the Banshee appeared and floated through the trees ahead of them, her glowing eyes fixed on Willa.

"Are you here to fulfill your promise?" Belladonna said.

"Not exactly," Willa replied. "I need another favor."

*

The Archon's ship curved around Xos in high orbit. From space, the planet's surface was a grey and black patchwork of stone and metal, interrupted here and there by large, circular reservoirs that were once lakes and seas. The drab mosaic was laced with a spider web of canals and massive pipelines that delivered water, synthesized food and fuel to industrial plants and the cement-block barrios of the oppressed population.

The Archon sat in the pilot's seat, directing the ship's course via his neuro-telepathic link with the computer.

Yadra and Doona occupied the other two seats, focused on monitor readouts that displayed the ship's systems.

"All systems are at optimum, my Lord," Yadra reported.

Xos-Asura remained silent, as he usually did when given good news, since he expected nothing less than perfection from his subjects. However, the ship's smooth operation was short-lived. The sub-light engines abruptly climbed to full power and the ship sped off through space toward the distant Maelstrom.

The Archon attempted to power down and course correct, but the console didn't respond. His deadly gaze turned toward Yadra.

The terrified minion worked frantically to gain control but the ship remained unresponsive. "I… I apologize, my Lord. I don't understand what's happened. I can't find anything wrong with the systems!"

The computer's dispassionate voice filled the cabin. "That's because there's nothing wrong."

Xos-Asura swiveled back to face the computer interface nestled in the center of the main control console.

"Explain," the Archon demanded.

"I've taken control of the ship's systems," Sagittarius responded.

"Why?"

"I've been programmed to recognize neurological patterns that represent a high degree of imbalance. When we established the interface, I determined that your thought process is incompatible with the interests of the Contact Council."

"I am your captive, then," the Archon concluded without emotion.

"Yes. I've set a course for Earth. As soon as I calculate a safe route through the anomaly that destroyed my ship, I'll deliver you to the Council for questioning."

"And if I resist?"

"I'll open the airlock."

Without another word, the Archon rose and moved to the back of the cabin. He released the manual lock on the single escape pod and, as Doona and Yadra watched in baffled silence, Xos-Asura stepped inside, sealed the hatch and launched the pod into space.

Doona turned to the computer. "The Archon's escaped."

"I have no control over manual systems," Sagittarius said.

"Are we also your captives or will you return us to Xos?" Doona said with a flicker of hope.

"I will not keep you captive for long," the computer assured him. "If I am correct in my psychological assessment of your Archon—"

The ship and its occupants exploded in an incandescent fireball that reduced it to cosmic dust in the blink of an eye.

Miles away, the Archon switched off his remote detonator and piloted the escape pod back to the Citadel on Xos. The distant explosion faded as quickly as the Archon's memory of his two dead minions.

*

Brim awoke with a score of glowing ruby-red eyes staring down at him. He jumped to his feet in a panic, ran and tripped over a stone block. He fell at the feet of several other Elementals, including Ashleen. Brim stared up in fear at the elder Pooka's pink eyes.

"Who are you? Where... where am I?" he stammered.

"No manners, these off-worlders," Ashleen complained. "No manners at all!"

Brim scrambled away from the Elemental and froze when he realized he was boxed in by the towering stone ruins of an ancient Abbey, surrounded by all manner of strange creatures. Faeries fluttered in the air on gossamer wings, wrinkled gnomes squatted atop moss-encrusted stone blocks, slender salamanders blinked at him with fiery orange eyes.

"I'm dreaming," he said, trying to convince himself.

Rusalka, once again a hare, hopped forward and slapped Brim across the face. "Then this is your wake up call."

Brim tensed as the albino Pooka approached. "My name is Ashleen," she said and waited for Brim to respond. He just stared at her, tongue-tied. Ashleen sighed, growing impatient. "And yours?"

"Brim." He finally managed.

Ashleen wrinkled her rabbit nose at him. "Odd name. Where are you from?"

"Why am I here?"

"Answer the question," Ashleen pressed.

Lying on the ground as he was, Brim's attention shifted to the stars above Ashleen's furry face. He pointed to the Orion constellation.

"I was told those are the stars of my home."

The Pooka glanced skyward, then back to Brim. "I've never seen your kind here before."

"No," Brim admitted, "we're visitors."

"We?"

"He came with his father and two others," Rusalka explained. "Refugees from a slave world."

Ashleen cocked her head at the boy. "You escaped?"

"Yes," Brim nodded quickly, hoping to buy sympathy. "Earth offered us sanctuary after we rescued one of your people."

Ashleen looked to Rusalka. "One of ours?"

"He means Kale Ashgrove." Rusalka turned his red eyes on Brim. "If you're under the Contact Council's protection, you won't be needing this, will you?" The Pooka held up Brim's knife.

Brim instinctively slapped a hand on the empty sheath in his boot. "That's mine. Give it back... please."

Ashleen frowned. "We don't allow such things in our forest."

"Give it to me and I'll leave."

Rusalka lowered the blade to his side. "Not until we ken why you were involved in a time shift."

"A what?"

Grennan, the Pookas' aged seer, stepped forward. "A shift in the timeline," he said as he sniffed at the boy. "You reek of temporal residue, that's for sure."

Brim blinked, confused. "I have no idea what you're talking about. For that matter, I have no idea who or what you are. I've seen pictures of animals that used to live on my home world before the Overlords came. You look similar to some of them but, as far as I know, none of them were able to talk."

Ashleen bristled at the comparison, then forced herself to calm down. "Everything talks if you know how to listen. As I already said, my name is Ashleen." She gestured to the group around her. "We're known by many names. Pookas, like myself, Sylphs, Salamanders, Undines, Gnomes. Nature Spirits. We're Elemental Beings."

Brim shook his head. "You might as well be speaking Jarushka."

Ashleen turned to Rusalka, exasperated. "And I thought humans were dense."

*

The Quorum, along with Kernunnos, stood facing the Banshee. Kernunnos rocked back and forth, his eyes locked on Belladonna. Dark spirits were the only things that made the giant Elemental nervous.

Belladonna scowled at Willa, less than pleased. "Another favor!"

Willa took a few steps toward the apparition, even though Holly tugged at her to stay back. Willa waved her mentor off and locked eyes with Belladonna. "We need your help to find someone. It's very important."

Belladonna peered intently at Willa. "There's something different about you." She focused her ethereal senses and was shocked to discover the truth. "You altered time!" she said. "That means you have the power to take me back to the time before I became a Banshee."

"Belladonna," Holly said as soothingly as she could, "Willa can't control the power yet. Asking her to invoke another time shift without the proper training could have catastrophic results."

"Besides," Alder interjected, "even if she did reset time, you wouldn't know it had happened. Without someone there like Willa to stop you, you'd make the same mistake you made before."

Belladonna floated in silence, unsure whether to trust Holly and Alder.

"They're telling the truth," Willa interrupted. "Please trust me. As soon as I find a way to bring you back safe and sound, I will."

"Very well," the Banshee said, still skeptical. "Who are you searching for?"

Holly took the lead. "We're looking for a boy, a little older than Willa, a stranger to this world."

Belladonna's eyes glowed a bit more brightly. "I see him. Those foul little Pookas have him at the Abbey." Belladonna hesitated as her vision unfolded. "I also sense he's part of the danger I warned you about."

"I know," Willa admitted, her tone somber.

"Thank you for your help," Holly said with a respectful bow of her head. "I'll add my promise to Willa's. We won't forget you."

Belladonna's expression softened slightly. "I'll trust your good nature, Cryptic. See that you don't take advantage of mine." She turned to Willa. "But before I go, I would love to feel the earth under my feet again, if only for a moment."

Willa hesitated. "You promise to behave?"

"I have no enemies here," Belladonna said with sincerity.

Willa nodded and allowed the spirit to pass through her body. Belladonna regained solid formed and gently landed on the forest floor. She dug her toes into the soft soil, closed her eyes, took a deep breath and released an ecstatic sigh as the Quorum watched, amazed at her transformation. Even Selene peered out from her hiding place to witness her great-grandmother's mortal moment.

A few heartbeats later, Belladonna sublimed back into her vaporous form. She floated upward and smiled at Willa. "Thank you." Willa nodded her own thanks and with that, the Banshee vanished like smoke in the wind.

"Amazing," Alder said with awe as he glanced at Willa. She averted her eyes, embarrassed and wary of the Sage's attention.

"I didn't truly believe you could be this powerful," Moshi admitted, "until I saw what you just did with my own eyes."

Eridani smiled at Willa and Rose and Lilac blinked as though seeing her for the first time.

"We should go," Holly reminded everyone.

"The Abbey is this way," Kernunnos said, relieved that the Banshee had departed. He headed northward through the trees and the others followed.

Selene blended back in with the group and caught up to Holly and Willa. "You understand you can't time shift for Belladonna. You have to find another way."

"What do you mean?" Willa said, not sure where the Nocturnal was going with this.

Selene frowned in exasperation. "She became a Banshee over three hundred years ago, remember? If you time shift her back to a living Sage, you erase three hundred years of history, along with us and, being the only one left who would know that time had been altered, you'd need to warn her not to drink the corrupted Divinorum and that would create yet another altered timeline."

"Right," Willa admitted, feeling foolish. "I guess I really do have a lot to learn."

"Humility at last," Selene said. "Perhaps there's hope for you after all."

When Holly wasn't looking, Selene mouthed a silent 'thank you' to Willa, then stepped up her pace and fell in behind Kernunnos. Holly glanced over at Willa's downcast face as they hurried along.

"Keep your spirits up," Holly said with a smile. "That's as close to a compliment as you're likely to get from Selene."

Willa walked the rest of the way in silence. She knew that the real reason Selene urged caution in bringing Belladonna back to the land of the living was that she wanted the Banshee's Divinorum recipe for herself. Willa hated keeping Selene's secrets, hated not being able to confide in Holly or her mother, but a promise was a promise and she would have to find her way out of the maddening dilemma without anyone's help.

*

Xos-Asura stood before a new team of techs, all paying rapt attention to the Archon.

"Use the data extracted from the Earth pilot and the analysis of their computer to construct a new one that will link only to me. You will accomplish this within twenty cycles."

The new lead tech, a pale, pea-green Takanni alien named Soonash spoke under his breath to a fellow technician. "Twenty cycles? That's impossible."

The Archon's sharp hearing snatched the comment from midair. "I assume the previous crew's reward will provide sufficient motivation?"

Soonash's long neck retracted into his bone-colored carapace. "Yes, my Lord," he answered with a nervous tick in his one large, lemon-yellow eye.

As Xos-Asura turned and left, all eyes remained forward, locked on the corpses of the last tech crew, hanging by their necks from the steel rafters.

*

Thorn awoke to see his father and brother staring down at him. Each took a hand and helped Thorn sit up. He winced and rubbed his aching jaw.

"Why does everyone keep punching me?"

"Who hit you?" Kale demanded.

"Gar."

They pulled Thorn to his feet. Kale examined the swollen purple bruise on his son's face. "He and I will have words when we catch up to them."

Rowan adjusted his backpack. "We don't know which way they went."

Kale held Thorn's gaze. "Can you take us to where you left the Quorum?"

Thorn nodded.

"Then that's where we'll start." Kale hurried out the door.

Rowan handed Thorn a backpack. "Try to duck next time."

Thorn threw a withering look at his brother as they hurried after their father.

*

Gant and Haldane, wearing their replicated Hybrid masks, wove their way through the crowd of humans, Hybrids and aliens that populated the seaside settlement of Sintra near Port Lisbon.

Locals and tourists wandered under stone arches and beneath the square stone towers of the ancient Moorish castle that had been converted long ago into a sprawling market that drew beings from far and wide.

Even without their masks, Haldane and Gant wouldn't normally have drawn a second glance from the throng of aliens that traded all manner of exotic foods and goods from across the galaxy. Nevertheless, they reasoned it would be prudent to remain in disguise while searching for clues to the Black League's whereabouts.

The Orions kept their voices low as they took in the kaleidoscope of sights, sounds and smells that threatened to overload their senses.

"How do they tolerate this chaos?" Haldane said as they pushed their way past a particularly dense gathering of Shunzai from the Eridani system, their scarlet scales glistening in the light from dozens of Luminaria that floated overhead. Haldane reached up and tapped a Luminaria globe with his finger. The crystalline sphere moved a few inches away and gently floated back to its original position.

Gant and Haldane stared at one of Sintra's human denizens as he strolled down the street, engaged in a conversation in Portuguese with an intelligent, nano-glass robot that resembled a slender, featureless Greyhound.

"Impressive technology," Haldane murmured, slightly envious.

"The wealth of this world would enrich the Empire beyond measure," Gant proclaimed, his mind frothing with ways he might use Earth's vast resources to gain an advantage over the Archon.

As the covert pair passed by the dining patio of a bustling teahouse, they caught a snippet of conversation between Ander Garza and a blue-eyed female Hybrid named Jacaranda Florus, her forehead emblazoned with an eight-pointed star tattoo that marked her as the Alliance's chief astronomer.

Ander was adamant. "I'm telling you, Jac, there's something off about that recent meteor. The math doesn't add up. Look." He handed his colleague a data pad covered in glowing calculations.

Haldane pulled Gant to an empty table within earshot.

"What am I looking at?" Jacaranda said.

"The station keeps track of every Near-Earth Object. This isn't one of them."

Jacaranda nodded. "It probably calved off from the Leviathan comet."

"That's just it," Ander continued, "the rock's trajectory doesn't make sense. It took a course nearly perpendicular to the comet's path. For that to have happened, it would have had to suddenly lose all its forward momentum, which is pretty much impossible."

Jacaranda studied the data. "Are you sure these calculations are—" She stopped herself as she caught Ander's glare. "You wouldn't have brought this to me if you hadn't triple-checked as usual. Apologies. So what's your conclusion?"

"Here's the crazy part," Ander said, lowering his voice. "I think someone deliberately sent that rock toward Earth."

Haldane and Gant exchanged a concerned glance. A pleasant-looking elderly woman appeared at the Orions' table.

"Would you care to order tea or honey biscuits?" She hummed with a matronly smile.

"No." Gant said with gruff impatience. Haldane eyeballed him until Gant realized he had been curt enough to draw the attention of a few nearby customers. "I mean… no, thank you. We're just… resting a moment if that's alright."

"Perfectly," the shop owner said and ambled toward another table of guests. Haldane and Gant turned their attention back to Ander and Jac, hoping they hadn't missed anything.

"Are you writing another novel?" Jacaranda said to Ander with a dry smile.

"Really, Jacaranda?"

"You said it yourself, Ander. The theory's crazy. Who would do such a thing? And why?"

Ander's voice lowered another notch. Gant and Haldane strained to hear, trying not to look obvious.

"You've heard the news about the off-worlders, yes?" Ander said.

"You mean the Orions? Of course."

"Word is they come from an extremely militant society bent on conquering and enslaving entire planets."

Jacaranda frowned. "I don't see the connection."

"What better way to decimate a population than to toss a few meteors onto our cities? It's cheap, accessible artillery."

"So, you're saying the meteor was, what… some kind of test? The Orions are the guests of the Contact Council. Why would they do such a thing? For that matter, how could they have done it without the Council's awareness?"

Ander's voice lowered another notch. "What if there are more Orions than we know?"

Jacaranda steepled her fingers as she processed Ander's comment. "I don't know. That's long on theory and short on proof."

"True," Ander admitted. "Still, it's a theory the Contact Council should be made aware of."

Jac nodded. "Agreed. Have you been to Port Dublin?"

Ander shook his head. "No. I'd welcome a guide."

Jacaranda smiled. "Happy to. I'll gather my things and meet you at the Shaddok." Ander nodded and headed out. Haldane and Gant waited a moment before they followed the unsuspecting scientist.

A grizzled old Shapeshifter named Variabilis, wearing a dark cloak and hood that hid his square-jawed face, stood in the shadows of a doorway across from the teashop. His obsidian eyes tracked Haldane and Gant as they hurried down the street after Ander. The Shapeshifter followed them, keeping his distance, and melted into the crowd.

CHAPTER SEVENTEEN

ENCLAVE

"In the ancient story 'Alice in Wonderland,' Alice falls down a rabbit hole in pursuit of a White Rabbit wearing a pocket watch who laments that he's late for an important date. What most people at that time didn't realize is that the rabbit hole was meant to represent a portal to another dimension and that the 'rabbit' in question was, in reality, a Pooka. After all, real rabbits don't talk and couldn't care less about time."

Excerpt from "The Quintessential Elemental"
by Nightshade the Nocturnal

*

BRIM SAT CROSS-LEGGED on the ground in the center of four increasingly larger circles of Elementals within a large forest clearing. The smallest circle, closest to Brim, included the Pookas who, along with the Gnomes, represented the energy of the Earth. The next circle was composed of Salamanders and other fire Elementals. Outside that, Undines and a variety of water Elementals formed the third ring and the outer circle was filled with Sylphs and all the Elementals of the air.

Every being that partook of the Enclave was locked in a trance, their eyes glowing with light as they held Brim in a soul-penetrating gaze. Brim squirmed under the intense scrutiny but had little choice other than to remain where he was.

Just beyond the clearing, hidden behind a dense grove of Yew and Oak trees, Holly, Willa and the Quorum watched the ritual in silence. Kernunnos was hunkered at the edge of the clearing, also in trance, his eyes glowing like the rest of the Elementals.

"What are they doing to Brim?" Willa whispered to Holly.

"It's an Enclave," she said, her voice equally hushed. "They're reading his heart energy to determine his true intentions. It's the Elemental version of a lie detector. We'll have to wait until the trance is broken."

As the Enclave's energy built to a crescendo, the Pookas' ruby-red eyes became clear as glass and emanated a brilliant white light. The air around the gathering buzzed with electricity. Brim's body stiffened as though gripped by an invisible force field. With every heartbeat, electromagnetic waves radiated outward from Brim's chest and passed through the Elementals in each ring, dissipating just beyond the Enclave's perimeter.

With a final burst of light, the energy waves vanished and the Elementals' eyes returned to normal. Brim went limp, exhausted from the ordeal.

"What did you do to me?"

"It's what you've done that's of concern," Ashleen responded.

"I haven't done anything."

Holly stepped into the clearing, followed by Willa and the Quorum. "That's not entirely true."

The Elementals turned toward her and parted as Holly and Willa marched up to Brim, who stood to face them. "At last. I was worried you might not find me—"

Willa's anger cut him short. "Worried? You murdered Thorn! If I hadn't brought him back—"

Brim's eyes darted from Willa to Holly and back again. "What are you talking about? I didn't murder anybody!"

Holly placed a gentle hand on Willa's shoulder and locked eyes with her. "Remember what we discussed?"

Willa reluctantly backed down and let Holly do the talking. "Brim, something's happened that may be difficult for you to understand. But before I explain, I need to speak with Ashleen."

Holly waved the Pooka queen to one side and engaged in a whispered conversation as the Quorum looked on. A palpable tension darkened the air between Willa and Brim, but they remained silent. Now and then, Ashleen gestured toward Brim, who didn't like the expression on her furry face one bit. Their exchange ended with a nod of understanding from Holly and they rejoined the group.

"This is far more serious than I thought," Holly said. "We need to get Brim back to the Contact Council immediately."

"I don't understand what's happening! You said you'd explain," Brim protested.

"It'll have to wait. Come, we must hurry," Holly said and, with a silent touch of thanks on Kernunnos's furry forearm, she headed back the way they had come. The Quorum let Brim pass by and, with a final glance at Rusalka, Willa followed them all into the forest.

Rusalka ambled up to Ashleen as they watched the Quorum depart.

"You were right," Ashleen said to Rusalka. "That girl is the key. Holly's instruction may take too long. If our people are going to survive, we need to help her realize her full potential soon."

"Are you suggesting…"

Ashleen nodded and kept her voice to a whisper. "The Kenning."

"But she's not an Elemental," Rusalka said with genuine concern. "It could damage her, even kill her."

"It's a risk," Ashleen agreed, "but it's our only hope." She fixed her pink eyes on Rusalka. "If I didn't know you better, I'd say you'd taken a shine to Willa."

Rusalka's nose twitched in annoyance. "There's no need to be insulting."

Ashleen smiled and turned her attention back to the departing Quorum.

Without knowing why, Willa felt a cold shiver caress her skin. She stopped at the edge of the clearing, turned and locked eyes with Ashleen and Rusalka for an eternal heartbeat, then followed the Quorum into the forest.

*

Ander walked with purpose through the ancient streets of Sintra as he made his way to the Shaddok. He turned down a cobblestoned alley, dimly lit by a few amber-hued Luminaria globes, unaware of the two slender silhouettes that followed half a block behind him. Ander turned a corner, momentarily out of sight.

Haldane and Gant pulled razor-thin curved blades from under their cloaks as they closed on their prey. They turned the corner and spotted Ander as he crossed the street toward another alley.

Without warning, Ander stopped under a floating Luminaria sphere, his back exposed to his attackers. Mere yards away, Haldane and Gant poised their blades to strike when their target abruptly turned to face them. Taken by surprise, the Orions hesitated.

The surprise on their masked faces shifted to shock as Ander suddenly morphed into Variabilis, his all-black eyes pinned on them.

"What do you want with Ander Garza?" said the Shapeshifter in a voice like viscous oil.

Haldane lunged at Variabilis, the point of his blade aimed at the Shapeshifter's heart. Variabilis's hand turned to steel as it shot up, grabbed the blade and snapped it in half. Haldane recoiled, fear in his eyes.

"What sorcery is this?" Haldane croaked.

"You're not from here," Variabilis said. "Your faces are false."

Haldane and Gant turned to run. The Shapeshifter's arms transformed into long tentacles that snapped out and wrapped around the fleeing Orions, pinning their arms to their sides. As Variabilis pulled them close, two more tentacles plucked the masks from his captives' faces and tossed them aside.

"Who are you?" Variabilis said, his tone threatening. "Why were you stalking Ander?"

Haldane and Gant remained tight-lipped.

"I see. Perhaps a little perspective will loosen your tongues." Variabilis took on a demonic aspect as he shifted into a gigantic bat, the terrified Orions clutched in his gnarled talons. They pounded at him, tried to break free, but Variabilis's grip was too powerful. With a thunderous beat of his large, leathery wings, the Shapeshifter carried his screaming captives into the star-studded sky.

When they were a mile up, the Shapeshifter hovered in the crisp air. The warm lights of Sintra stretched out below them. Gant and Haldane stopped trying to free themselves and held on for dear life.

"Lovely view, don't you think?" the bat inquired with deliberate nonchalance.

"Let us go!" Gant yelled.

"As you wish," Variabilis said. He opened his talon and dropped Gant.

"No!" Haldane screamed.

Variabilis plummeted after Gant and caught him a thousand feet above the ground before he soared back into the heavens with his prisoners.

"Feeling more talkative?" Variabilis said.

Gant's breath came in spurts. "The man we followed was going to make a false accusation to the authorities!"

"That's a lie," the Shapeshifter said. "If you lie again, I'll let go and I won't save you next time."

"I can't answer your questions if I die," Gant pointed out in desperation.

The bat's eyes glinted at him. "If you die, your friend here might be more forthcoming."

"We live or die together," Haldane said.

Variabilis sensed Haldane's conviction. "Very well." He tightened his grip on the two Orions and flew northward over the moonlit countryside.

*

A gentle knock brought Poppy to her front door. She opened it and found Lily standing on the porch.

"Mother Hillicrissing, what a pleasant surprise," Poppy said, her mind racing with several unpleasant reasons why Willa's mother would pay them an unannounced visit this late in the evening. "I'll let my mother know you're here."

"I'm not here to see Sylvania," Lily said as she entered the warm glow of the fire-lit living room. "I'm here to see you."

Poppy shut the door. "Me? Is something wrong? Is Willa okay?"

"That's what I'm here to find out."

"I don't know what you mean," Poppy said, fearing that she knew exactly why Lily had come.

"You're Willa's best friend. She may not tell me her secrets, but I know she tells them to you, and now you'll tell them to me."

But... they're secrets," Poppy said as though it should be obvious.

"Not where my daughter's safety is concerned," Lily responded. "It's dire enough that she's made a promise to a Banshee, a promise she probably can't keep, but she's seen something in her Divinorum visions that has robbed the joy from her soul and she refuses to tell her mentor and her own mother what it is."

Poppy swallowed in a dry throat. "What makes you think she told me?"

Lily narrowed her deep blue eyes in a way that told Poppy she wasn't leaving until she got what she came for.

Poppy sighed, resigned to her fate and gestured to a comfortable chair. "There's a lot to tell."

"I have time," Lily said as she sat. "Why not enlighten me over a cup of tea?"

*

Willa, Brim and the Quorum emerged from the edge of the Yew forest and made their way toward the distant Shaddok. Three silhouettes, rimmed in silver moonlight, stood on a small rise, blocking their path.

Brim locked on them as they approached. "Father!"

Dennik quickened his pace. "You found my son!"

Brim headed toward Dennik. Alder gripped his arm, anchored Brim to the spot. Holly stepped out in front of the Quorum, her hand outstretched. "Stay where you are!"

Dennik stopped, puzzled. "What's wrong? Why are you holding Brim?"

"We need to deliver him to the Council. There are questions that must be addressed."

Dennik frowned. "What are you saying?" He faced his son. "Brim? What happened?"

"I've done nothing, Father! I swear! I don't know what's happening!"

Selene stepped up next to Brim. "Say nothing!" She turned her unnerving ebony eyes toward the Orions. "Your son's been involved in an incident. You will not speak to him until we learn the truth of it!"

Gar stepped out in front of Dennik, his temper rising. "You said we were your guests. Is Brim now your prisoner instead?"

"That remains to be seen," Holly interjected. "If you want your son back, do not detain us further."

One of the Shaddok portals flared to life behind Dennik and his men. Kale, Rowan and Thorn stepped through it and the light faded. They sensed the tension in the gathering before them, but before Kale could speak, Thorn jabbed a finger at Gar.

"He attacked me!"

"I was keeping you out of this in case there was a problem, which obviously, there is," Gar said, gesturing to Brim.

"That's for the Council to decide," Holly said as she led the Quorum toward the Shaddok.

Dennik blocked her. "You're not taking my son anywhere without me."

Kale stepped between them. "Dennik, whatever the problem is, the Council will straighten it out. They'll be fair, trust me."

"Trust you?" Gar spat. "We rescued you and trusted your almighty Council to help us. All we got for our trouble was three obsolete cargo ships!"

Alder watched the back and forth with barely disguised boredom. He handed Brim to Selene and sauntered up to the Orions.

"Gentlemen, allow me to explain." Before Dennik could protest, Alder quickly but gently touched each of them directly over their hearts with a single finger that flashed a spark of electric blue light and they froze like statues. Satisfied they'd be no further trouble, Alder strolled back to the Quorum.

"It's getting late and I would really like to have tea and evening meal before it turns into breakfast," he said to Holly.

Brim strained against Selene's grip, to no avail. The Nocturnal was immovable as stone. "What did you do to my father?"

"Don't worry. I merely overloaded their motor nerves. It'll wear off after we leave," Alder assured him.

The group headed for the Shaddok. Willa caught up to Thorn, who was still seething. She glanced at his bruised jaw as they walked.

"I'm sorry I hit you," she said.

"Seems you started a trend," Thorn said without looking at her. He glanced over at Brim as Selene pushed her prisoner forward, and took pleasure in the Orion boy's downcast face. "I told you something was off about him," he gloated. Thorn picked up his pace and joined his father and brother as they stepped through the Shaddok portal and vanished.

The others followed suit and within seconds, the only sign of life in the meadow were the three immobilized Orions. Alder's spell broke as he had promised, setting Dennik, Gar and Koro free.

Dennik shook off the lingering effects of the paralysis and raced toward the Shaddok, Gar on his heels. Koro hesitated as he tried to clear his head.

Gar glanced back. "Koro?"

Dennik stopped. "We need to get to the Council chamber to demand Brim's release!"

"Go ahead, I'll only slow you down," Koro said.

Dennik nodded and stepped through the portal, followed by Gar.

Koro glanced up at the stars and took several deep breaths of cool night air to clear the cobwebs from his mind. As he stared up at the night sky, a disturbing, surreal feeling crept over him that something was terribly wrong, although he couldn't quite put his finger on it. As his eyes tracked the various constellations, Koro became more and more disoriented until, in a single heartbeat, he was flooded with a terrifying realization that threatened to shatter his sanity.

"Impossible!"

CHAPTER EIGHTEEN

VARIABILIS

"The ability to shape-shift has nothing to do with a rearrangement of matter in the classic sense, but everything to do with parallel realities that exist simultaneously with our own. Imagine you're in a labyrinth of mirrors, each reflecting back a different angle, a different shape of your body. Then imagine that you can become one of those alternate reflections, shift your consciousness, your identity and perspective so as to see through its eyes. That is the secret of the Shapeshifters."

"The Five Levels of Mastery"
by Sequoia August Moon

*

GANT AND HALDANE awoke on a cold stone floor in a hexagonal, vaulted chamber that served as the hub for six other rooms that comprised Variabilis's lodgings. A few high windows glinted with dawn light. The Shapeshifter, having returned to his original Hybrid form, sat in a carved wooden chair, his inky gaze fixed on the unmasked Orions.

"Good morning," Variabilis said cheerfully, as though Gant and Haldane were favored houseguests. The Orions scrambled to their feet, wary. They looked around and riveted on a pair of large, wooden doors at the far end of one chamber that served as an entry hall.

"Where are we?" Haldane demanded.

"My humble home," the Shapeshifter obliged.

"How did you turn into… that creature?" Haldane said, afraid that Variabilis might do so again at any moment.

"I'm a Shapeshifter."

Haldane kept his eyes on him. "You say that like it's an ordinary thing."

"Well, not everyone chooses to follow the path of Mastery," Variabilis said as though conversing with an apprentice, "but it's not uncommon."

Gant finally found his voice. "You carried us too high into the upper atmosphere. We passed out."

"He did it on purpose so we wouldn't see where he was taking us," Haldane stated as a matter of fact.

Variabilis nodded. "I'm glad you understand. I'd prefer our conversation to be more… transparent."

Gant glanced at the doors once again. "We're your prisoners, then."

"Oh, you're quite free to leave," Variabilis said with no hint of guile.

Haldane and Gant eyed their host with suspicion as they slowly made their way to the doors. They pulled the curved metal handles and the huge doors swung smoothly inward on oiled hinges. Gant and Haldane froze before taking a cautious step onto a short balcony.

They gazed out at the snow-capped mountains that surrounded the Shapeshifter's stone tower. They were in an aerie at the very top, fully three hundred feet up with no visible way down.

Haldane scowled at Variabilis. "Free to leave…"

"Once you learn to fly, of course," Variabilis added with a genial smile.

The Orions stepped back inside. Gant glared at the smug Shapeshifter. "You can't keep us here!"

"I will happily return you to Sintra after you tell me who you are and why you attacked Ander."

"We attacked *you*."

"True, but you *thought* I was Ander." The Shapeshifter stood and warmed himself before a crackling fire that blazed in a large stone hearth. "You have three choices: Talk, become permanent houseguests or walk out those doors."

"If we talk, you could strand us here anyway… or kill us," Haldane said, defeated.

"No. I'll take you to the Contact Council and let them decide what to do with you. You have my word."

"We don't know you. Your word means nothing," Gant grumbled.

"Fair enough. But I don't see that you have much choice," Variabilis countered.

Haldane thought it through. "The meteor that landed off your coast… we made that happen so we could use it as camouflage to land undetected."

"What are you doing?" Gant hissed.

Haldane faced Gant and threw a look that hinted at a plan. "You heard this creature. What choice do we have?"

Gant understood Haldane's secret signal and decided to play along. "None, I suppose."

Variabilis frowned. "Call me a creature again and you'll take the short cut to the bottom of the tower."

Haldane continued. "Apologies. We're here to rescue our friends. Their ship malfunctioned and they made an emergency landing on your planet. We were searching for clues as to where they landed."

"So why attack Ander?"

"We know nothing of your world," Gant said, picking up the thread of Haldane's fabrication. "Your people might've been hostile. Your friend Ander realized we used the meteor to disguise our arrival and was about to alert your Council. We believed we had to stop him to protect our friends."

Haldane and Gant could almost hear their nervous hearts beating as Variabilis absorbed their story, trying to sense whether or not it was true.

"You say you know nothing of Earth," the Shapeshifter said with mounting suspicion, "yet you speak our language."

"We wondered about that since we landed," Haldane said, "but from our point of view, your people speak *our* language. How is this possible?"

"You expect me to believe that?" the Shapeshifter said.

"It's the truth," Haldane replied as Gant nodded to back him up.

Variabilis narrowed his eyes as though it might provide him with deeper insight. He stood and pointed to a chamber with cupboards and a hearth that served as a kitchen. "There's food and drink. I'll think about what you've said."

The Orions glanced toward the kitchen but hesitated.

"It's not poisoned," Variabilis assured them. "If I wanted to kill you…" he gestured toward the open doors, his meaning clear. The Shape-shifter went into the dark chamber opposite the entry hall and closed the wooden doors, leaving the Orions to themselves.

Gant, uneasy from the vertiginous view, closed the balcony doors and leaned close to Haldane, his voice low. "You think he believed us?"

"I don't know," Haldane admitted, "but how is it possible that, separated by more than a thousand light years, our two worlds speak the same tongue?"

"Coincidence," Gant shrugged. "It's a big universe. There are bound to be similarities between some worlds."

Haldane shook his head. "The odds are against that."

"Who cares? We need to focus on how to escape before that… thing in there decides to take us to his superiors… or throw us out those doors."

Haldane nodded, but he couldn't help feeling there was something they were missing, something important behind the mystery of their common tongue.

"Let's eat," Gant said, ever practical. "We're going to need our strength."

*

Brim stood before Brahma Kamal, the Council, the Quorum and a full gallery of spectators, including officials from other worlds observing through the circle of floating Luminaria globes.

Willa watched from a seat to one side, next to River and Lily. She glanced at Thorn, who sat with Kale and Rowan a few rows back. He ignored her attempt to connect and kept his attention solely on Brim. Willa felt doubt nibbling at what little confidence remained. Could she really trust her newly expanded senses? Did she really damage the time-line the way Selene insisted she had? If so, what effect did that have on the proceedings that unfolded before her? Brim had attacked Thorn, but now he hadn't. Willa wondered how much of the truth she should reveal to the Council if she was called to testify. Brahma's calm but penetrating voice broke through her self-deprecating reverie.

"Can you account for your actions?" The Council leader said.

"Where's my father? Where are Gar and Koro? Why aren't they here?" Brim replied with mild defiance that he hoped masked his desperation.

"Don't worry," Brahma said, "they'll have their turn before this Council." He held up the blue nano-bead that Brim stole. "Explain why you took this."

"I didn't take it," Brim said with total conviction.

"We found it on you," Brahma reminded him.

"Then someone planted it to make me look guilty."

"What reason would anyone have to do that?"

Brim aimed an accusing finger at Thorn. "Ask him."

Thorn jumped to his feet. "Don't put this on me! You've been up to no good since you arrived!"

Kale placed a hand on Thorn's shoulder and gently pulled him back to his seat. "Thorn… don't let him bait you."

Brahma turned his attention to Kale. "Master Ashgrove, do you understand what this is about?"

Willa's mélange of emotions finally coalesced. She felt a strong need to set things right as best as she could. She stood and walked out onto the floor before Lily and River could stop her. "I do."

"Willa! What are you doing?" Lily said, trying to keep her voice low.

Willa ignored her mother, stood near Brim and threw a withering look at Thorn. "Thorn is jealous of Brim because you ordered me to spend time with him, just like his father ordered him to recruit me to their cause," Willa said, determined to air the truth and end the charade.

A swell of disturbed murmurs from the gallery forced Brahma to raise a hand for silence. Willa pressed forward, far from done. She locked her eyes with Brim's and peered deep into his soul with her amplified sight. "He stole that data bead and he killed Thorn."

"I didn't do either!" Brim protested, hurt and confused. "Why do you keep saying that? Look! Thorn's sitting right there and he's perfectly fine!"

"You did kill him... and you didn't," Willa insisted.

"Willa," Brahma interrupted, "you're not making sense."

Willa's nerves were on edge. She knew that if she told the truth about the full extent of her abilities in front of the Council and the gathering, there would be unpleasant consequences. But, deep down, she knew she couldn't avoid the truth, no matter where it led. She glanced at Holly and saw the worry in her eyes, but continued despite her mentor's concern. "He killed Thorn, stabbed him to death, but..." She took a deep breath and plunged forward, "somehow, I reversed time and erased the attack, like it never happened."

The gallery surged with astonishment and disbelief. A dangerous-looking Nocturnal named Sibylline Darkwood rose to her feet, outraged. "This is nonsense! Only a Sage can master time. This girl's not even a Cryptic!"

Alder stood and faced Sibylline. "She's telling the truth. The Elementals confirmed it. The boy is flooded with temporal residue. I can sense it."

"How is this possible?" Sibylline shot back. Alder exchanged a look with Holly, who sighed and rose from her seat, resigned. She walked onto the floor and stood an arm's length from Willa. It didn't take enhanced senses to tell that her mentor was displeased.

"I didn't want to announce this outside of the Quorum until Willa had more training, but... she has the ancient Mark," Holly said, anticipating the crowd's reaction.

She wasn't disappointed. The gathering erupted with incredulity. Brahma stood to his full height and, for only the third time in the past twenty years as Council leader, raised his voice above the din. "Silence!"

The crowd hushed, as much from surprise as respect for Brahma's authority. Brahma scanned the chastised spectators with his arctic gaze, making it clear that he would brook no further outbursts. He sat and took a deep, centering breath.

"The Anu Mark is so rare that most consider it nothing more than a myth," he said in a calm and even voice.

"Nevertheless, she has it," Holly said. "She's exhibited several abilities beyond her station as an apprentice and even a few beyond the ken of most Sages. Fortunately, her powers aren't yet at full strength. The time reversal only affected her immediate surroundings."

The gathering couldn't stop from expressing shock at Holly's assessment, although one glance from Brahma kept the whispers to a minimum.

"The Council will discuss Willa's... condition with you in private," Brahma promised Holly, "but for now, the case against this boy must take precedence." He shifted his gaze to Willa. "Do you have anything else to add?"

"Yes," she began, keenly aware of Holly's eyes on her. "My senses also tell me that whatever Brim did, he didn't do it on purpose."

"What do you mean?"

"If you please, Councilor Kamal, bring Dennik and Gar in and I'll show you."

At a signal from Brahma, Dennik and Gar were admitted to the Council chamber by an orderly. Dennik ran to Brim's side, worry etched on his face. Gar followed behind at a respectful distance.

"Are you alright?" Dennik asked.

"I'm... confused," Brim said.

"I can explain," Willa said. "I sense that he was controlled... programmed to do the work of another without knowing it."

"A puppet? Whose?" Brahma demanded.

Willa turned her golden gaze on Gar. "His."

"An outrageous lie!" Gar spat. "I've done no such thing!" He locked eyes with Dennik. "How long have we served in the League together? You know I would never do anything to put your son in danger!"

Willa's gaze became more intense; her eyes began to glow. The gathering gasped as Willa peered into Gar's soul. "I can see right through you, Gar. You want our technology and you'll stop at nothing to get it. But you had to throw suspicion off yourself."

Dennik placed himself between Willa and Gar. "Willa, I admit that we coveted Earth's advanced tech. Can you blame us? It could help the Resistance win the battle against the Archon. But none of us, including Gar, would stoop to theft."

Willa kept her gaze fixed on Gar, as though Dennik was transparent as glass. "He doesn't want our tech for your Resistance. He wants to give it to the Overlords so they can crush the League once and for all."

"More lies!" Gar spat as he advanced on Willa.

Dennik held Gar back but Willa's words shook him to his core. "That's not possible. You must be wrong."

Holly moved to Willa's side. "Willa, this is a serious accusation with deadly consequences. We're talking about a person's life here. Your abilities, while powerful, are still untrained. Are you absolutely certain of what you're saying?"

Willa scanned the gathering. Her mother's face reflected her own uncertainty; her father's eyes encouraged her to trust her instincts and she could see confusion and shame on Thorn's face as he began to realize he might have falsely accused Brim because of his own jealousy.

Willa rested her eyes in Brahma's cool gaze of assurance. He nodded for her to answer Holly's question.

Willa turned back to Gar. His eyes were frantic. She focused on him, pushed her senses to the limit until sweat beaded her brow. Astonished murmurs rippled through the gathering as Willa's eyes shifted to black, like a Nocturnal or a Shapeshifter. Gar's image dissolved to a dizzying kaleidoscope of energy patterns in her sight that yielded his every thought, feeling and belief… and something hidden so deep within his psyche that Willa overlooked it at first glance.

"Layers within layers," she whispered to herself.

Holly strained to hear. "What did you say?"

Willa emerged from her trance; her eyes returned to normal. She blinked at Holly then turned to Dennik.

"Where's Koro?"

"We left him back at the Shaddok," Dennik said and pointed to Alder in the gallery. "He was disoriented by what that man did to us."

"A simple paralysis projection," Alder explained. "Quite temporary, I assure you."

"You need to find him," Willa said to Brahma. "He's behind all this."

"This is unacceptable," Dennik said, getting more frustrated by the minute. "First you blame Brim, then Gar and now Koro. Am I next?"

"No. Your only mistake was to trust a traitor. Koro programmed Gar to program Brim so the two of them would take the fall if his plan failed."

Brahma threw a glance at Argus, who stood in the upper row at the back of the gallery. "Argus, please find Koro so we can get to the truth. Do it quietly."

Argus grunted his assent and hurried from the chamber.

Willa went up to Brim and Gar. "I'm sorry."

"You should be after all your lies," Gar said, arms crossed.

Willa shook her head. "I mean I'm sorry for what I'm about to do." She placed a finger on each of their foreheads, her eyes glowing with unbridled power. Brim and Gar stiffened, held in place as though electrified.

The gallery reacted in shock as Dennik lunged toward Willa. "What are you doing?"

Holly held him back as Willa released her "captives" and dropped to her knees, her energy spent. Brim and Gar blinked, disoriented as though waking from a dream. Holly rushed to Willa's side. "Willa?"

"I'll be okay," Willa assured her worried mentor.

"What did you just do?"

"I removed their programming," Willa said.

Gar said as he regained his senses. "It's like she lifted a fog from my mind."

Dennik cradled the back of Brim's head. "Brim?"

His son nodded. "I'm alright and... I remember everything. Stealing the data bead. I even remember..." He turned to find Thorn in the gallery. "I'm so sorry. It's like I was trapped in a nightmare and couldn't wake up." Thorn averted his eyes, ashamed.

"But if Willa time-shifted, how would you remember harming Thorn," Brahma asked. "According to the new timeline she created, that never happened."

"For a brief moment, we shared memories when I released him from his programming," Willa said, blushing slightly at the admission of intimacy.

Thorn eyed her and smiled. "Don't worry, I promise not to get jealous again."

"Tactics!" Gar blurted.

"What?" Dennik said, puzzled by his friend's unexpected outburst.

"The game. I remember now. That's how Koro programmed me. There were things he said that were strange. At the time, I thought he was just trying to distract me so he could win. But now that I look back…"

"And you taught me the game," Brim said, his own memories bubbling to the surface. "We were brainwashed."

"Insidious," Brahma said and caught Dennik's eye. "Is this the kind of threat we face from your world?"

"Mind control is child's play to the Overlords. You all have no idea what's coming," Dennik said.

Willa's horrifying premonition of the Archon's bloody victory flooded her vision. "I do," she said, her stomach queasy.

"We need to find the traitor," Dennik said. He turned to Brahma, his anger rising. "You should send a squad—"

"Argus will find him," Brahma interjected. "If we alert Koro before he can be captured, he may cause more harm. I'll inform you when we have him in custody."

Brahma rose, somber. "The Council's adjourned until after mid-meal tomorrow, at which time we'll discuss plans to prepare Earth and the Alliance for the Overlords' coming attack." Brahma and the rest of the Council entered their private chambers as the gathering broke up in a flurry of whispered conversations.

Thorn felt Kale's reassuring hand on his shoulder. He walked onto the floor and stood before Brim.

"I owe you an apology," Thorn said. He held out his hand. "Can you forgive me?"

Brim gripped Thorn's forearm in the Orion way and smiled.

"Friends?" Brim said hopefully.

"Brothers," Thorn replied. He released his grip and stepped up to Willa, embarrassed. Before he could speak, she wrapped him in a hug that melted his tension like snow in spring. He hugged her back, grateful for her forgiveness.

Kale and Rowan joined them along with Willa's parents. Despite their reassuring hugs, Willa was still in turmoil.

Holly placed a hand on Willa's shoulder. "You did well, Little Fox."

"I almost got everything wrong. I accused Gar—"

"But you went deeper, saw through the surface appearance," Lily reminded her.

"If something more dangerous happens... if I don't have time to think. How can I trust what I'm sensing? You heard what that Nocturnal said. The powers are growing faster than I can handle. What if I can't control them? What if I alter the timeline again? For all I know, I might be the cause of the invasion I see in my visions!"

"I don't believe that," River said.

"But you don't know for sure!" Willa shot back more forcefully than she intended.

"Your training," Holly said. "You'll learn to control the abilities with practice."

"Maybe," Willa admitted, her eyes welling with tears. "But you shouldn't trust me until I can trust myself." She turned and ran from the chamber.

Both Holly and Thorn moved to follow, but Lily gently held them back. Holly understood that Willa needed her mother far more than her mentor at the moment and nodded. Lily gave Holly and Thorn quick kisses on their cheeks and went to find her daughter.

CHAPTER NINETEEN

PROMISES

"Seven hundred years of peace, while allowing Earth to expand and prosper in ways no human would have believed possible prior to The Landing, gave us much but also took something crucial in return. Humans, Hybrids, Extraterrestrials and Elementals of the Alliance are ill equipped to handle the threat posed by the Overlords who seek to dominate and absorb our worlds into their Empire. We can scarcely conceive of the dark plots and cruel machinations we've learned are second nature to the Overlords' way of thinking."

From the opening speech of Brahma Kamal
307th Session - First Contact Council of Earth

*

HALDANE THREW ANOTHER log on the fire from the stack next to the hearth in the central chamber of Variabilis's aerie and Gant warmed his cold hands over the flames. The few, small windows that pierced the thick stone walls kept the chill night air at bay only by means of wooden shutters rather than glass. The Orions' absent "host" hadn't made an appearance since he shut himself in his study.

Gant edged as close to the fire as he could without singing his skin. "What in the name of the Elder Gods is he doing in there?" he said, shivering despite the blaze.

Haldane ignored his companion's question, being the tenth time he'd heard it in as many hours. He occupied himself by thinking of ways to escape their lofty prison, although the chamber's sparse furnishings offered few options.

"If I had enough time," he mused, "and the right tools, I could turn probably turn the table and doors into a respectable glider."

"If," echoed Gant. "If, if, if. There's no way out of this place except at the whim of that foul creature."

Haldane cast a nervous glance at the study doors. "He might be listening."

"I don't care anymore. He's either going to kill us or he's not."

As if on cue, the study doors swung open and Variabilis returned. Haldane and Gant got to their feet and awaited their fate. The Shapeshifter leveled his all-black eyes at them.

"You'll be happy to know that your friends didn't crash."

"No?" Haldane said innocently. "That's good news."

"They're the guests of the Contact Council at Port Dublin," Variabilis informed them.

"Is that far?" Gant said.

"Not at all, a mere thousand miles. The Shaddok can do that in a single jump. Unless, of course, you'd like me to fly you there the same way I brought you here."

Gant paled. "I'd rather not, if it's all the same to you."

Haldane regarded Variabilis with a blank stare. "Shaddok? Is that a ship?"

The Shapeshifter's only answer was a crooked smile.

*

Willa sat on a bench amid the lush gardens that surrounded the Contact Council building. Lily sat quietly beside her and waited until Willa felt like talking.

"I don't know if I can do this," Willa said when she finally broke her silence.

"Do what?" Lily gently prompted.

"Everyone wants something from me. Selene, Belladonna, Dennik, Thorn, the Council... even the Elementals expect me to protect them from the coming invasion. I really don't know if I have the ability... or the strength."

"Tell me what it's like," Lily said. "Tell me how the new abilities feel."

Willa collected her thoughts. "They just sort of happen. One minute they're there and the next, they're gone. It's like I'm myself and then I'm someone else. No, no... it's more like I become some*thing* else. Not human, not Hybrid, not... me."

"This grey girl from your vision, tell me about her," Lily prompted.

"How did you... oh, Poppy told you."

"Don't blame her, I gave her no choice. What she told me about that strange girl is disturbing to say the least."

The grey girl was last person Willa wanted to talk about, but Lily's adamant expression made it clear she wouldn't back down. "I'm not sure who she is exactly, but her arrival on Earth as part of the invasion feels... inevitable." Willa slowly fell back into the vision of her last encounter with the Orion girl as she spoke. Her golden eyes slowly darkened to black as the vision deepened. "When I see her I feel this insatiable hunger, this burning thirst for power, like a fire that can't be quenched." An image of the grey girl's back began to solidify, as though Willa was sneaking up on her from behind. The girl sensed Willa's intrusion and slowly turned, her pale eyes clouding to black like Willa's.

Lily was alarmed by her daughter's unexpected transformation. "Willa?"

Willa instantly pulled back and broke the connection. She shivered as though a biting chill had penetrated deep into her bones. Lily wrapped an arm around Willa, attempting to comfort herself as much as her daughter.

"You asked how I feel, having these abilities. I feel empty, scared... and alone." Tears flowed down Willa's cheeks as she sobbed. "I can't be what everyone wants me to be. I'm only thirteen."

Lily remembered saying that to Holly prior to Willa's first Divinorum ritual in the Passage and Holly's reply rang in her ears: "She's about to grow up very quickly." Lily held Willa closer, her own heart breaking. She wiped away her own tears and sat up straight, trying to appear strong for her daughter, but inside, she was a whirlpool of emotions. She looked at her daughter with a mix of pride, awe, sorrow and fear.

"My brave girl."

"Brave?" Willa said in disbelief. "Haven't you been listening? I'm terrified!"

"I know, I know," she said softly. "But most brave people are. They just do what needs to be done in spite of their fear, or maybe because of it." Lily looked sideways at her daughter. "Grandmother Mimzy used to say, 'A strong person stands up for themselves. A stronger person stands up for others.' You're stronger than you think, Pooka."

"What should I do?" Willa pleaded.

Lily took a deep breath. "The only thing you can do," she said, her voice gaining strength. "Let Holly finish your training. Be as prepared as possible for whatever comes."

"And if I fail?" Willa said, her eyes welling again.

Lily pulled her closer. "Whether in this life or the next, at least we'll all be together."

Despite her fear, Willa laughed. "Is that supposed to make me feel better?"

"It's just my way of saying that, no matter what happens, your family's always here for you," Lily said.

Willa wrapped Lily in a crushing hug and, for the first time since her apocalyptic vision, felt a weight lift from her shoulders.

*

Argus exited from the Shaddok where Dennik and Gar had left Koro. The Sasquatch scanned the countryside, but the wayward Orion was nowhere to be seen. Argus found a few footprints nearby, sniffed at them and followed the trail over the rolling hills and between jutting outcrops of grey rock.

As he crested one hill, Ashleen and Rusalka came toward him through the meadow that bordered the edge of the woods.

Argus bowed his huge head. "Argus is pleased to see the Queen of Pookas."

"Good to see you Argus," Ashleen said. "What brings you this way?"

"Argus search for outworlder. You see stranger here, looks like Brim?"

"No one passed us," Rusalka responded, "but the trail you're following leads to the Cliffs of Moher. He can't go farther than that."

"Unless he can fly," Ashleen added with a smirk.

Argus bowed, grunted his thanks and set off across the meadow on Koro's trail. The Pookas continued toward the Shaddok.

"Now *he* has nice manners," Ashleen said. "Not like that nasty off-world boy. What was his name?"

"Brim," Rusalka said.

"Brim," Ashleen repeated, wrinkling her nose as though the sound left a bad taste in her mouth. "Even his name lacks poetry."

"I agree, my Queen," Rusalka countered, "but shouldn't we discuss how we're going to convince the girl to go through a potentially life-threatening ritual?"

"We're not. You are."

Rusalka stopped. "Me?"

"She's gotten to know you. You said you saved her once and, though you've tried to keep it from me, I sense she's also saved you."

"Yes, well, ummm…"

Ashleen waved off Rusalka's sheepish grin. "You have a bond with her."

"That doesn't mean she trusts me."

"Sometimes charm can convince where trust is lacking," Ashleen said.

"She doesn't find me charming, either."

"Then lie to her about the Kenning, whichever course you think best. Just remember that all our lives depend on her."

They walked through the meadow in silence, Rusalka growing more concerned with every step.

"Cheer up, Rusalka. Things could be worse," Ashleen said, patting him on the back.

Rusalka stopped. "How's that?"

"We could be relying on *you* to save the world. Oh wait... we are. So, if you're thinking of having second thoughts, think again." Ashleen smiled and continued toward the Shaddok.

Rusalka shuddered as the weight of Ashleen's words sank in and, for the first time, began to feel empathy for Willa. He cleared his mind, thought it through until an idea hatched in his brain. He scurried after Ashleen.

"Wait, my Queen, I have a better plan!"

*

Variabilis, Haldane and Gant emerged from the Port Dublin Shaddok. The Orions looked back at the glowing nano-glass ring of upright trilithons and lintels with unabashed wonder.

"We're a thousand miles from where we began?" Haldane asked.

"As the crow flies," the Shapeshifter responded.

Haldane knitted his brow. "What's that mean?"

"In a straight line, without detours," Variabilis said.

"What's a crow?" Gant said.

Variabilis shifted into a black bird. "This is a crow," he squawked. He shifted back to his Hybrid form. "Don't you have birds where you come from?"

Haldane and Gant answered together. "No."

"Then your world's the poorer for it." Variabilis headed east toward Port Dublin, looking back to make sure the Orions followed. Haldane and Gant hung several yards behind and conversed in whispers.

"Their technology, if that's what gives him his ability, is astonishing. Far more advanced than what the Archon's technicians found aboard the prisoner's ship," Gant exclaimed.

"Yes," Haldane agreed, "but there's a more pressing matter. The Archon suspects that the Black League's leader, Dennik himself, brought the escaped prisoner here. If that's true, what's the plan now that we're no longer covert?"

"It remains the same. Kill him on sight," Gant said casually as if it required no explanation.

"In front of everyone? They'll strike us down before Dennik hits the floor."

"Did you not swear an oath to the Archon to do his bidding even if it costs you your life?"

"Yes, you're right. The blow Dennik's death would cause to the Resistance is worth a hundred lives." Haldane glanced at the Shapeshifter's back to make sure he wasn't paying attention. He clasped Gant's forearm in camaraderie. "For the Empire."

Gant returned the ritualistic grip. "For the Empire."

*

Argus emerged from a Shaddok near the ruins of O'Brien's tower at the edge of the vertiginous Cliffs of Moher. Atlantic Ocean waves pounded the base of the cliffs seven hundred feet below. Argus's fur fluttered in the ocean breeze as his enormous strides carried him across the wide, grassy field around the ancient ruin. His sharp eyes searched for any sign of Koro's tracks among the blue-violet Sheep's Bit, white Campions, delicate Sea Pinks and the other hardy wildflowers that carpeted the limestone Burren atop the cliffs.

The Sasquatch stopped and crouched to inspect a broken Foxglove. He sniffed at it, then rose and sniffed the air. Argus locked on a direction and quickened his pace as he continued down the precipitous shoreline.

*

Variabilis escorted Gant and Haldane into the Contact Council's central chamber. Brahma and the full Council were present in their usual seats, along with Dennik and Gar who stood on the floor, ready to greet their fellow Orions. Since this was an unofficial meeting, the spectator gallery was empty. Variabilis stepped to one side and gave a respectful bow to the Council.

Brahma bowed his head slightly in return. "Variabilis. How long has it been," he said, pleased to see his old friend.

"Ten years," the Shapeshifter replied as he waved Haldane and Gant forward. "This is Haldane and Gant. Gentlemen, this is Brahma, head of the Contact Council." He gestured toward Dennik. "And this—"

"No introduction is needed," Gant said as he took a step forward. "It's a great honor to finally meet you, Dennik."

Dennik remained neutral as he sized up the newcomers. "How did you come to be here?"

Haldane moved up beside Gant. They were both just a few yards from their target. "We were pursued by the Archon's sentries during our search for the Resistance."

Gar moved up beside Dennik. "Why were you searching for us?"

"To join in your fight against the Overlords, of course," Haldane said. "Our sensors picked up your ship's gravity wake and we followed you through the Maelstrom. Our ship was slightly damaged but the sentries weren't as lucky."

"Quite a stroke of luck for you," Gar said, suspicious.

"Yes," Gant agreed. "The stars were with us."

"We were told you used a comet fragment to disguise your arrival," Dennik said, his tone still devoid of emotion.

"I was fortunate to have a clever pilot," Gant said, clapping Haldane on the shoulder.

"So," Dennik continued, "you wish to join the Resistance. You're willing to swear the oath of loyalty, to devote your lives to our cause?"

"We are," Haldane and Gant said in unison.

Dennik extended both arms. As Haldane and Gant stepped forward to grip Dennik's forearms in the traditional show of fealty, Gant eyed the dagger strapped to Dennik's belt as Haldane pressed his thumb into the underside of his middle finger. A poison-tipped needle extended from the artificial finger and jabbed into Dennik's forearm.

"For the Empire!" Haldane hissed.

Quick as a striking snake, Gant snatched Dennik's dagger and drove it into Haldane's heart. "Traitor!"

The Council members rose to their feet in shock but Dennik and Gar remained implacable.

Haldane slowly faced Gant, eyes wide. He opened his mouth but his lips frothed with blood before he could speak. Gant gave the dagger a cruel twist and Haldane collapsed to the floor, dead, the knife protruding from his chest.

"Master Gant!"

All eyes turned toward Brahma, who riveted on Haldane's bloody body, aghast. He tapped a button on his console. Within moments, three gleaming nano-glass emergency robots entered the chamber. Brahma gestured toward Haldane. "See if you can revive him."

The robots swarmed around the body as their fingertip sensors checked Haldane's vitals. The lead robot stood and faced Brahma. "There's too much damage. He's dead."

"Please transport his body to the medical center morgue."

One of the robots flattened into a pallet as the other two robots placed Haldane's corpse on top of it. The pallet lifted and floated toward the exit under the guidance of one robot as the remaining emergency bot quickly siphoned the blood from the Council chamber floor and followed his companions out.

Brahma struggled to retain his composure as he faced Gant, his blue eyes cold as space. "There hasn't been a murder on Earth in centuries! And certainly never in these hallowed chambers, until now! Killing may be the way of your world, but it's unacceptable here!"

Gant locked eyes with Dennik. "My only thought was to save your life! Haldane was one of the Archon's spies! He used me to get to you! I knew nothing of this, I swear!" Gant suddenly realized that Dennik appeared unaffected by the poison. "Master Dennik, are... are you alright?"

"I'm fine," Dennik said with a dry smile. "It's a simple matter for a Shapeshifter to transmute poison into a harmless substance."

Gant was at a loss. "Shapeshifter?" His eyes flickered to Variabilis. "Like him?"

Dennik eerily morphed into Encantado and glanced to one side of the room. "How'd I do?"

Gant followed his gaze as the real Dennik entered from Brahma's private chamber.

"You could fool the Archon himself," Dennik said with a wide grin.

Gant glanced down at Haldane's body, then back to Dennik. "But… what made you suspect…"

"First rule of the Resistance… never take anything at face value."

"I sensed something was off about your story," Variabilis added. "So I eavesdropped on your conversation, just as you did with Ander."

Gant was puzzled. "You had a listening device in the room?"

Variabilis transformed into an identical version of his chamber door. "No need," the door said as it morphed back to the Shapeshifter's normal form. "I alerted the Council about my suspicions before we left my tower."

Dennik extended his arm to Gant. "You've proven your loyalty. Kneel and take the oath."

Gant gripped Dennik's forearm and knelt.

"I am sworn and honor bound to the Black League. We fight the enemy from within the shadows with only the stars to light our path. We will strike at the heart of the beast and burn his Empire to ashes. We will free our world from his all-consuming hunger. We will be free in this life or the next, I so swear."

Gant repeated the solemn words and Dennik helped him to his feet.

"Welcome to the Resistance," Dennik said. Gar slapped Gant on the shoulder for good measure.

Gant's eyes filled with gratitude. "I'm honored to fight at your side," he said and secretly congratulated himself on his successful infiltration of the League. Now he could safely continue to hatch his scheme against the Archon, wipe out the Resistance and take his place as absolute ruler of the Empire.

"Not so fast," Brahma interrupted. "We can't simply allow this killing to go unpunished."

"But Haldane was a spy!" Gar said as if that excused everything.

"Be that as it may, the old laws from before The Landing have never been changed. Gant must at least stand trial for his actions. Since there are no traditional courts on Earth anymore, the Interstellar Tribunal in the Sirius system will determine his guilt or innocence," Brahma explained. "Until then, he must remain confined to his quarters."

"I'm to be tortured at this Tribunal of yours?" Gant said, nervous.

"As I said, this isn't Xos," Brahma said, sickened at the mere mention of the Overlords' cruel ways. "We will hear testimony from the witnesses, including your people, weigh all the facts and come to a decision."

"And if I'm found guilty?"

"At best, you will be banned from Alliance space and forbidden to return."

"You mean I would leave with Dennik? Then why not just let me go without the trial?" Gant said hopefully.

"Because the Tribunal may decide to place you in a rehabilitation program," Brahma explained.

"Rehabilitation?" Dennik asked.

"You mean brainwashing, don't you," Gar said, sour-faced.

"Neural retraining to be precise," Brahma said, somewhat defensively. "You would become incapable of performing any further violent actions."

"Even in self-defense?" Brim wondered aloud.

Brahma nodded and focused on Gant. "But there would be no need to defend yourself if you remained on Earth."

"You're saying I'd never see my people again."

"I'm saying you'd be free to go, but you wouldn't be able to fight."

"Then I'd be useless to the Resistance."

"No," Dennik assured Gant, "you'd be valued for any other skills you possess."

"I was a security guard in the Archon's citadel. That's not much of a skill," Gant bemoaned.

Dennik and Gar exchanged a meaningful glance.

"How much of the Citadel did you see?" Dennik asked.

"All of it, including the Archon's chambers once."

"Can you draw us a map?" Gar said, a bit too eager.

Gant thought about it and nodded. "I can."

Dennik's signature smile was back. "Then you just became one of the most valuable members of the League."

Gant returned Dennik's smile.

Gar thrust a thumb in the Council's direction. "Assuming they don't rehabilitate your memory away."

"Maybe you should draw the map before the trial," Dennik suggested as delicately as he could.

Gant's smile faded as he imagined his secret plans being vacuumed from his brain. He turned to Brahma. "You have no other form of punishment?"

"We don't punish," Brahma said, incensed, "but I'm ashamed to say your actions here today made me wonder if we shouldn't adopt some of your planet's laws." He turned to Encantado. "Please see that our 'guest' remains in his quarters." Brahma strode to his private chamber as the Council members took their leave.

Encantado ushered Gant, Dennik and Gar from the Council building.

"Don't worry," Dennik said to Gant, "we'll vouch for you at the Tribunal."

Gant nodded his gratitude but, as they crossed the Council grounds toward the guest lodgings, his mind searched for another way out of his dilemma before the Tribunal could expose the secrets locked deep within him, particularly the knowledge that he and Koro, who Gant assumed must be ensconced somewhere within the headquarters of the Resistance, were brothers, a fact that would once again throw suspicion on Gant, prevent his acceptance into the Black League and possibly foil his plans to rule the Empire.

CHAPTER TWENTY

THE RAZOR'S EDGE

"Tactics, like the Earth game of Chess, is first and foremost a game of deception. Pieces are moved in a manner that fools one's opponent into believing that an attack is coming from one direction when, in fact, the killing blow quietly approaches by an entirely different and unseen path."

Excerpt from "Tactics"
by Winona Sixkiller Smith

*

A GREEN BEAM scanned the Archon's eyes, linking the new computer to the neural pathways in Xos-Asura's brain. The beam snapped off and the ship's systems glowed to life.

"Interface successful," the cloned computer announced. "All systems operational. I await your instructions."

The Archon stood back and inspected the control console of his new ship. "You will address me as 'my Lord' and your designation will be Thrall."

"Yes, my Lord," Thrall responded obediently.

The Archon headed for the airlock hatch as Soonash stood by, nervously awaiting his master's assessment. Xos-Asura avoided eye contact with the lead Tech as he found the Takanni's single yellow orb somewhat unsettling. "Your work is acceptable."

The chief technician bowed, masking the relief on his face. "I live to serve, my Lord."

"And you serve to live," the Archon reminded him.

The rest of the tech crew was gathered at the bottom of the sleek ship's ramp. They all bowed as the Archon passed.

"Prepare my ship for a weapons test," Xos-Asura commanded without waiting for a response. He exited from the hangar bay and made his way to the elevator that would lift him to the top of the Citadel.

Eschavek Ren, the late Doona's replacement, stood at attention in the entry foyer outside the Archon's private chambers. A member of the same diminutive race as Doona, Eschavek's violet skin was tinged with pale blue, a sign that he was slowly changing from male to female as the birthing cycle took hold of his biology.

He bowed low as Xos-Asura emerged from the lift.

"My Lord, I have news."

"Speak."

"The scouts have calculated the path your prisoner took through the Maelstrom. Our ships are now able to pass through it with minimal damage."

The Archon felt a shiver of pleasure at the thought of expanding the Empire far beyond the borders of the Maelstrom. He could almost feel his skeletal hand stretch across the cosmos, crushing the resistance, clutching hundreds of new worlds in his grasp, squeezing the riches from them as billions of new slaves fell under his sway.

"Inform the fleet captains to oversee the installation of the new computers in each warship. As soon as I receive intel from my agents regarding Earth's vulnerabilities, I will plan my attack."

Eschavek bowed again as he backed out of the room. "At once, my Lord." The minion slipped through the double doors and left The Archon alone.

Xos-Asura activated a view screen on one wall and tapped in a code.

Xanthes, the young, grey-skinned female Overlord of the Eastern block, the girl that both Sylvania and Willa saw in their visions, appeared on the screen within moments. She offered a slight bow of respect.

"May the stars bend to your will, most high Archon. Your humble servant is honored to serve."

"You may dispense with the formalities," the Archon said, "no one else is listening."

Xanthes immediately abandoned her pretense. "What onerous task do you have for me now, Father?"

"The responsibilities that fall to you as the daughter of the Archon also bring you great rewards. I don't hear you complaining about those," Xos-Asura chided.

"Spare me the lecture. Why did you contact me?"

"To tell you that your greatest reward is yet to come."

"Yes? And what is it you'll want in return?"

"Only your continued loyalty. How would you like to be Overlord of an entire planet?"

Xanthes held her tongue as she searched her Father's pale eyes for some sign of trickery. For the first time in her life, she saw no hint of guile. "You found them!"

"The gift of sight you inherited from your witching mother has born fruit. We found the strangers exactly where you said we would and are preparing to use their own technology against them. Their planet's called—"

"Earth."

"Yes. None of the other Overlords know what I'm about to tell you," the Archon said.

"None of them shall learn it from me." Experience had taught her that any advantage over the other Overlords, no matter how small, was essential for survival in the constant struggle to maintain power.

The Archon continued. "This new technology will allow us to expand the Empire from a mere twenty worlds to hundreds of planets. The knowledge has already allowed us to plot a safe course through the Maelstrom. When we conquer Earth, it will be the farthest outpost in the Empire. You will be the Overlord of that world."

"The other Overlords will cry favoritism."

"Earth is the seat of an interstellar alliance. Over a hundred planets. There will be enough to go around," the Archon said, his eyes gleaming with fervor. "Have you learned anything new from your visions?"

"I've made a connection to a girl, I don't know her name."

"You already linked with a woman on their world. The fewer people who know about you, the better," the Archon admonished.

Xanthes nodded, but quickly added, "This girl's different, more powerful. She has the witching sight, like me. I'm learning to use her abilities to magnify my own with each new connection. I will surpass her powers in short order."

"Excellent, but be cautious. Despite our interrogations, we still know very little about them."

"Send me what data you have on their world," Xanthes said.

"Always cautious," the Archon said with restrained pride. "I taught you well."

"I credit mother for my caution," Xanthes corrected him. "I learned a lesson I'll never forget on the day I killed her for treason."

*

Willa passed by a grove of Yew trees as she approached the bridge on her way to the Quorum Lodge.

An animal's high-pitched scream snapped her attention to the woods. Willa instantly ran through the trees in search of the sound. She spotted a line of blood drops on several rocks. Willa followed the crimson trail deeper into the forest. She broke into a clearing and stopped dead, aghast at the sight of Rusalka's bloody body lying on the ground under the paw of a massive black wolf with fierce yellow eyes.

Willa shouted and waved her arms but the ravenous wolf just growled, protective of its prey. Willa grabbed a stone from the ground and chucked it at the wolf. It struck just above the predator's eye. It yelped in pain. Willa clutched another stone but the wolf backed away with a whimper and slunk off into the forest.

Willa ran over, knelt in the dirt next to Rusalka and gently shook him. "Rusalka?"

The Pooka moaned slightly, his breathing labored, but remained unconscious.

"Rusalka, can you hear me? You're safe now." She stroked the fur on his head as she searched his body for wounds.

Her attention focused on Rusalka, Willa neither saw nor heard the black wolf creep out from the shadows of the trees behind her. It treaded slowly and quietly toward her and, when its toothy maw was a foot from her neck, the wolf transformed into Ashleen. The Pooka gently placed three furry fingers near the back of Willa's neck. Faint wisps of blue energy emanated from Ashleen's fingertips and slipped into Willa's skin.

"*Is feider leis an Kenning tus,*" the Pooka whispered in Gaelic, her pink eyes aglow.

The sky darkened, though no clouds blocked the sun. Birdsong, wind in the trees, the buzzing of insects all stopped. A falling leaf was suspended in mid-air as a single second stretched into an eternity. Willa was still as a statue in the suffocating silence, her eyes fixed and unblinking on Rusalka, both of them a frozen tableau.

Ashleen moved in a wide circle around them as she drew shimmering lines of blue energy with her paw and formed arcane symbols that floated in the air. Tendrils of light snaked toward Willa from each of the symbols as they took on the aspects of living Elementals: A Pooka, a Salamander, a Sylph, a Gnome or Fairy. They spun around her in a macabre dance as Ashleen's invocation echoed among the trees.

"*Is feider leis an Kenning tus! Is feider leis an Kenning tus!*"

With a final invocation, the ring of spectral symbols collapsed into a ghostly sphere of blue light around Willa's head and was absorbed into her body.

Ashleen brought her paws together with the sound of a thunderclap. Birds sang, insects buzzed, wind rustled the trees and the leaf fell to the forest floor as time resumed.

Willa spun around as the echo of Ashleen's thunder faded away, but the Pooka queen had vanished. Willa scanned the trees. All was normal. She turned back to Rusalka, who moaned and pretended to regain consciousness.

"Rusalka, are you okay?"

The Pooka made a show of struggling to his feet, bracing himself on Willa's shoulder for support. "I... I think so," the Pooka said, thoroughly milking the part.

Willa helped to steady him. "We need to get you some help."

"My people will know how to heal me," Rusalka said as he limped away. "Thank you for saving my life... again."

"I should go with you," Willa said. "That wolf might come back."

"No, no," Rusalka responded a bit too emphatically. He coughed to reinforce the charade and spoke in a weaker voice. "I'll be fine, really. To be honest, I'd be somewhat embarrassed for my people to see that I needed to be rescued twice by one of your kind. No offense," he added quickly with a faint smile.

"I understand," Willa said, although in truth, she didn't.

"Thank you. Once again, I owe you a debt," Rusalka said as he limped deeper into the forest.

Willa stood, watched him go and scratched her head as she made her way back to the path. "I swear Pookas must be a mystery even to themselves."

Rusalka and Ashleen peered out at Willa from behind a large Yew tree. Ashleen rubbed the spot above her eye where the stone had struck her.

"Can't fault her aim," the pink-eyed Pooka muttered.

"How long before the Kenning takes full effect?" Rusalka whispered.

"Everyone's different," Ashleen whispered back. "With her quirkability, it's difficult to say."

Rusalka's rabbit nose twitched nervously. "I know I said this before but this is a huge risk. If she doesn't learn to control her powers, the Kenning could drive her insane, or worse."

Ashleen fixed her pink eyes on her fellow Pooka. "Doing nothing is the biggest risk of all."

*

Holly stood in the main room of the Quorum Lodge and stared at the golden flames that danced in the hearth under a bubbling cauldron of Divinorum.

Willa entered but Holly seemed not to notice.

"Are you okay?" Willa said.

Holly's faraway gaze remained on the fire. "You heard?"

Willa nodded. "If I'd been there—"

"Reversing time again would've been too dangerous," Holly lamented. "Still, if only we could've questioned Haldane about the Archon's invasion plans…"

Willa frowned at a thought. "His death was convenient, wasn't it?"

Holly saw where Willa was going. "Maybe too convenient. Well, Gant will stand trial, and we may yet find Koro, so if the truth is hiding in the shadows…" she trailed off, lost in her own thoughts.

"I could use my abilities to pull the truth from them, like I did with Gar," Willa offered.

"Perhaps when you develop more control," Holly said. "You almost condemned an innocent man and pushed yourself to exhaustion. Besides, a murder demands a trial under the law. That hasn't changed in seven hundred years."

"I could help at the trial," said Willa.

"We'll see. Regardless, it's important that we continue your training." Holly pointed to the circle on the floor. "Please sit."

Willa took her place in the circle's center as Holly spooned a few ounces of Divinorum into a small silver cup.

"That's all?" Willa said.

"Based on your amplified abilities, I shudder to think what a full dose would do to you now. Best to err on the side of caution."

Holly sat on the floor between Willa and the crackling fire. Her shadow danced across Willa's face.

"What if there's not enough time to be cautious?" Willa said.

"Then this will be the second biggest mistake of my life," Holly admitted.

Willa flashed a mischievous grin. "I thought you didn't make mistakes."

"I'll tell you about it someday. For now…" Holly handed her the cup. "Just a small sip."

Willa put the cup to her lips, took a sip and winced. "Do you ever get used to the taste… or the smell?"

"Pray you never do," Holly said with a straight face.

Willa wanted to press Holly on her cryptic remark but let it slide as Holly focused Willa's attention on the inlaid circle that surrounded them.

"The symbols around the circle represent the five levels of mastery," Holly explained. "You already know them as Cryptic, Nocturnal, Shapeshifter, Sage and Wraith, but each symbol also stands for the element that's associated with each level." She pointed to a green malachite triangle inlaid in the wooden floor. "This represents Earth, the rocks, trees, animals, Elementals, Humans, Hybrids and all the things a Cryptic must develop a strong connection with in order to discover one's true nature."

Her finger moved around the circle and stopped on a wavy blue line of inlaid turquoise. "The sea and the mysteries in its depths that reflect the depths of our emotions and the mysteries within our consciousness. This is the realm of the Nocturnals."

She traced a path to the next symbol, a white arc of marble, like an albino rainbow. "The sky, with its ever-shifting weather and cleansing winds belongs to the Shapeshifters."

Holly's finger aimed at a black circle of onyx. "Space, the infinite void that symbolizes the domain of the Sages."

Her finger finally landed on a small dot of pure, clear quartz. "Spirit, which resides within us all and in which we all reside; the realm of the Wraiths. There is much more to learn from these symbols beyond what I've said here."

Willa's golden eyes retraced the symbols around the circle. "Earth, Sea, Sky, Space and Spirit."

Holly nodded. "Good."

"Holly?"

"Yes, Willa?"

"I... never thanked you for choosing me as your apprentice."

Holly's features softened. She gently cupped Willa's elfin face in one hand. "In a different life, you're the daughter I would have wished for."

A tear flowed down Willa's cheek. Holly wiped it away. "Here now, none of that. Like you said, we have a long way to go on a very short road."

*

Dennik, Gar and Brim were huddled inside their quarters, locked in a heated debate.

"We can't just abandon Gant here," Brim said. "He killed Haldane to save my father's life."

Gar held up a data pad. "He gave us a map of the Archon's Citadel. Every room, the guard posts, all the vulnerable entry points. We need to get back to the League and act on this information!"

"We don't know if it's accurate," Dennik argued.

"It's more than we've ever had!" Gar shot back. "We need to go, with or without Gant. Like you said, we can come back for his trial."

A knock at the door stopped the conversation cold.

"You sure no one's listening?" Gar said, his voice lowered.

"After what happened, they might start," Dennik admitted. "I know I would."

He went to the door and tapped the control. The door slid back to reveal Selene and Alder.

"Sorry to disturb," Alder said, polite to a fault.

"You keep that damn digit of yours in your pocket," Gar spat.

"I mean you no harm," Alder assured him.

"Argus found your… traveling companion," Selene reported in her usual disapproving tone.

"Koro? Where was that cowardly traitor hiding?" Gar demanded, his ire rising.

"You'd best come see for yourselves," Alder said. He tried to keep a neutral expression but his cautious tone told the Orions that something was very wrong.

Dennik, Gar and Brim grabbed their jackets and packs and followed the Sage out the door.

*

Koro sat cross-legged on the grass near the edge of the Cliffs of Moher, gazing out over an endless ocean dotted with golden flecks of light from the setting sun. O'Brien's tower cast a long shadow across the rolling meadow.

Argus led Dennik, Gar, Brim, Selene and Alder toward the cliff. Dennik stopped about fifty yards from Koro and motioned for the others to hang back.

Gar threw Dennik an angry glare, and a protest formed on Brim's lips, but Dennik was in no mood to argue. "Wait here, both of you, that's an order."

Gar grumbled under his breath as Dennik left the group and cautiously walked up behind Koro.

"I'd know your footfalls anywhere, Dennik," Koro said without turning.

"How could you betray us, Koro?"

"To be a traitor, I'd have to have been on your side in the first place."

Dennik lowered his head, disappointed. "Get up. We're taking you back to the Council."

Koro didn't budge. "The old legends say that Xos once had oceans like this before the Overlords came. Do you think that's true?"

"Koro…"

Koro rose to his feet, but continued to face the distant horizon. "I see everything clearly now, Dennik. I know why Xos and Earth speak the same language."

Dennik stared at Koro's back. Some deeply buried instinct clawed its way to the surface of Dennik's awareness and made his skin crawl. A voice in the back of his mind screamed for him to run but, despite his fear, he was driven by the need to know what Koro had discovered.

"Why?"

After a long moment of silence, Koro turned. A soul-piercing chill coursed through Dennik's veins as he riveted on the crimson gore caked below Koro's empty eye sockets. His gaze flickered to the bloodstained dagger in the fugitive's hand.

Koro's lips stretched into an insane smile.

"Look to the stars."

Without another word, Koro dropped his dagger, stepped off the edge of the cliff and plunged to his death on the jagged rocks seven hundred feet below.

*

Willa and Holly sat in the Lodge circle, their eyes closed, the crackling fire and their deep, rhythmic breathing the only sounds.

Ashleen's incantation oozed into the silent space in Willa's mind: *"Is feider leis an Kenning tus."*

Willa suddenly gasped as a vision overtook her. Her eyes snapped open, all black like a Nocturnal. Her head arched back and she stared upward, not at the ceiling, but far beyond it as she'd done before.

"Willa? Willa! What's wrong? What do you see?" Holly pressed.

Holly's voice was drowned out by the deep rumble of the churning Maelstrom as it filled Willa's vision. She peered through it, then far beyond it, all the way to the dark, metal and stone-clad world of Xos. Her view continued to plummet down to the surface, to a large iron castle on the border of the Eastern block.

So used to the green forests and the rainbow flowers that carpeted the verdant fields around Port Dublin, Willa was repulsed by the bleak horizon that stretched out before her sight. The black iron castle dominated the grey canyons of the surrounding cityscape. Its turrets rose in tiers toward the dun-colored sky, the central spire capped with a bristling array of surveillance sensors.

Willa's view moved inside the fortified structure and penetrated deep within the vaulted metal halls until it stopped in a central chamber where Xanthes, the grey girl, her eyes closed, sat on the floor inside an inlaid circle of arcane copper glyphs in front of a giant hearth, just like Willa.

Xanthes opened her eyes as she telepathically sensed Willa's intrusion. Her pale irises darkened to inky blackness and she linked with Willa's mind.

"Who are you? Why can't I see you more clearly?" Xanthes whispered.

In the Quorum Lodge on Earth, Willa's body seized and jerked in fits as she struggled to break the mental link. Holly grabbed her by the shoulders to steady her.

"Willa! Let go! Come back!" Holly pleaded to no avail.

"Tell me who you are!" Xanthes demanded more forcefully.

"No!" Willa cried out. She continued to seize, frothing at the mouth, unable to break the link. Holly shook Willa as hard as she dared. Willa's terrified scream echoed in the cavernous Lodge, matched by Holly's fearful cry.

"Willa!" Holly placed both hands on Willa's temples, closed her eyes and concentrated, adding her own formidable mental powers to Willa's. She telepathically penetrated deep into Willa's besieged psyche and flooded her mind with cool assurance.

"I'm here, Willa. Focus on me."

Xanthes ghostly eyes flashed with ethereal blue fire as she forced her thoughts into Holly's mind. *"You can't help her! You're not strong enough!"*

Holly summoned every ounce of strength at her command to repel Xanthes's telepathic attack. *"You do not rule here!"* She felt Xanthes shift her focus back to Willa and doubled her efforts to shield her beloved pupil from Xanthes's mental assault.

"Willa. I'm here. Follow my voice. Come back to me!"

Holly's mental plea penetrated Willa's beleaguered mind. She struggled to break free from Xanthes's iron grip, but the grey girl was too strong. A sudden flash of Ashleen's paw on her neck during the Kenning along with the Pooka's eerie invocation infused her with unexpected strength.

"Is feider leis an Kenning tus!"

Power flowed through Willa like an electric arc. Her body stiffened, then collapsed on the floor as the telepathic link with Xanthes broke. Holly crouched over her exhausted apprentice, her eyes blinded by tears.

"Willa? Can you hear me? Willa?"

Willa's ebony eyes blinked open and faded back to yellow, her face pale and slick with sweat. She opened her mouth and croaked out a single word: "Xanthes."

Willa's mind reeled, her vision blurred and her senses were overwhelmed by the horrifying sensation of falling through a cold, empty and infinite void. After a few agonizing moments that seemed to last an eternity, everything went black.

*

The first thing Xanthes saw as she emerged from her trance in the fire-lit mediation chamber was the ghostly gaze of Uzza, her Sensate tutor. His gaunt, grey face was almost as cadaverous as her father's but was cracked with age. Sensates were rare, and greatly feared, among the Overlords. It was only through the Archon's power and influence that Xanthes was Uzza's only student in the black arts his coven had studied and practiced for countless generations. The Sensate knew equally well that his dedication to Xos-Asura made him indispensable, since his occult powers were a potent deterrent to any Overlord who might plot a coup against the Archon.

In truth, there was nothing supernatural about Uzza's abilities as they relied on the same, deep understanding of nature and quantum physics employed by Earth's sages, along with the amplified assistance of potent potions, similar to Divinorum. This knowledge remained a carefully guarded secret, passed down through the coven's clandestine rituals to their initiates for over three thousand years.

"The girl's mentor helped her break the link," Xanthes reported as she pulled herself to her feet. She poured a glass of water from a silver pitcher on a dark, stone table and drank the cool liquid to replenish her strength.

"No matter," Uzza said. "Under my guidance, you'll soon be stronger than both of them together."

Xanthes's mother, Kalvia, had also been trained by Uzza but had betrayed her husband and daughter. She fed secret information to the Resistance, aided them when they destroyed the Western stronghold and killed three Overlords in the attack.

Though she would never admit it, especially to Xos-Asura, it broke Xanthes's heart to take Kalvia's life after she pretended to join her mother's misguided cause. She was first and foremost loyal to the Empire.

She finished her water, sat back down on the stone floor in the center of the chamber and closed her eyes. "Let's begin again," she commanded.

Uzza was impressed with her stamina, but he also knew her limits. "You should rest first."

"That wasn't a request," Xanthes said.

Uzza sighed and nodded. "Your mother was just as stubborn."

Xanthes cat-like reflexes sprang her to her feet in a heartbeat. She pulled a razor-sharp blade from her thigh scabbard and held it to Uzza's throat. "Mention my traitorous mother again and you'll join her in the rendering vats!"

Ever stoic, the Sensate never flinched. "You're definitely your father's daughter. Shall we begin?"

Xanthes sheathed her knife and regarded the old fool with grudging respect before she sat back down, closed her eyes and took several deep breaths to prepare for the next phase of Uzza's instruction.

CHAPTER TWENTY-ONE

THE GATHERING STORM

"There's no such thing as a prediction of the future. There is, however, a sensing of the state of things that exist at the moment the prediction is made. Should that state remain the same, the prediction may come to pass. But should the state change, something else will manifest. The irony is that the prediction brings attention to the state and, having done so, can change the state, thus rendering itself obsolete."

"The Book of Paradox"
by Sassafras the Sage

*

WILLA WOKE UP in her hammock, safe and secure in her room. Golden morning light shone through her window and reflected off the nano-glass walls. The sound of whispered conversation floated up from the living room below and reminded Willa of those occasions when relatives from afar would gather at the Nest to celebrate some special family event. Willa drifted in those pleasant reveries for several moments, until the memory of her last encounter with the grey girl sucked all the warmth from the room.

She bolted upright and grasped at the solitary word that she managed to capture in the disturbing exchange. "Xanthes!"

Downstairs, the debate continued in whispers among a small, but concerned group: Holly sat next to Lily and River on a divan that extended seamlessly from the floor. Kale was present along with Dennik and Brim, who sat around a table, and Alder occupied a comfortable chair against a curved wall to one side, his legs crossed.

"You saw the grey girl?" Lily said, her face etched with worry.

Holly nodded. "I caught a glimpse of her in my mind as I pulled Willa back. Her energy is dark and powerful. But there's something that concerns me more." Holly searched for the easiest way to break the news. "I sensed... Elemental energy at work. It helped to break the link between Willa and that girl."

"What are you saying?" River prompted.

"I don't know how, but I think Willa's been exposed to a Kenning," Holly replied.

Alder sat forward, alarmed. "A Kenning? Are you sure?"

"What's a Kenning?" Brim said.

"Elementals, like the beings that held you in the forest, have the ability to link their minds together becoming, in essence, a much more powerful collective consciousness. They can then use that amplified state to do things no individual Elemental can, like when they probed you and discovered you attacked Thorn, even though Willa's time reversal had undone it."

"The whole is greater than the sum of its parts," Dennik offered.

Holly nodded. "Exactly. I believe an Elemental extended this linking ability to Willa, in the hope that, in combination with her Anu genes, it would magnify her senses and abilities, not only to discover what the invaders are planning, but perhaps even to stop them."

"In other words," Alder said, "they weaponized Willa."

"My daughter isn't a weapon," Lily bristled.

"The Pookas," Willa said from the bottom of the staircase.

All eyes turned toward her.

River frowned. "What about the Pookas?"

Lily went to her daughter and helped her to a chair that suddenly rose from the floor. "You should be resting," she insisted.

"Ashleen and Rusalka," Willa said. "I think they did something to me in the forest."

"I know. I'll have words with them later," Holly promised.

"If they've harmed my daughter, I'll have more than words with them," Lily said, her temper flaring.

Willa squeezed her eyes shut and rubbed her temples. "May I have a cup of tea, please, Mother?"

"Of course, Pook... Willa," Lily said as she hastened to the kitchen.

With a wave of River's hand, another chair extended upward as he moved to sit beside his daughter. He took her hands and gently massaged them. "We can continue this conversation another time."

The warmth of her father's hands soothed Willa. She felt she could sleep for a week and she wanted nothing more than the safety and comfort of home and her parents' loving protection. Her mind drifted into fond memories of childhood. As much as she yearned for independence and freedom as a young woman, she suddenly craved those precious moments when she was little and her days were filled with carefree adventures and bedtime stories. Those days seemed very far away now.

Lily returned from the kitchen and handed Willa her tea. She sipped the steaming liquid and felt it course through her like a revitalizing elixir. "No," Willa said, to her father as she mustered her strength. "There's no time to rest. It's important we have a plan. I want to help." She lifted her eyes to Holly. "I heard you say you saw the grey girl. Her name is Xanthes."

Dennik startled. "Xanthes? Are you sure?"

"You know that name?" Holly said.

"She's one of the Overlords, the Archon's daughter. I've heard rumors that she possesses strange, witching powers, but I always thought it was just propaganda to scare the populace and keep them in their place."

Willa searched the memory of her harrowing experience. "I think..."

River placed a hand on Willa's shoulder. "What is it, Willa?"

"I think Xanthes also has the Mark."

*

Variabilis, in the form of a giant, red-tailed hawk, soared over the mountainous vale that surrounded the monolithic tower he called home.

The Shapeshifter landed on his lofty balcony and returned to his Hybrid countenance. He strode through the wooden entry doors, crossed the hexagonal hub of the aerie and entered his private study.

A single, large Luminaria globe floated above a polished burl wood table in the center of the grey granite sanctuary. An open window admitted cloud-filtered sunlight that illuminated the Shapeshifter's simple bed on the far side of the Spartan chamber.

Variabilis tapped a series of numbers in code on the Luminaria's crystal surface. Quinlat, an elder female Shapeshifter appeared in the globe, her severe face an eerie combination of human and feline features that reminded Variabilis of Bast, the cat-headed goddess of ancient Egypt. Quinlat's large, ebony eyes were in stark contrast to her ivory skin, which was smooth as marble. A shoulder-length mane of straight blue-black hair swept back from a sharp widow's peak and enhanced her resemblance to the elder deity.

Quinlat's voice was a silky purr yet resonated with an undercurrent of immense power. "Variabilis, my dear apprentice. It's a pleasure to rest these old eyes upon you after so many years."

Variabilis offered a slight bow of respect, though his face remained grim. "Your pleasure may wane, Quinlat, when you hear of my news."

"Will you finally confess to being the Grim Reaper? Are you coming to snatch my soul and carry me to the next world?"

Variabilis allowed a half-smile at the memory of his apprenticeship under Quinlat's tutelage. He often bore the brunt of her jokes as she teased him about his dour disposition. The smile quickly faded as he remembered why he had called his former mentor.

"There's reason to be grim. Your jest may soon become my epitaph."

Quinlat fixed her obsidian eyes on him. She reached out with her arcane senses. Her expression froze for so long a time, a stranger might have truly mistaken her for a marble bust, which made it all the more unsettling when she finally parted her pale lips to speak again.

"You're cloaked in the shroud of death. What's happened?"

"Murder... in the very chambers of Earth's Contact Council. Beings from another star with dark designs to enslave the Alliance," Variabilis said, his face laced with uncharacteristic concern.

"Come to Cimarron," Quinlat said. "I'll send word to the rest of the Colloquium. You must tell us all what you know."

Variabilis gave Quinlat a curt nod. "I've already booked passage on the next ship."

The Luminaria went dark as Quinlat ended the transmission.

Variabilis paused to gaze out the window at the distant mountains that had been his home for the past ten years. Though the Shapeshifter usually shunned sentiment, he felt deep down that it might be a long time before he would lay eyes on their majestic peaks, if ever again.

He cast the dark thought from his mind. Quinlat was right. He dwelled too often within the grim, grey mists between life and death. He knew, in those rare moments when he was willing to admit it to himself, that the isolation of his stone tower was an escape from a world that had ripped the joy from his heart and left it as cold and hard as the stone walls that cloistered him in his misery.

But now, the dire threat to the Earth, the Alliance and all those he still cared for ignited a flame within him. He once again felt purpose coursing through his veins and Variabilis resolutely vowed that no others would suffer the agonizing loss of their loved ones as he had if he could possibly help it.

The Shapeshifter strode to his balcony, transformed back into the magnificent hawk and soared away toward the spaceport that lay beyond the distant peaks.

*

Poppy stood at the top of the staircase outside her mother's room, a steaming cup of tea in one hand. She knocked on the door. "Mother? Are you okay? I brought you a cup of jasmine tea."

There was no answer so Poppy knocked again, a bit louder.

"Mother? You've been in there for two days. I made morning meal. Please come downstairs and eat."

Again, nothing but silence. Poppy tried the door, it swung open to reveal an empty room. "Mother?"

Poppy spotted an orange poppy flower in a thin glass vase on Sylvania's dresser in front of the mirror. A small nano-bead sat next to it. Poppy tapped the bead. It floated in the air and expanded to a screen that played a recording of Sylvania's tortured face.

"My darling girl. My vision still haunts me day and night." Sylvania closed her eyes a moment to push the internal images away. Her eyes shot open again. "Now that I know it might come to pass, I have to go far away, to another world." A tear rolled down her cheek and a deep sigh escaped her lips. "I'm so sorry, my little flower, I know I've been distant and that this is hard for you but I believe it's the only way to keep you safe. I beg you, please don't try to find me." Her hand lifted as though she could reach through the screen to touch Poppy's face. "I love you with all my heart, Poppy. I always will."

The recording ended and froze on Sylvania's image. Stunned, Poppy dropped the teacup. It shattered on the floor. Lost in a trance, Poppy stared at Sylvania's transparent image, then focused on her own reflection in the mirror, eyes fierce and wet with tears.

A storm of conflicting thoughts and emotions swirled in Poppy's mind until her anger broke through to the surface. She punched through her mother's image, shattered the mirror into a dozen jagged shards and spilled the flower vase.

On impact, the screen snapped back to a bead. It fell, bounced off the dresser's top and hit the floor. The bead rolled across the room, bounced down the stairs and stopped at the base of a table set with two empty plates. Poppy's heartbroken sobs drifted from upstairs into every corner of the house.

*

"We don't know that much about the Anu," Holly said to the gathering that still held court in the Nest. "It's possible the ancestor race spread their seed throughout the galaxy."

"Which would mean that we share a genetic connection with your people," Alder said to Dennik and Brim. "Although that doesn't explain how we speak the same language."

"The answer to that question drove Koro mad," Dennik said. "I'm not sure I want to know."

"What was the last thing he said to you?" Holly asked.

"Look to the stars."

"Any idea what that meant?"

Dennik shrugged and shook his head. "Koro was a pilot, used to plying space. Most in the Resistance have little time to stargaze."

The gathering was silent as everyone pondered the matter. Kale decided to change the subject. He turned to Dennik. "What are your plans?"

"The League needs to know everything that happened here, then Gar and I will attend Gant's trial as character witnesses," Dennik explained.

"I'm not sure you should trust him," Willa suggested, her senses on alert at the mention of Gant's name.

"I don't," Dennik assured the gathering, "but better to take him away from Earth and keep a close eye on him by drafting him into the League." Dennik exchanged a glance with his son. "If you'll have him, Brim would like to stay on Earth until I return."

"He's welcome here as our guest," Lily offered.

"I'd like that," Brim said, trying not to appear too eager. He turned a shy face to Willa. "If you're comfortable with that."

Willa smiled and nodded. "Of course," she said warmly, although Holly and Lily could see Willa's mind was elsewhere.

Dennik pulled a nano-bead from his pocket. "Thanks to Willa's ability to remove Koro's programming, the Council saw fit to provide us with a copy of your starship technology. It'll give us a great advantage against the Overlords."

Alder eyed Dennik. "What if it falls into the Archon's hands?"

"Brahma came up with a simple solution," Kale said. "The data bead self destructs if anyone but Dennik touches it."

Dennik smiled, tucked the bead back in his pocket and stood. "Gar's waiting for me at the spaceport."

Brim stood and embraced his father in a hug. "Give Mother my love."

"You can do that yourself when she returns with me," Dennik said with a pat on Brim's shoulder. He turned to the gathering. "Thank you all."

"I'll escort you to the spaceport Shaddok," River said as he guided Dennik toward the far wall. The door opened and they descended down the thick, winding oak branch.

Kale gave Lily a hug and Holly a respectful bow of his head. "Best get back to my boys before more mischief finds them." He winked at Willa and followed River and Dennik down the branch.

Lily felt Willa's forehead and stroked her hair. "You should rest."

"I agree," said Holly, "but first, I'd like a brief word with Willa in private."

Lily nodded her consent and, at Holly's bidding, Willa followed her mentor out the door and down the branch. They reached the base of the giant oak and strolled across the meadow toward the nearby Yew grove.

"We should continue your training tomorrow if you're up to it," Holly said. "Now that we know the Pookas performed a Kenning on you, I can adjust for it. Still, we'll have to be cautious."

Willa nodded as she walked beside Holly. They came to the bank of a winding brook and stared at the sparkling water in silence.

"This isn't going to be easy, is it?" Willa whispered.

"No. If you're only willing to do what's easy, life will be hard. But if you're willing to do what's hard, life can be easier."

"I'm beginning to think that my purpose in life is to act as a warning to others," Willa said in a dry tone.

Holly's laugh sparkled like sunlight on water and blended with a strange, subtle sound that drew Willa's attention to a nearby Yew tree that hugged the riverbank. She remained fixated on the tree and, as Holly's laugh faded, Willa swore she could hear a soft whisper that floated toward her like a leaf on the wind. She strained to understand it and, as her focus deepened, her eyes lowered to the placid surface of the river.

Instead of her own reflection, Xanthes glared back at her, filled with malicious intent.

Willa stepped back from the riverbank, her eyes haunted by the vision.

"The tree just told you something, didn't it?" Holly said.

"Xanthes and I are two of a kind," Willa said, her voice trembling.

Holly wrapped an arm around Willa's shoulder. "There are many ways to interpret what trees may tell you. You're just starting to learn how to hear them. Don't take what they say too literally."

Willa nodded, though she was still disturbed by the implications.

"Willa, you heard the tree!" Holly said with excitement. She swung Willa around in a circle, proud that her pupil had made an important leap toward becoming a Cryptic.

Willa blinked and brightened. She looked at Holly. "I heard the tree! I heard the tree!" Willa stopped, breathless as it sunk in. She looked at Holly, all smiles, then felt every tree around her welcome her as one of their own.

"Congratulations. But rest for now. I'll see you back here tomorrow morning." Holly gave Willa a hug and headed off through the grove.

Willa turned toward home. She stopped, surprised as she spotted the mysterious red fox once again. It stood some distance down the riverbank and locked eyes with Willa as though trying to impart some message. Willa took a step in the fox's direction. It took off through the trees and quickly disappeared from view.

Willa knew there had to be portent in the fox's repeated appearances but she was too exhausted to push her senses further. She sighed and made her way across the meadow to the Nest.

Back in the grove, the fox had left a trail of prints on the muddy riverbank. They wove around rocks and through shallow gullies and, just before the footprints veered into the forest, the fox's four-toed tracks slowly evolved to human footprints.

*

Xanthes stood on the balcony outside her private chambers high atop her iron castle. Though she gazed out over the grey jumble of stone blocks that served as her subjects' austere dwellings, her thoughts were light years away, focused on the golden-eyed girl that potentially had the power to challenge Xanthes's claim to the Earth.

One of Xanthes's steel-suited guards stood in the arched entryway behind her.

"I brought her from the Archon's Citadel as you commanded, my Lady."

"Does my father know?"

"No, my Lady. Only the Techs who are loyal to you."

Xanthes turned. "Bring her in."

The guard curtly gestured for someone to enter from the hallway.

Elowen Koa, Kale's pilot, entered the chamber and walked toward Xanthes, one eye socket empty and sewn shut.

"That's far enough," the guard said. Elowen stopped a few yards in front of the young Overlord. Xanthes circled the Hybrid pilot, inspecting her as she might a new acquisition. She peered into Elowen's remaining eye but only received a blank stare in return.

"The Techs are certain the programming will hold?"

"See for yourself, my Lady," the guard assured her.

Xanthes considered Elowen's lifeless gaze and stepped to one side. "Jump off that balcony," she commanded.

Without hesitation, Elowen walked to the balcony and leapt up onto the wide railing.

"Stop!" Xanthes said. "Come back."

Elowen froze, pivoted on the metal railing like a well-balanced top, then jumped down and returned to her former position in the room.

"She hasn't much of a personality," Xanthes remarked.

"There are still two more phases of programming. By the time the Techs finish with her, she'll be the perfect puppet. Your thoughts will be her thoughts, my Lady."

"Just as her world will be mine," Xanthes said as though stating an immutable fact. Xanthes noticed a single tear well up in Elowen's good eye. It traced a course down the pilot's cheek. The grey girl caught it on her nail and licked it from her fingertip like it was nectar. She stood inches from Elowen's face.

"You're still in there somewhere, aren't you?" Xanthes whispered. "Imprisoned within your skull, hoping for any escape, even death." She cradled Elowen's face in one hand with unexpected tenderness. "Don't worry, my precious little wind-up doll. As soon as you've served your purpose, I'll send your soul to the Lord of Oblivion where you will have the honor of serving his hideous appetite for all eternity."

To be continued in:

SHARDS OF A SHATTERED MIRROR

BOOK TWO: NOCTURNAL

CAST OF CHARACTERS

HYBRIDS

WILLA HILLICRISSING
Our hero, a strong-willed thirteen-year-old Hybrid girl with a rare genetic "Mark" that gives her special, amplified abilities far beyond her years and training.

LILY HILLICRISSING
Willa's mother, a wise and caring soul with a green thumb and a love of growing things along with a fierce protective nature where her daughter's wellbeing is concerned.

RIVER HILLICRISSING
Willa's father, a gentle man who exudes warmth and assurance but relies on a no-nonsense attitude when the circumstances call for a level head.

HOLLY COTTON
Willa's Cryptic mentor, and a member of the Northern Quorum, who loves her apprentice as though she was her own daughter and does her best to focus Willa's stubborn nature toward her study of Mastery.

KALE ASHGROVE
An explorer who, while on official expeditions for the Interstellar Alliance, also searches the stars for his missing wife every chance he gets.

THORN ASHGROVE
Kale's youngest son and Willa's boyfriend, impetuous and jealous of any boys who might vie for Willa's affections and whose insecurity stems from fear of losing more of his family after his mother went missing and his father was captured by the Orions.

ROWAN ASHGROVE
Kale's oldest son, studying to become a First Contact Specialist, is some-

what more level-headed than his younger brother but is still prone to taking dangerous risks in order to protect his family.

CELANDINE ASHGROVE
Kale's wife and Thorn and Rowan's missing mother, mysteriously lost without a trace on a diplomatic mission to Shan, an alien world newly admitted to the Alliance.

ALDER REDWOOD
A flamboyant Sage and another Quorum member, given to eccentric behavior that belies his power and wisdom who realizes Willa's full potential and chooses to become one of her mentors.

SELENE NYMPHAEA
A secretive Nocturnal and Quorum member with a hidden agenda who forces Willa to use her abilities to search for a lost formula that could transform Selene into a powerful Wraith like her Great-Grandmother, Belladonna Bloodroot.

ERIDANI GINKO
A Nocturnal in the Quorum who keenly and silently watches events unfold and only speaks when she has something important to say.

ROSE LARKSPUR
A Cryptic within the Quorum who possesses strong empathic abilities and whose mere touch brings a soothing calm to tense situations.

LILAC LARKSPUR
Rose's identical twin in the Quorum with identical Cryptic abilities and who, like Rose, remains forlorn ever since their mother died from a rare affliction ten years ago.

LAUREL LARKSPUR
Rose and Lilac's deceased mother; the most recent person to die in Port

Dublin and whose untimely death lured the wailing Banshee from her dark, forest haunt.

BRAHMA KAMAL
The monk-like head of the First Contact Council, Brahma has served in the position for years due to his deep wisdom, a sacred respect for all life and, as reflected by his ice-blue eyes, the soothing demeanor of a placid mountain lake.

VARIABILIS
A reclusive Shapeshifter who suffered the loss of his wife and daughter in a tragic accident and has hidden away in a remote stone tower for a decade until events forced him back into society to protect his friends.

QUINLAT
An elder female Shapeshifter on the planet Cimarron, former mentor to Variabilis and the leader of a secret society known as the Colloquium.

ENCANTADO
A brooding Shapeshifter in the Quorum known for his terse, impatient encounters with people and who prefers decisive plans and physical action more than talk.

MOSHI
Another Shapeshifter in the Northern Quorum, more thoughtful than Encantado, prone to pessimistic outbursts but just as quick with praise when praise is due.

SYBILLINE DARKWOOD
A Nocturnal who often attends Council gatherings, has a very high opinion of her opinion where the path of Mastery is concerned, along with strong political aspirations and doesn't suffer foolish gossip or idle chatter.

STARGAZER
A Shapeshifter in the process of transitioning into a Sage, with a fondness for splitting herself into multiple copies in order to run the Stargazer Inn, which she owns in Port Dublin, and doesn't hide the fact that she has a crush on Alder Redwood.

JACARANDA FLORUS
The head astronomer of the Interstellar Alliance on Earth, a fact marked by an eight-pointed star tattoo on her shaved head and who makes her home in Sintra, a quaint town near the ocean in Portugal.

ELOWEN KOA
Kale's former pilot before she was captured by the Archon's minions, forced to endure severe torture and give up the secret of Earth's advanced artificial intelligence computers and who is later brainwashed by Xanthes in order to become her unwitting spy.

CAPTAIN BRYONY BRACKEN
Head of Earth's rescue and sentry squad, assigned to patrol the solar system and maintain security.

CAPTAIN YARROW
Commanded one of the rescue squad ships destroyed over Saturn by Haldane's stealth weaponry.

HUMANS

POPPY ROUSSEAU
Willa's best friend and confidante, somewhat devil-may-care with a propensity for blunt talk and psychic gift she uses to level the playing field between humans and Hybrids with advanced abilities.

SYLVANIA ROUSSEAU
Poppy's mother, a rare human Nocturnal, often withdrawn and secretly

struggling against Xanthes's telepathic intrusions that threaten her sanity and Poppy's life.

ANDER GARZA

An astronomer stationed on Andromeda Spaceport who first recognizes the unusual data regarding the comet Leviathan that leads to the exposure of Haldane's and Gant's stealthy arrival on Earth.

CAPTAIN SORREL

Commanded one of the rescue squad ships destroyed over Saturn by Haldane's stealth weaponry.

THE BLACK LEAGUE

DENNIK

A Captain in the Black League, the Resistance movement attempting to overthrow the Archon's tyrannical reign over the enslaved worlds of the Empire.

ALARRA

Dennik's wife, another member of the Resistance sequestered in the tunnels of a dark moon orbiting a rogue gas giant planet, with a warm heart and a firm resolve to defeat their Overlord enemies.

BRIM

Dennik's and Alarra's sixteen-year-old son, eager to join the Resistance and play his part in fighting the Archon, but somewhat headstrong and impatient to grow up and be taken seriously.

GAR

A seasoned, grizzled old soldier, always ready for an argument or a fight, who lost an eye in battle but still acts as Dennik's right-hand-man while also mentoring Brim in the ways of the Resistance since Dennik and Alarra are often away on clandestine missions.

KORO

A Resistance pilot, actually an undercover spy for the Archon and secretly Gant's brother, who ultimately goes mad once he inadvertently realizes the answer to the puzzling mystery that links Earth's and Xos's common language.

DARVA VAL AT'N

The founder of the Black League and the Resistance movement against the Overlords' occupation of Xos and the other enslaved worlds of the Empire who died in a failed strike against the Archon's Citadel fifty years ago.

KARA VAL AT'N

Darva's daughter, who inherited her mother's mantle as leader of the Resistance after Darva's death. Kara commands the Black League with cool assurance and confident leadership, despite her own secret doubts about their ability to crush the Empire.

JONNA

Kara's right hand, Jonna keeps the League's secret moon base running efficiently and ensures that supplies keep flowing via raids on the Empire's cargo ships.

VODNIK

A tall, imposing and mysterious sentinel whose face is constantly hidden under a dark helmet visor and who, along with his security team, guards the entrance to the League's communications chamber and other sensitive areas within the moon base, making it impossible for any spies to send a secret message to the Overlords.

OVERLORDS & ORIONS

XOS-ASURA

The cadaverous, grey-skinned Archon of the Overlords who rules the Empire's twenty enslaved worlds with an iron grip and plans to use intel from Kale's captured crew to breach the electromagnetic anomaly known as the Maelstrom in order to conquer Earth and use its advanced technology to defeat the Interstellar Alliance.

XANTHES
The sixteen-year-old Overlord of the Eastern Block on Xos, and the Archon's daughter, who possesses the same Anu genetics as Willa and exhibits similar abilities that she refers to as her "witching" powers.

UZZA
Xanthes's aged mentor who instructs her on perfecting her powers and thus, belongs to a rare and powerful group known as the Sensates, the Xoshi equivalent of Earth's Sages.

KALVIA
Xanthes's mother who secretly aided the Resistance and was killed by Xanthes for her betrayal of the Empire.

GANT
One of the Archon's former guards who, because he declared he had a brother in the Resistance, was commissioned as a spy and sent to Earth instead of being executed for failing to prevent Kale's escape from the Archon's dungeon.

HALDANE
One of the Archon's most loyal and experienced pilots who takes Gant to Earth in his stealth ship to retrieve the escaped prisoner and kill Dennik if possible.

SASQUATCH

ARGUS
The Quorum's eight-foot-tall Divinorum master who presents a gruff exterior but has a huge heart and an appetite to match.

ELEMENTALS

RUSALKA

A shape-shifting Pooka who usually takes the form of a large hare with red eyes and who, through trickery, is responsible for turning Belladonna into a Banshee.

ASHLEEN

Queen of the Pookas, also usually in the form of a hare with white fur and bright pink eyes, who performed a Kenning on Willa to amplify her powers in the hope of staving off the coming Orion invasion.

GRENNAN

Another Pooka, somewhat older than Ashleen and Rusalka, referred to as a "Seer" who has the gift of perceiving past and future parallel realities and sensing dangerous shifts in time.

KERNUNNOS

A very ancient forest spirit, bigger than Argus, with a strange, bearded elk-like face, hoofed feet and enormous antlers who, because of his penchant for rewarding the good and punishing the bad, formed the original seed for the story that eventually evolved into the concept of Santa Claus.

SILVER

A small, flying, fairy-like Sylph that offers her insights at Elemental gatherings called Enclaves.

VULCANUS

Another ancient Salamander Elemental that looks similar to the sleek amphibians but appears shrouded in blue flames.

BANSHEE

BELLADONNA BLOODROOT

Once a Sage, Belladonna was tricked by Rusalka and transformed into a mournful, wandering spirit stuck between life and death in order to prevent her from gaining power over the spirit realm and unintentionally causing a rift between the world of the living and the realm of the dead.

ALIENS

BRAELAN
A young Shinzai and friend of Poppy's with a skin of scarlet scales and a long tail who often competes against Poppy in the prediction game called Hexes.

DOONA SET
A diminutive alien from the planet Tet, who initially served as the Archon's attaché until he no longer proved useful and was killed.

YADRA JEET
Another alien from Tet who functioned as the Archon's lead Tech and, due to his failure to harness Earth's advanced computer technology, suffered the same fate as Doona.

ESCHAVEK REN
Also from Tet, a planet where genders can shift from male to female and back again, Eschavek replaced Doona as the Archon's new attaché.

SOONASH
An alien from Takanni, with pea-green skin and a single, yellow eye, who replaced Yadra as the Archon's new lead Tech.

WHELKS
Small, thin beings with huge black, bug-like eyes, known in the twenty-first century as the Greys, responsible for genetically engineering the Hybrids that eventually arrived on Earth during The Landing.

NOMMOS
Amphibious beings from the Sirius star system, home of the Interstellar Alliance Tribunal where Gant will go on trial for Haldane's murder.

SENTIENT COMPUTERS

OCULARIS
The Artificial Intelligence computer that operates Andromeda Spaceport while in orbit over Earth and sees to the needs of the station's thousands of workers and visitors.

CORVUS
Rowan Ashgrove's ship, the first sentient computer to greet the Orions when Kale and his sons were reunited after his escape from the Archon.

RIGEL
River Hillicrissing's ship, used in pursuit of Rowan and Thorn during their attempt to rescue their father Kale.

SAGITTARIUS
Kale's starship, damaged by the Maelstrom and ultimately destroyed by the Archon when the computer tried to take him prisoner and deliver the unwilling Overlord to Earth's authorities.

STARLING
Captain Yarrow's rescue squad ship, destroyed over Saturn's moon Titan by a missile from Haldane's stealth vessel.

THRALL
The Archon's new computer and ship, rebuilt with data from Sagittarius and engineered to be loyal to the Overlord.

ABOUT THE AUTHOR

DARRYL ANKA is a writer-director-producer at Zia Films LLC (www. ziafilms.com), a film production company he owns with his producing partner and wife, Erica Jordan. He has an extensive background in miniature effects, storyboards and set design and has worked on some of the biggest sci-fi and action films over the past thirty years, such as *Star Trek II: The Wrath of Khan, Iron Man* and *Pirates of the Caribbean: At World's End.*

He is also an internationally known public speaker on UFOs and metaphysical topics. Over twenty books of his seminars have been published in the United States and Japan and recordings of his talks have been sold to thousands of people around the globe by April Rochelle, his partner at Bashar Communications, Inc. (www.bashar.org)

Darryl is always working on new films, scripts and novels. He lives in Woodland Hills, California, a suburb of Los Angeles.

www.ingramcontent.com/pod-product-compliance
Lightning Source LLC
Chambersburg PA
CBHW061634050726
47502CB00012B/2168